KANSAS KID

OTHER FIVE STAR WESTERN TITLES BY LAURAN PAINE:

Tears of the Heart (1995); *Lockwood* (1996); *The White Bird* (1997); *The Grand Ones of San Ildefonso* (1997); *Cache Cañon* (1998); *The Killer Gun* (1998); *The Mustangers* (1999); *The Running Iron* (2000); *The Dark Trail* (2001); *Guns in the Desert* (2002); *Gathering Storm* (2003); *Night of the Comancheros* (2003); *Rain Valley* (2004); *Guns in Oregon* (2004); *Holding the Ace Card* (2005); *Feud on the Mesa* (2005); *Gunman* (2006); *The Plains of Laramie* (2006); *Halfmoon Ranch* (2007); *Man from Durango* (2007); *The Quiet Gun* (2008); *Patterson* (2008); *Hurd's Crossing* (2008); *Rangers of El Paso* (2009); *Sheriff of Hangtown* (2009); *Gunman's Moon* (2009); *Promise of Revenge* (2010)

KANSAS KID

A WESTERN DUO

LAURAN PAINE

FIVE STAR

A part of Gale, Cengage Learning

Detroit • New York • San Francisco • New Haven, Conn • Waterville, Maine • London

GALE
CENGAGE Learning˙

LIBRARY OF CONGRESS CATALOGING-IN-PUBLICATION DATA

Paine, Lauran.
   Kansas kid : a western duo / by Lauran Paine. — 1st ed.
     p. cm.
   ISBN-13: 978-1-59414-829-3 (alk. paper)
   ISBN-10: 1-59414-829-5 (alk. paper)
   I. Paine, Lauran. Border Dawn. II. Title.
   PS3566.A34K36 2010
   813'.54—dc22   2010007208

First Edition. First Printing: June 2010.
Published in 2010 in conjunction with Golden West Literary Agency.

CONTENTS

★ ★ ★ ★ ★

BORDER DAWN

★ ★ ★ ★ ★

I

Where Blue River left the mountains, the cut was deep, the mountain slopes dark-colored, and the serrated skyline was sere and forbidding. The only moving thing as far as a man could see was the river itself, and through those rocky cañons of barren stone, rusty-looking and ageless, where the river was confined and pressed close between unyielding rock bluffs, arose the only sound, too. Here, the water surged with awesome force and angry power. Farther along, beyond the mountains, the river widened and became less fearsome. Out there, it even nourished willows and riverbank grasses. For half the length of the Blue River—the half that lay beyond the barren mountains— riverside communities of flourishing life had been in existence for millennia. Entire cultures existed, some nearly as old as time itself, some more recent, but all completely dependent for survival upon the Blue.

Those cultures even included tribesmen, Pimas, Hopis, Zuñis, and farther north Paiutes, but there were never many of those people, so, for the most part, the cultures that existed the length of the Blue had to do with trees and grasses, undergrowth that was peculiar to particular areas, and every conceivable manner of desert wildlife. The Blue was life. Basically that was exactly what it was: life. Without water on the north desert there just simply would have never been a green belt of inhabitable land on both sides of the riverbed, or even back a few miles from the Blue. If that had been the case, then the north desert would have been as dead and unworkable as was the south desert lying east and south, down where the Blue never reached even in flood season. It was the river that gave value and meaning to all existence on the upper desert. Centuries earlier, the tribesmen had observed a simple but very significant phenomenon—water did not run uphill, but if a man walked backward, dragging a wide, pointed stick, the water would follow him like one of the domesticated wolves; it would follow him for miles, for as long as he wanted to drag his stick and make a shallow trench for the water to run in. A few generations later when the fundamental, natural laws of irrigation were understood more fully, the tribesmen led water through their ditches in all directions from the Blue, and the whole north desert flourished.

Water ditches like veins went from maize patch to squash field to grassland, to the fort-like adobe villages. Trees grew where there had never before been any kind of man-high shade. The desert yielded up forms of new life no one had ever seen before. Water changed the entire structure of life on both sides of the Blue for miles, and once this natural wonder was known to men, it was never allowed to wither completely. Not even when the tribesmen, for reasons no one ever fathomed, suddenly disappeared from their fields and villages. Even then, water continued to flow through their ditches for centuries, even though it no longer watered crops.

For centuries, there was no one to take the place of the tribesmen, but eventually there were the Mexicans and the transplanted, sedentary Indians. Again the north desert bloomed and flourished. Then another blight appeared—two-legged blights; deadly, savage, unpredictable Apaches and Kiowas and Comanches, the worst destroyers ever to arrive in the Southwest. They massacred and murdered, burned and destroyed out of hand. They were primitive, war-like, and far inferior in most ways to the simple people they broke and scattered.

Again, the ditches ran but the water irrigated fallow fields, except that the grass returned. Always, there was grass wherever there was water. It was a lowly growth to everyone except the people who came next. Cattlemen. They did little to improve the ditches beyond keeping them open, and they were also mounted on war horses and willing to kill. Finally the north desert Indian marauders had met their match. Even so, it took a long time, several generations, in fact, before the cattlemen rode down the last of the redskin raiders.

They then created their culture; superimposed it over those previous cultures, brought cattle to eat down the graze and browse. Ignored the haunted, old earthen remains of the previous cultures, drove their wicked-horned, evil-dispositioned, slab-sided cattle over the ancient fields where people had cultivated crops, staked claims, and marked off boundaries, and shot those who ignored them. They were six-gun arbiters. Their law was simple, basic, and deadly. They themselves having employed force to resolve all difficulties relied upon force to maintain their methods. In most ways they were the most aggressive, interesting, and colorful of all the riverside cultures. They built towns, created vast cattle ranches, patrolled their country inadvertently, but, nonetheless, adequately, and every man among them was the law even though they denied that this was so. When some of them caught a thief, they hanged him on the spot. When they were challenged, they charged. When their institutions were endangered, they turned out all together armed to the teeth. Every one of them was a law unto himself even though they invariably insisted their particular lawmen were the only real officials empowered to enforce their legal edicts.

Their period of flux was between the period when the last of the raiders were vanquished and the advent of the bad side effects of their own epoch, a matter of perhaps fifteen years. In those early days no one fought over the land itself; they rode across it, grazed their herds upon it, built and organized and supervised it, but there was far too much of it to fight over. When they claimed they were warring over the land, they were really warring over something else—one man's inability to tolerate another man, usually. Eventually, with most of the real dangers gone, more settlers arrived. Not many, but to people accustomed to riding two or three days before meeting another human being, any growth was a threat.

Not all trouble arrived with the newcomers, although in some cases it could be attributable to the imaginary peril these newcomers presaged. The big cowmen sought to reach out and control more land. Not because they needed it or even wanted it, but so that no one else could encroach. This happened even among the old-timers. It was the threat, real or imagined, of the newcomers that drove some of the old-timers to encroach upon each other. It did not make much sense; few things that caused range wars ever made much sense.

There was an ancient ditch that had at one time, in centuries past, been a wide, deep, main ditch leading inland from the Blue. It was called Funnel Ditch in English, and in Spanish it had been the same—*embudo*. It was one of those arduously created central ditches from which the prehistoric Indians had led off in all directions with their vein-like, smaller bleeder ditches. Its course had been improved down the centuries until its grade was exactly right to carry the maximum amount of water at the swiftest rate to the largest areas of the land. Over the centuries men had widened and deepened it, first by hand, then through the use of oxen, mules, and horses. It became a man-made river, a time-hallowed tributary from the Blue. No one could remember when it had not furnished water. Along its raised, wide shoulders grew willows, and berry bushes as thick and thorny as barbed-wire entanglements. It housed birds by the score and every imaginable variety of small animal life. Also, there were larger four-legged animals who existed in its thickets, as well as great-winged predators who lived in the hollows of tall trees. It had been there for so long generations of people had come and gone who did not consider the ditch man-made at all; it was a creek to them. It had been considered a creek for hundreds of years. It even had a name—Acequia Creek. And that was perhaps a little ironic because *acequia,* the name given it generations ago by its Spanish-speaking benefactors, meant in Spanish simply a ditch, usually an irrigation ditch, but to the most recent lords of the north desert, the Americans, most of whom did not speak or understand Spanish, *acequia* was the name of their creek and had no particular significance at all.

A lot of things had no special significance to the *Norteamericanos* who had inherited all the vast Southwest from their forefathers who had fought a war with Mexico to get title to it. One other thing that had no significance to them were the old-time native titles and rights, called in Spanish the *fueros*—the privileges. An example was the hundred irrigated acres of José Alvarado, known locally around Sangerville as Joe Alvarado. His father and his grandfather had been entirely content to hold their small piece of land, and to develop it until its grass would support seventy-five head of cattle ten months out of the year.

The Alvarados were quiet, industrious, peaceful men, kindly and tolerant and usually understanding. Also, they had fenced in their hundred acres. The earliest Alvarado had come to the Southwest with one of the missionary expeditions, as a soldier of Spain. He had secured title to the land. His son had begun the development that had lasted through the succeeding generations. He had also begun the faggot fence that other generations had added to, painstakingly, over the generations, rebuilding and adding to it until the entire Alvarado small holding was fenced in. Where the other neighborhood cattlemen had thousands of wild, unfenced acres and bunkhouses full of wild horsemen to police their ranges, the Alvarados with their small but highly developed holding made a fair living, and, generally, the people around Sangerville respected both the Alvarados and their thriftiness.

Of course, they were Mexicans. Anyone of Spanish descent in the Southwest was a Mexican to the *Norteamericanos,* and that of course included people of Mexican descent as well as those of Spanish descent. The difference, which was a very great and real difference, was not understood at all by the new lords of the Southwest. It was not significant to them at all. Anyone who spoke Spanish and who still affected the traditions and even to some extent the attire of old Mexico was a Mexican if the *Norteamericano* using the term were sober, and, if he were not sober, they were Mexes or greasers, or a number of other appellations including beaner and pepper belly.

What all this meant, clearly, was that the Spanish-speaking people were inferiors. As a matter of fact, some of them were; some of them were just as treacherous, dishonest, devious, and thieving and murdering as *Norteamericanos* claimed they all were. In fact, some of them were just as evil as some of the *Norteamericanos* were, but there were just as many who were not dishonest at all, exactly as there were *Norteamericanos* who were honest and self-respecting people. The difference was that there were many more of the *Norteamericanos.* They owned the towns, the laws, most of the land and herds, and they were indisputably the masters. When one of them decided in a drought year Joe Alvarado had no right to the irrigation water from Acequia Creek, that this water should by all rights of the Mexican War conquest go to water and nourish the land of his own *Norteamericano* cow outfit, why then he could invoke a dozen rights and reasons and most of his neighbors would support him because he was a *Norteamericano* and old Joe Alvarado was a greaser.

II

Joe Alvarado was not a young man. He was sixty years of age, and, although his gray eyes were as piercing as ever, his hair was no longer dark, and the bronzed, lean features had coarsened a little, had settled with age. He had been a widower thirty-five years. He had had a son and a daughter. The son had died in a freak lightning storm one terrible night many years ago, and his breathtakingly beautiful daughter had died thirty years earlier in childbirth, over in Arizona. Nothing aged a man like having more of himself on the other side than on this side. For as many years as most folks could recall, Joe Alvarado had gone every Sunday to the mission church out back of Sangerville.

For as long as a man lived, he was here, which meant he had obligations to himself and to the things he worked around and existed beside. Joe worked his little brood of cattle, his few heads of horses, and cared for his small band of sheep. He kept the water flowing in measurable amounts across his lush fields. He never took more than he needed and he never neglected to change its flow when a particular area had been adequately watered. In other places along Acequia Creek there were water hogs but in all Joe Alvarado's many years no one had ever accused him of being such a person, not even old Grant Mitchell who had steadily put together twelve thousand acres, most of it beyond reach of the Blue River's life-giving force and most of which encroached on both sides of the Alvarado holding. In fact, Mitchell's great cattle empire had Joe Alvarado cut off on three sides. The only area old Grant Mitchell did not yet claim title to was the half mile or so of open country between Alvarado's land and the limits of the town.

Mitchell was a second-generation inhabitant of the north desert, but he had acquired nearly all the land his Big M cattle and horses ranged over, his parents having been content desperately to cling to their first piece of deeded land a mile east of Joe on Acequia Creek. They, too, had been content to water a few small fields. It had been their son whose avarice and ruthless drive had created Big M, one of the largest cow outfits of the north desert country. You gave the devil his due. Grant was not just a cattleman; he was also a restless innovator. He had been accumulating the land lying below Acequia Creek for years. His purpose was sound, even admirable. When Big M cattle came off the desert in good health and shiny, but not really fat, Mitchell finished them on his miles of irrigated pasture. He was the first cowman in the entire Sangerville area to do this. When Big M cattle went down the trail to rail's end and were sold, even with the inevitable shrink from being trailed, they brought more money year in and year out than anyone else got.

Grant Mitchell did not ride over and visit Joe Alvarado. Once he probably would have, but Grant was a wealthy and influential man now. He and José had known each other all their lives. Grant Mitchell had gone on, had grown very powerful and rich. Joe Alvarado still sat in the shade of his walnut trees at the back of the same added-to ancient adobe house his family had lived in for more generations than anyone now recalled, and read books, or nursed ill and injured animals, or laughed at the antics of his colts and calves or lambs, and made a living, which contented him, and never tried to do more than that. Mitchell understood people like Joe Alvarado. He had grown up among them. They were naïve, trusting, not terribly ambitious, fond of pointless things like laughter and Saints' days and old friendships. They never had a financial reserve; they never bothered their heads about things like updating ancient land titles.

Grant Mitchell went down to his bunkhouse one early evening, took his range boss, Cliff Habersham aside, and gave the order: "Send one of the men down along the creek and tell him to plug old Alvarado's outlets."

Habersham was a large, dark man, a good range cowman. "All the outlets?" he asked.

"Every damned one of them," answered Mitchell, and looked steadily at his foreman. "He's got no right to that water. We Americans got them rights when we whipped the Mexicans in the war of 'Forty-Eight. Cliff, Big M needs that additional water to open up more grassland to finish off more cattle. You understand?"

Habersham understood perfectly because he had been in Mitchell's employ six years. He said: "All right, but it'll take two men. Most of old Alvarado's taps've been open for so many years they're a yard wide. One feller could be shoveling all night long."

"Then send two men. Just make sure they understand those outlets are to be completely filled in, and they got to do it so well the old man couldn't dig them open in a week. By that time the claim I filed yesterday for his water should be back in Sangerville, approved, but it's based on the old man not using his water right . . . if he ever had any such a thing . . . so you've got to make certain those outlets are plumb filled up."

Grant Mitchell studied his range boss from a pair of gunmetal eyes set in a craggy face that had a slash for a lipless mouth. Cliff gazed back. He was a powerful man, thick and strong as an ox. He had ramrodded the Mitchell interests without reservation or hesitation since first signing on. He knew his employer very well, so now he said: "Mister Mitchell, old Alvarado will go to the law in Sangerville. Or else he'll lie out there with his old rifle. I ain't finding fault. I'm just warning you what could happen."

Mitchell smiled. "You don't have to do my thinking for me," he told the range boss. "I'm plumb able to do that, Cliff. I think I know that old greaser as well as anyone knows him. As for the law in town . . . it's not going to lift a hand. We got the right.

That water by rights belongs to us. He's just been using it because we was tolerant all these years. Now we need the water and that is all there is to it. You understand?"

Cliff understood perfectly. "I'll tell the men to ride over after supper. They ought to arrive along the creek above Alvarado's place when it's dark. Just one question. If the old man happens to walk up on to them . . . ?"

Mitchell shrugged coldly. "Everyone's got a right to defend themselves."

Cliff stood in the barn shadows, watching Grant Mitchell walking back in the direction of the fortress-like owner's residence, a magnificent, great, sprawling *hacienda* with bright red roofing tiles. For the range boss it was never a matter of right or wrong; it was a matter of the Mitchell interests. He turned back in the direction of the bunkhouse, and around him the soft, late springtime evening steadily darkened along toward full nightfall.

It was the best time of year on the desert. There was, as yet, no heat, and later, when the hot time of the year arrived, it would not be as sweltering on the north desert that had green fields and trees and blessed water, as it would be on the south desert that had a bare minimum of those blessings. The nights were warm even in early springtime. This time of year, when it lacked only a few weeks of being total summertime, a man could lie out on the ground with only his saddle blanket to cover him, and sleep comfortably.

Dawn came a little earlier each week, it seemed, and dusk was as tardy at arriving upon the other end of the day. When there was a moon, animals continued to graze and people, especially in the sparse few north-desert settlements, neglected to retire early. It was a very fine time of year. On the nights when there was no moon, such as the night those two Big M riders walked their horses silently along the bank of Acequia

Creek, star shine cast adequate, soft light earthward to provide the means for those horsemen to make their way.

In the winter there could be Santa Anna winds that filled the air with sharp particles of sand and mica, or there could be deafening thunderstorms with deluges of rain water. People ventured out less in wintertime. This more benign time of year men arose early to witness the rebirth of the new days. Joe Alvarado had been an early riser all his life. It was the best time of day, he was convinced, for a man to go abroad and it influenced his mood for the balance of the time there was sunshine. It also tended to influence his feeling toward other living things. No man, he had said in the past, who first saw the works of his Maker at dawn before other men appeared to soil things, or to destroy them, could possibly begin his day doing wrong.

Maybe Joe was right. He walked up through the dew-damp grass under the drowsy gaze of his animals heading for the slightly elevated, broad shoulder of Acequia Creek to check his flow of water and to make changes in his irrigation settings. When he got up there in the pearly, cool dawn light and saw his empty bleeder ditches—for the first time in his entire memory without flowing water in them—he was stunned into immobility.

He strolled along the broad bank in among the willows, where disturbed birds in the upper limbs drowsily complained, looking at one outlet after the other. They were all filled in. Not just roughly shoveled full, but carefully and laboriously tamped full of earth. There was no way for water to leave the ditch and reach his fields. It was the first time he had ever seen this. He leaned upon his shovel and looked left and right along the full, visible distance of the creek where water flowed silently and with a steely quality right on past his outlets heading toward Big M's irrigated big fields on eastward.

When the light improved a little, Joe Alvarado read the sign

19

of shod horse marks where two booted men had ridden along, dismounting at each of his outlets to work very diligently at filling them in completely. It had been no accident, of course. No one made accidents of this magnitude.

He stood a long while forgetting that he had not eaten, that he had come forth to become part of God's fresh new dawn, forgetting that in all his life he had never seen anything like this before. All he thought of was that the man behind this was ruthless, was clearly going to dry up Alvarado's fields, starve his livestock, destroy him personally, and do it all for no real reason. He knew exactly who that man was. He had been told before, over the years, that sooner or later Grant Mitchell would move to gobble up the Alvarado land exactly as he had gobbled up other land. It was not that Joe had disbelieved this; it was simply that he did not see why Mitchell would need the Alvarado pasture, which was infinitesimal in comparison to the land Grant Mitchell already owned or controlled.

Now, it made him feel miserable to come to the conclusion that Grant Mitchell's reason for starting his campaign against Joe Alvarado was nothing better than greed. There was no other reason. They had never been enemies. They had never been friends, either, but they certainly had never been actual enemies. It was easier to understand a man's motive if he were antagonistic or if he had even avowedly hostile feelings, but this was different. Grant Mitchell and Joe Alvarado had never exchanged a single word in anger. They had attended school together many years earlier, as children, and they had been cowboys together in their yeasty teens and early twenties.

Mitchell had appeared in a new black suit at the funeral of Joe Alvarado's wife. He had sent gifts, earlier, when Joe's children had been born, and, although Mitchell had never married himself, he had once said to Joe out front of the marshal's office in Sangerville that, if he ever saw another woman like

Joe's wife, he would marry.

Finally, with the sun coming, Joe turned and looked in the direction of Big M. Of course, those nocturnal riders were no longer visible. They had come and gone in total stealth. Joe leaned a long while upon his shovel, then he started back without making a single attempt to dig out any of the blocked outlets. The fields could survive for a week or so without wilting. He always did that kind of a watering job.

He had a few days to work something out. Breakfast did not taste good this morning and the magnificent golden sun, when it finally arose above the faraway flat edge of the earth, lacked its usual appeal. Joe drank some chocolate, smoked a brown-paper cigarette, fed the animals that were close by, in the adobe barn, then he stood in the center of his yard goading himself to get dressed for the ride over to town to the marshal's office. He did not want to go over there. He did not like to make complaints. He also happened to know that, now, there was no other course open to him. If he rode to Big M, either Grant Mitchell would not see him at all, or, if he did consent to see him, Grant would not relent. This much he was sure of—Grant Mitchell would not relent and the fact that they had known each other all their lives would not mean a thing.

III

Town Marshal Greg Hudson listened to everything Joe Alvarado had to say, then arose to draw off two cups of coffee at the little rickety table across the jailhouse office near the wood stove. Marshal Hudson was a man of average height but as thick through as an oak tree. He was half Joe's age, and, when he returned to hand over one of the coffee cups, he said: "Did you talk to Mister Mitchell? Maybe it wasn't any of his men did that, Joe."

Alvarado looked askance. "Who, then? Who would ride along

the ditch in the night with a shovel . . . two of them . . . to work so hard at filling in water outlets?"

Hudson shrugged massive shoulders. "I've got no idea, but it didn't have to be Big M riders."

Joe sipped the bitter black coffee while solemnly studying the racked-up rifles, carbines, and shotguns across the room. As he lowered the cup and swung his attention back to the younger, thicker man, he half smiled. "Greg, I know what happened. I think I know why it happened. I don't want to think about something like that happening. All I want is for the law to uphold me in what is right."

Hudson nodded slowly. "Sure, Joe. That's the purpose of the law." Hudson looked down into the coffee cup. "You got a legal paper on your water right from the creek?" Hudson did not lift his face.

Joe sat gazing across at the younger man. A sinking feeling assailed him. After a moment he said: "What legal paper? All my life my land has been irrigated from Acequia Creek. All the life of my father and grandfather."

Marshal Hudson raised his eyes. "Yeah, I understand. All I'm saying is that for me to ride out and tell someone to quit meddling with your turnouts, I've got to have a legal document."

They exchanged a long look. Joe said: "There is no such paper, Greg. No one on the creek ever had such a paper."

The marshal leaned back. "Mister Mitchell's got such a paper, Joe. He's got a fistful of 'em from each piece of land he's acquired that lies below the ditch. That's how folks know who is entitled to water from the creek, and how much they're entitled to."

Joe leaned to set aside the half empty cup. "I have never seen any such paper," he averred. "I've never even heard of such a paper."

Marshal Hudson was unrelenting. "Joe, if folks using water

from the creek don't use it during the season, there is a rule that says they forfeit their right ever to take water from the creek again. Did you know that?"

Alvarado hadn't known it, had not in fact ever heard of such a thing, and, as he sat now staring at the law officer, his earlier sinking sensation returned. They had closed his outlets for this purpose. He did not know this. He was not even sure which of Mitchell's range men had filled in his outlets. In fact, if he had been called upon to prove the allegation that Grant Mitchell had anything to do with his blocked-off water outlets, he could not even have done that. A man who has lived most of his life among animals develops the same kind of sixth sense, instinctive warning capability. He did know. He could not prove it, but he did know. Now, sitting in the cool old adobe jailhouse gazing across the room at the burly lawman behind his table, Joe Alvarado also knew something else.

He arose, feeling as old in every joint as he really was. "Do you remember, before your parents died, and your father would bring you out to my house, Greg . . . we used to saddle horses and go riding together? I taught you things."

Hudson squirmed slightly, then arose. His heavy features, though, were unrelenting. "Joe, just find your paper. If you'll fetch that back here to me, I'll try and find out who's messing around your turnouts and. . . ."

"No you won't," retorted old Alvarado, pulling himself up erectly at the door. "I stand here and look over there at you. . . ." Joe slumped slightly, then turned and walked out of the office without completing his remark.

Marshal Hudson gazed a long while at the closed roadside door, then took his cup back to the stove for more coffee. His face was closed down in an expression of unrelenting doggedness.

Joe crossed to Merrill's general store, bought some tobacco, and went over to the tie rack out front of the jailhouse to step aboard the handsome colt he had ridden to town. The horses of Alvarado had been legendary in all the north-desert cow camps and communities for seventy-five years and this black colt was no exception. There were two range riders leaning over there, admiring him. When Joe turned the colt and stepped up, one of those cowboys called to say: "Hey, *viejo*, you want to sell that horse?"

Joe forced a smile when he replied. "No. Maybe someday, but not now."

The other cowboy grinned boldly. "You may change your mind in a couple of weeks, when your grass dies and there's nothing for that horse or any of your other livestock to eat."

The office door behind those two range men opened. Marshal Hudson stepped through, looking furious. Without warning he lunged for the pair of riders. One of them saw him in time and sprang clear, but the second man was still taunting Joe Alvarado when Hudson's powerful fist closed over his shoulder and heaved the man with tremendous force off the boardwalk. He fell in a heap in the roadway. Dust burst up from where he fell.

Marshal Hudson stood poised to launch himself a second time. He said: "Get your horses and get out of town! Don't let me see either one of you back here!"

The man in the dirt got splotchy red in the face. As he rolled to arise, his right hand moved, but his partner caught that arm and spun the cowboy half away in the direction of the opposite sidewalk. He herded his partner with curses and pushes.

Joe Alvarado sat in the saddle ignoring the pair of riders and concentrating upon Greg Hudson. "What was so wrong?" he finally asked in a soft tone of voice. "They simply asked if this colt was for sale."

Hudson, still venomously glaring up where the range men were beating off dust as they headed for the saloon, did not

24

answer for a while. When he turned, eventually, to face Alvarado, he gestured. "Go on home, Joe. It wasn't so much what they said. I heard 'em through the front window. It was how they said it . . . 'Hey, old man, you want to sell your horse?' What kind of manners are those?"

Joe continued to gaze thoughtfully at the lawman for a moment, then turned without another word and headed for home. Men who lie should be much younger. Older men did not make believable liars unless they had been lying all their previous lives, and Greg Hudson hadn't been.

Greg knew who had filled in Joe's outlets. So did Joe know the answer to that—now. He had just met them out front of the jailhouse office. They were unknown to him by name, but he knew the brand on the horses they rode and he had seen them before. They worked for Grant Mitchell.

It was no surprise who they rode for. The surprise was how violently Marshal Hudson had reacted to those range men revealing themselves, their knowledge of the outlets and their cow-outfit affiliation. Greg had been furious. Why? Because he knew as much as those slack-mouthed cowboys also knew?

Grant Mitchell was a man of considerable power and influence, and, if that would not be enough to sway Marshal Hudson, Grant was also a very wealthy man. One way or another, he had managed to put Greg Hudson and the law of Sangerville in his pocket.

Disappointments were nothing new in the life of Joe Alvarado, not even when they were of such magnitude as this latest one, but they hurt him; they saddened him and made him melancholy.

He put up his colt at home and draped his saddle from the wall peg by one stirrup, then he rolled and lit a cigarette from the fresh sack of Durham he had bought at Merrill's store, and sank down upon the bench out front of the ancient adobe barn in the utterly still and silent air of mid-morning. There had been a time when he could have dug out those outlets in a couple of days. Well, a man ages, and, although he can still accomplish the same things, some of them anyway, it takes longer.

He went to his shed and honed the edge of his shovel at the grinding wheel, then, with mid-afternoon arriving as he trudged northward through the lush grass and beyond tree shade, he doggedly went out to the first water tap that fortunately, because it was hot in the afternoon, was in the shade of creek willows. The men who had filled in the tap must have been young and strong. It would require two days for Joe to re-open it. He began digging, and, when some aggravated birds in the treetops complained at this intrusion, he told them tartly that he would be here for at least two days, and, if that interfered with their family raising or their bug hunting, they were just going to have to live with it.

Joe was a wiry man, sparse and sinewy and as tough as old rawhide. Also, being desert bred, he knew how to pace himself at anything he did. He did not work fast; he just simply did not stop working. It took a lot of time to get even a third of the obstructing dirt out of the tap. The sun was dropping away and reddening by the time he stopped to lean upon his shovel and gaze off in the direction of Mitchell's Big M cow outfit. He was not tired because he had not worked fast, had rested often, and had made a satisfactory slow and steady progress. But he was beginning to turn resentful.

Finally, hungry and with chores to do, he stopped work and hiked back to his barn where he sluiced off at an ancient stone trough out back, then fulfilled the obligations every livestock man has in the vicinity of his barn, did all his menial, little time-consuming chores.

Dusk was coming, the land was cooling off, and there was a noticeable fragrance in the evening air arising from creosote

26

bush and all the other varieties of desert undergrowth, when a horse out back of the barn nickered. Joe straightened up to turn. It was too late; they were already entering the yard from the northeast. He recognized them at once. The pair of range men Marshal Hudson had lit into down in Sangerville.

Joe shuffled to the doorless, wide opening of his barn, and leaned there on a long-handled fork. The horsemen saw him but did not make a sound or pick up the slow gait of their horses. They never took their eyes off him, though, and, when they were in front of the barn tie rack, they dismounted, still wordlessly, looped their reins, then stood a moment removing their ropers' gloves and looking around.

Joe said—"I still don't want to sell that colt."—and smiled.

They came around the tie rack from opposite ends and one of them looked pleased about something but they still said nothing.

Joe straightened up, tightened his grip on the manure fork, and waited. He did not wear a gun. He hadn't worn a gun and bullet belt in thirty years, but both of those range riders were armed, and both had their holsters tied down. Joe eased his weight off the pitchfork. "Whatever you want," he said, no longer pretending to be friendly, "you say it right now." He raised the tines of the fork.

The range man halted, eyed old Joe, eyed the poised manure fork, then one of them finally spoke: "Put down the damned fork, you old bastard."

Instead of obeying, Joe took a forward step, raising those five tines as he did so, holding his weapon as though it were a lance or a javelin.

One of the range men licked his lips and looked quickly at his companion. Evidently he did not like facing steel tines.

The other rider methodically drew his Colt and cocked it. "Put down the pitchfork, you old son-of-a-bitch," he said to Joe

Alvarado. "We owe you for gettin' us into trouble with the law in town today. We come to pay you in full. I said put down the damned fork!"

The cowboy tipped up his six-gun and squeezed the trigger. Joe was incredulous even before the bullet hit him with stunning force, half knocking the wind from his chest. He did not believe it, could not believe these range riders would shoot him over something he had had nothing to do with. He felt the blazing, sudden eruption of heat inside his body somewhere, felt his legs turning loose, and he even saw the ground coming up, but he did not feel its hardness when his body struck it and rolled. Nor did he hear one of the range men say: "For Christ's sake, what did you do that for?"

IV

As a nurse Leona Gomez had the best possible qualifications. She had been caring for injured people ever since the death of her husband fifteen years earlier. She had also successfully raised three exceptionally handsome daughters, and had got them all married before there was any trouble. She was forty or more, was not very tall but was abundantly female, and solidly strong and hefty. When they came for her to go out to the Alvarado place, it was her second time out there. Four years earlier when Joe had broken a leg riding a green colt, she had gone out, but that time all she'd had to do was cook his meals and scold a man of his age who had no better sense than to ride green colts.

This time she was bitterly silent as she took over and went to work. When she was cleaning up the kitchen and Town Marshal Hudson strolled out for coffee, she got him a cupful and handed it to him accompanied by a reproachful look. He saw the look and turned defensive.

"They heard the gunshot down in town. That's all I know, Leona. Several people told me, so I came out here and found him. Leona, I can't manufacture the gunman. All I know is that Joe got shot in the chest and by rights, according to Doctor Ward, he should have died." Hudson sipped coffee for a moment and stood in the doorway, gazing out a shiny window. "There were two of them."

Leona Gomez turned back to scrubbing the old iron stove and speaking bitterly as she did so. "Why? For his money? He had none and everyone knew it. Did they steal one of his horses, then, *jefe*, maybe some of his sheep or cattle?"

Greg scowled. She was baiting him. She was being bitterly sarcastic. He finished the coffee and slammed down the cup, then turned and went back across the parlor where Dr. Arthur Ward was just emerging from a quiet coolly shadowed bedroom on the far side of the house. Marshal Hudson said: "Well . . . ?"

Dr. Ward was young and slight of build with very dark eyes and hair that was already receding and turning thin. This was his first practice after medical school and he was very wary about committing himself, so he ignored the lawman to walk farther into the parlor and place his black satchel upon a little table, then fondle his gold watch chain as he slowly spoke, his back to the town marshal.

"At that range, a Forty-Five usually tears a hole in human flesh you can push your fist through. This time, the old man had a big, old watch in his shirt pocket. The bullet was miraculously deflected. Even so, the shock must have been monumental, like being struck head-on with a sledge-hammer."

"Will he live or die?" asked Hudson.

Dr. Ward went right on recapitulating as though he had heard nothing. "The damage was extensive, even though the watch undoubtedly turned aside the major force of the gunshot. The old man's breastbone is cracked. He also has a couple of broken ribs, and, where the bullet actually penetrated, he has a gory wound in the side. He lost a lot of blood before he was found.

He might even have bled to death if you hadn't got right out here, Marshal."

Hudson strolled closer. "Doctor, just tell me . . . will the old man die?"

Arthur Ward turned. "I doubt it, Marshal, but he certainly will be unable to leave his bed for a long time. Even if he were younger, he wouldn't be able to leave his bed for perhaps three or four weeks."

Greg Hudson faced halfway from the doctor and remained gazing at the closed sick room door until Arthur Ward picked up his satchel and muttered something about walking back to town, then Marshal Hudson roused himself from his reverie and turned also to depart. He looked more troubled over the shooting than relieved over the probability that Joe Alvarado would survive.

It was not an especially long walk from the Alvarado place back to the center of town, and, when a man had something on his mind—on his conscience, actually—the distance seemed a lot less than it was. Marshal Hudson and Dr. Ward talked as they walked. When they had exhausted the physician's involvement, they turned upon the lawman's responsibility, with Arthur Ward saying: "Back East, Marshal, where I come from, every city has its force of detectives. Murderers ordinarily do not escape."

Hudson looked up, reddening. "Who said this was a case of murder, Doctor?"

Ward was not cowed. "All right. Attempted murder. The old man was not armed."

"Who told you that?"

"He did. In his one, very brief moment of lucidity."

Greg Hudson stared. "What else did he tell you?"

"Nothing," answered the medical practitioner. "Just that they were armed and he was not." Ward raised dark eyes. "But I'm sure he'll be rational enough for you to talk to within a day or two. About that woman named Gomez . . . ?"

Hudson muttered his response: "She's a local nurse. Folks have been using her since before I was around here."

Ward accepted this. "It was good of you to think of her because that is exactly what the old man will need from now on, someone to look after him. Does he have any kinsmen?"

Greg Hudson did not answer. They were upon the northernmost section of plank walk when Dr. Ward asked that, and Greg Hudson was already widening his gait to leave the doctor as he headed across in the direction of the saloon where a number of horses were drowsing out front at the tie rack.

Ward shrugged and correctly assumed the lawman's incivility was the result of his concentration on the attempted murder of old José Alvarado.

When Greg entered the saloon, a moon-faced barman with pale eyes and a turned-up nose looked in his direction with frank interest, but Greg did not approach the bar. He veered in the direction of a table where two men were seated with glasses and a bottle, quietly speaking back and forth. He went over, pulled out a chair, sat down, then glared.

"Mister Mitchell, maybe you haven't heard yet, but a couple of riders went into old Alvarado's yard and shot him."

Big M's range boss never allowed his eyes to leave the angry countenance of the lawman as he said: "Did they kill the old bastard?"

Greg glared. "No, they didn't kill him. I just walked back from up there with the doctor. He said Joe'll be able to talk within another day or so."

Grant Mitchell's hard stare showed nothing. "Why tell us?" he asked.

Greg answered curtly: "Because I ran those two troublemakers of yours out of town only a short while before two men rode into Alvarado's yard from the direction of your range, and shot the old man. Now by God . . . !"

"Wait a minute," snapped the cowman. "Just hold your damned horses for a minute, Greg. Don't go flying off the handle at me. Like I told you, the old man's been taking water that don't belong to him. I had a right to send those fellers over there last night to plug his outlets."

"You never said a god-damned thing about shooting anyone!" exclaimed Marshal Hudson.

"No one was supposed to get shot," retorted the wealthy cowman. "But now that the old man's flat on his back, so much the better. He's got to forgo using water from the creek, to make my claim against his water right valid. If he's unable to. . . ."

"Mister Mitchell," stated Greg Hudson, "you're not paying attention. What I'm telling you is that within a day or so, when the old man comes around, he's going to be able to name those men who shot him, or at least describe them."

Cliff Habersham was indifferent to this peril. "What of it?" he growled at Marshal Hudson. "What can he say except that it was a couple of range riders? He don't know who they were by name and he don't know where they work."

"You're damned well wrong on that," replied Hudson, and related the incident of his run-in with those two range riders out front of the jailhouse that early morning. "He not only knew whose ranch they came from, but when that damned idiot made his remark about the old man not having any water for his livestock from now on, old Joe knew who sent them and that they were the men who had plugged his outlets. Listen to me, Cliff, old Alvarado is no fool. Maybe he's just another greaser to you, but I know a damned sight better."

Grant Mitchell looked annoyed. "What are you getting upset about?" he demanded. "What can the old bastard do even if he knows I sent those two riders over there last night, even if he says they are the men who shot him? What can he do about any of it?"

"He can talk, that's what he can do," replied Hudson vehemently, but holding his voice low with effort. "He'll tell all his Mex friends in the lower end of town, and any other folks up along this end of town who'll listen."

Mitchell showed scorn. "What difference will that make? Who pays any attention to what some old pepper belly says? And even if some of his greaser friends believe him, what of it?"

Hudson rolled up his eyes before answering that, then he quietly said: "Mister Mitchell, I'll tell you what of it. Maybe it won't make a bit of difference to you, but it's going to raise hell with my reputation all over town, not just down in Mex town, unless I go after those men and bring them in, and charge them."

Cliff looked thoughtfully at his employer. "We could pay 'em off," he suggested. "They done all they can do around here, anyway. One of them . . . the feller named Hanson . . . is too damned hair-triggered. I've been figuring to let them go."

Mitchell rolled a cigarette as he spoke. "Then pay them off," he instructed his foreman. "I didn't send them over to shoot Joe, anyway. That was a damned stupid thing to do." He lit up and smiled at Greg Hudson. "We'll fire them and they'll leave the country, and that'll take you off the hook. All right now?"

Hudson said—"I guess so."—and rose to depart.

Grant Mitchell's hard gaze raised a little. "You get upset too damned easy," he quietly told the lawman, showing contempt in his face as he said this. "I told you when you took the money from me, there wouldn't be no bad trouble. I keep my word. If I'd known those fools were going to stalk Joe and shoot him, Cliff and I would have intercepted them and done a little shooting of our own. But it's coming out all right. Joe will identify two men who are no longer in the country, and that'll be that."

"Not if he goes around saying you hired those two men, Mister Mitchell," retorted Marshal Hudson. "As far as most folks will be concerned, that pair of saddle tramps won't be the issue anyway. It'll be Big M."

Mitchell waved that away with a gesture of his hand with the cigarette in it. "Let 'em. Let folks say what they please. They been doing that about me for years anyway. Greg, I don't think you'll ever learn it by yourself, so I'll explain something to you. When a man gets to be a success, folks start hating his guts because they got someone right in front of their lousy faces every day to remind them that they're failures, that they aren't smart enough to succeed. So they nit-pick, they try to find things to hate you for. I'm used to it. As for what folks say, they can go to hell. As for Joe Alvarado. . . ." Mitchell flicked ash and turned in the chair to set his broad back to Marshal Hudson and reach for the whiskey bottle while Cliff Habersham also ignored Hudson, and smiled at his employer.

Hudson departed, and, despite the openly inviting smile of several customers up along the bar who were avid for details about the Alvarado shooting, he went out of the saloon into the golden daylight, his mood better suited to nighttime. The shooting may have been unplanned, and in this Marshal Hudson believed Grant Mitchell, but once it had happened, it did not really matter whether it was a deliberate attempt to kill Alvarado or not; what mattered was that the old man was in possession of some facts. He knew who the men were who had tried to kill him, and he knew with whom they had most recently been associated. Whether they were gone or not would make very little difference in the eyes of the people around the countryside who heard that they had worked for Grant Mitchell. It would not make much difference in the eyes of most folks, either, that Sangerville's town marshal had done nothing except arrange for a nurse for Joe Alvarado.

He returned to the jailhouse office, closed the door, and got his bottle of malt whiskey from the lower desk drawer and had himself a stiff, straight jolt. He had done a stupid, inexcusable thing. He had accepted money for the first time in his life to overlook something, and exactly what he had always been told occurred to lawmen who accepted bribes was now occurring: the whole damned thing was coming unraveled.

He had another jolt, then capped the bottle, put it back beneath the oily gun-cleaning rags in the desk drawer, and went to roll a cigarette while he leaned in a window and gazed unhappily out into the roadway. He had learned something else today. A man like Grant Mitchell was powerful and rich enough so that it did not make any difference at all what people thought of him. The people who could not function or survive without respectability were the less important, less wealthy and powerful people like town marshals; they had to have respect or they were ruined.

V

Joe was not just sore in every part of his body and weak from loss of blood, he was also very ill. There was heat and swelling and bad discoloration in his side where the deflected lead slug had torn through the flesh. Leona Gomez changed the bandage, saw the condition of the wound, wordlessly created the fresh dressing, then forced a smile when her eyes met those of Joe Alvarado. In Spanish she said: "Rest in comfort, *patrón*, you will recover." Then in English she turned shrewish: "Why do you have to get into things like this? Why can't you just sit out here in the shade and enjoy life?"

Joe considered her dark and troubled face through a small smile. "Oh, lover of incomparable passion," he said in slurred Spanish, and, when she reared back, dark gaze flashing, his wan, little smile strengthened.

She waited a moment, then laughed, showing beautiful white teeth. "You old fool," she replied. "What do you know of lovers, incomparable or any other kind? What have you done with your widowed years . . . rode horses and nursed old cows with new calves." She snorted. "And now this."

He considered her face. "Who found me, then?"

"Marshal Hudson. He said he heard the gunshot and was told of it also by other people over in town. He rushed out here and got you into the house and bandaged. Then he came for me. Well, *patrón,* who were they?"

"You wouldn't know if I told you," said Joe, and let his eyes drift around until he could see out the north wall window on to his stone-floored and roofed-over patio that ran the full length of the rear of his house. "They came to kill me," he mused, gazing out the window. "It is hard for me to understand that people would do such a thing over just water."

Leona frowned. "Over what? Water? You are out of your head, then."

He turned slightly and sought her face in the shadows of the bedroom. "It was Doctor Ward?"

"Yes."

"And Marshal Hudson?"

"Yes, and several other men." She leaned to smooth his blankets. "I think you should go down to Albuquerque."

That caught his attention at once. "What for? That is a very long distance to go."

"They have very good doctors down there," she retorted, pulling back and primly clasping both hands across her stomach while she put a dark glance upon him. "They even have two places where sick people stay . . . hospitals."

He disagreed. "The trip would be bad. Anyway, I have faith in Doctor Ward."

"He is young," stated Leona Gomez.

Joe smiled at her. "I wish I was." He sighed. "I'm not going to Albuquerque."

She accepted that. There were three reasons for her to accept it. One, he was her senior in years. Two, this was his house. Three, he was a man. So she shrugged round shoulders and pushed some hair off his forehead with a cool palm. He was going to die. She smiled softly, then left the room.

There was a large rosary upon the wall of the parlor near a picture of Our Lady of Guadalupe. Leona went over there on her way to the kitchen and was still standing there when a shadow fell across the wall on her right. She lost her breath for a second before she turned and saw the grave-faced man standing just outside the open front door. He was young; at least he had no gray in his hair when he removed his hat to smile and gently nod at her. He was clad in a dark coat with trousers to match; even his gun belt beneath the coat was black, and his boots. He was a handsome man, in a gray-eyed, lean, and rapacious, hawk-like manner.

In border Spanish he asked to see the *patrón*. Leona said the *patrón* had been badly wounded by an assassin and was presently confined to his bed unable to see anyone. She crossed to the door and leaned there, studying the stranger. When he looked surprised, she told him how Joe had been wounded and saw the abrupt stillness of his steady eyes. He asked a few questions, then bowed to her and walked out where a powerful, dappled horse stood waiting. She watched him mount gracefully and whirl away in the direction of town.

When she had been looking hard for a man like this one for her headstrong daughter, Létriana, where was he? *Humph!* She watched as he jogged across the little distance and entered town from the northwest, coming on to the main thoroughfare as though he had come out of an alleyway over there.

He had come a fair distance this day, but he must have

stopped along the way to beat off the dust and wipe his shiny boots. Even the liveryman who took his horse did not afterward recall anything unusual. For all he knew, he told folks, the man in the black trousers and coat could have ridden in from one of the outlying cow outfits, even though he certainly was not dressed like a range man.

Greg Hudson was sifting through some letters that had arrived on the late-day coach. He was out front of the jailhouse doing this when the stranger strolled up, smiling. Greg knew people. He knew a stranger when he saw one. He also had an instinctive ability to make shrewd guesses about people. He was sizing up the stranger now, when the man extended a bronzed, strong hand and said: "I'm John Gates, Marshal."

Greg spoke his name, pumped the hand, then reached and shoved open the office door, and gestured. As John Gates strolled in, Greg looked again at the bulge of the holstered black Colt on Gates's right thigh. It was a well-cared-for weapon. Cowmen, when they wore guns, usually took them down from a bunkhouse peg and carelessly buckled them on. They rarely cleaned their weapons or in any other way took any better care of their weaponry than they did of their saddlery.

Gates smiled easily. It made him look even younger. It also enhanced the rugged strength in his face and the stone-steady expression of full confidence in his eyes.

Greg went to the stove, tossing aside the letters as he passed the desk. "Coffee?" he asked.

Gates was agreeable. "Sounds like a good idea, Marshal."

As he worked at the stove with his back to the stranger, Greg asked an inevitable question. "Staying long in Sangerville, Mister Gates?"

The stranger strolled closer to the stove to accept the cup as he replied: "I doubt it, Marshal. I'm on my way out to California. To San Francisco."

Hudson was nodding his head as he turned. He had guessed John Gates to be a gambler. Mentioning San Francisco, the gambling capital of the West, confirmed this opinion.

Greg went to his table and sat down, then gestured for the lean, gray-eyed man to do the same. As Gates seated himself, he said: "So you had a near killing here in Sangerville." He hoisted the cup and drank a little of its contents, watching Greg over the cup's chipped rim. As he lowered the cup, his smile returned, easily and warmly. "Those things happen. It was an old man, wasn't it?"

Greg sighed to himself, and cursed the thought of the liveryman. "Yeah, an old man named Alvarado. I guess he antagonized a couple of range riders and they stalked him."

"How bad is he, Marshal?"

"Bad enough, but he had an old watch in his shirt pocket which deflected the bullet. He's not young, and even so the bullet tore up his side some."

Gates looked concerned. "And those men who shot him?"

Greg made a careless gesture. "Gone. Rode out right afterward."

"Range men, Marshal?"

Greg tasted the coffee as he nodded his head. He was lowering the cup when John Gates asked his next question, and now it suddenly dawned upon Marshal Hudson this stranger was not idly asking questions.

Gates said: "Who did those range men work for, Marshal?"

Hudson's gaze hardened toward the stranger. He was slow to answer, and, when he finally spoke, he offered no answer. He said: "For a feller who's got no interest, you're asking an awful lot of questions, Mister Gates."

The man in the dark clothing continued to look directly at Greg and to smile. He answered, eventually, in a disarming manner. "Well, a few years ago I was a deputy sheriff in northern

Arizona. A man keeps up his interest in the law, Marshal."

Greg Hudson softened a little. "Well, that'd make a differ-ence for a fact, Mister Gates." He softened a little more. "They were a pair of troublemakers, those damned range riders. They hired on with Grant Mitchell, the biggest cowman in these parts, early this spring."

Gates looked perplexed and leaned to set aside his empty cup. "Two range men against one old man who lived by himself out a ways? Maybe they had heard the old man had a cache on the ranch. Something like that. Maybe they meant to rob him, then kill him. Was the old man armed?"

Greg was tiring of this discussion. "No. I can't recall ever seeing old Alvarado carry a weapon, and I've known him since I first come to this place . . . maybe those men figured to rob him. Anyway, they're gone."

John Gates arose, hoisted his gun belt to resettle it, and kept smiling as he said: "Who has gone after them, Marshal?"

This, to Greg Hudson, was too much. As he also arose, he snapped his answer: "No one's gone after them, Mister Gates, and no one is going to go after them. I've worked up descrip-tions and forwarded them to have Wanted posters made. Otherwise, since the victim didn't die, it's attempted murder, and out here we don't kill horses trying to ride down men who have a hell of a big head start when the shot feller is recover-ing."

Gates opened the door, gazed pensively at Greg Hudson, then said: "All right, Marshal, it's your bailiwick." He closed the door and walked back across the road in the direction of the general store.

Something began troubling Greg Hudson. He could not define it; nevertheless it was a solid, weighty sensation behind his belt. He told himself Grant Mitchell had been correct; he worried too much and got upset too easily. He went over to the desk to riffle through for his bottle and get a long pull from it, when Hubert Townley, the stage company's Sangerville agent, walked in.

Greg straightened around a trifle guiltily and closed the desk drawer as he did so. Hubert was a bear-like man; he was about average in height but he was massively thick and slow-moving as a result of his vast powerful heaviness. It did not alleviate the impression he gave of a bear that he wore a full beard and his forehead looked to be no more than two inches wide, and there was more russet hair above it, sticking down from beneath his hat.

Greg peered, then said: "Someone stole horses out of your pasture?"

The stage company man shook his head. "Nope. Care to guess again? No? Well, I wondered if you'd seen a sort of tall feller dressed in black, good-looking man who wears a black shell belt and holster."

Greg had seen such a man. "Yeah. He just walked out of here. How did you not see him? He crossed to the general store."

Hubert Townley turned and grasped the latch as though he meant to rip the door from its casing.

Greg suddenly moved toward the front of the desk. "Hey, that man's name is Gates. John Gates. What do you want him for, Hubert?"

"There was a message for him on the late stage. It give his name, like you just said it, but it also give a description of him."

Greg held out his hand. "Let me see the letter."

Hubert stood balefully looking back from the open doorway. "What for? You ain't him." He pulled away and slammed the door.

Greg stepped to the window and saw him go rolling across in the direction of the general store. He would not have opened the letter but he would certainly have examined the outside of it very carefully. Not that he had misgivings, but that worried sensation was still troubling him a little. He could crystallize part of it: he did not trust John Gates. He had no feelings toward him otherwise; it had nothing to do with like or dislike; it was simply distrust.

The more he thought about all those questions the deeper that distrust became, and eventually, when he got that double swallow from the malt whiskey bottle from his desk drawer, he decided to look up John Gates and engage him in a fresh conversation to see if there was anything really worthwhile to be learned from Gates about himself.

VI

Old Pitts, the livery barn hostler, said he had seen that good-looking tall man dressed in black go past on his way down to Mex town, but when Greg Hudson got down there and talked to Gutierrez, the fat man who operated Mex town's *cantina*, he lost track of Gates. Gutierrez simply spread his hands, looking innocent, and none of the other men at the Mex saloon showed anything on their faces, either. They had no knowledge of a Señor Gates, for which they profusely apologized, and, as Marshal Hudson trudged back up toward the center of town, he got the same feeling he usually got after being in Mex town. He had been lied to. He had at least in part been lied to.

The men at the *cantina* had seen Gates. He had poked in his head and had asked one question in good Spanish: who in the *barrio* had been a friend of José Alvarado? Gutierrez had not answered Gates, but an older man had, who had been sitting near the door with a glass of thin wine, and John Gates had withdrawn. That was the extent of his visit to the *cantina*. They had seen him, but that was all.

Hudson went up to the harness shop and stood inside, facing the roadway window, watching people pass outside across the roadway, feeling uncomfortable. The harness maker was an old friend, but today they said little to one another and ultimately Hudson went along to the saloon.

Gates was there, leaning loosely upon the bar, listening to the bartender give his version of the various stories he had heard thus far about the shooting of old Joe Alvarado.

Marshal Hudson walked over, growled for beer, and twisted to face John Gates. "For a man who is a stranger hereabouts," he said bluntly, "you got a big interest in what's just happened around here, haven't you?"

Gates met Greg's stare with that soft smile of his. "I told you, Marshal, I used to be a deputy sheriff. I'm interested in things like shootings." He turned back to watch the barman deliver Greg's glass, then he faced half around again as the barman walked away. "What you told me at the jailhouse was just part of it, Marshal. Those men who tried to kill the old man . . . they worked for Mitchell, and Mitchell was after the old man's water rights."

Greg tasted the beer. It was tepid, as always. He put down the glass. "I'll give you some advice, Mister Gates. Since you're just passing through anyway, you'd do yourself a favor not to be so nosey. Folks hereabouts are friendly and helpful and all, but they don't take kindly to nosey strangers."

Gates chuckled. "I don't expect they do," he averred. "I don't blame 'em."

Greg picked up his glass and drained it. He heard the bartender say something about Big M, then the man ducked and rummaged below the bar for a bottle of private whiskey, and set it up. He saw it was Grant Mitchell and Cliff Habersham up the bar and wished they hadn't arrived right at the moment he was involved with John Gates. He hadn't said quite all that was on his mind yet. "Mister Gates, are you figuring on riding out this evening or in the morning?"

Gates looked back at Marshal Hudson, his gaze quizzical. He knew exactly what had just been said to him; he had not been asked a question; he had been delivered an ultimatum. "Maybe neither, Marshal, maybe neither." Gates straightened off the bar. "You know, I heard some talk a little while ago about why Alvarado got shot. Care to hear it? I heard he was shot because that man up the bar yonder, the older man, had filed on old Alvarado's water rights and wanted Alvarado cleaned out so's he could also get the old man's irrigated land."

Greg swore: "God-damned Mexicans down at the *cantina*."

Gates shook his head. "You're wrong, Marshal. You see that barman yonder? He's the one who told me that, just about the time you walked in." Gates studied Hudson's bleak profile for a moment before saying more. "You're a good officer, Marshal. You don't find many town marshals who track newcomers to their town to the *cantinas* and other places they visit." His easy smile was up again; it was always genuine-appearing and disarming. It was, in fact, a very nice smile, as Leona Gomez had noticed, and had reported to Joe Alvarado when she had described Joe's caller who she had sent away.

Greg Hudson finished his beer. He had not learned more about John Gates, but he had learned enough of the man's probable intentions to make him worry more. He also stood there having a bad premonition. Perhaps it was inevitable that some kind of rumor began circulating about the reason for Joe Alvarado's shooting. What bothered him most was how that rumor had come so close to the truth.

Then Gates made another remark. He said: "I also was told some Mexicans from the lower end of town were figuring to go up there to the creek out back of the Alvarado place tonight and dig out those closed outlets so's the old man's water right will still be in force."

Gates turned on his heel without another glance at anyone,

and strolled from the saloon. He went down to the livery barn to look in on his horse, and down there, finally, Hubert Townley caught up with him and tendered the letter that had come in on the stage. As he did this, Hubert said: "Now that's what I call knowing when to catch a man, mister. You didn't even arrive here on one of our stages, but, the same blessed day, this here letter comes for you. That's sort of like someone knew exactly when you'd be here, ain't it?"

John Gates laughed and handed over half a cartwheel and made a friend out of massive, bear-like Hubert Townley with his smile and his agreeable assent to Hubert's statement. Then Gates strolled toward the rear of the livery barn runway to get into the sunlight before opening and reading his letter.

Afterward, he and the day man sat on a bench out front of the harness room and squandered almost a full hour in conversation. Liverymen were just as liable to have good gossip as barbers or saloon men. In this instance the liveryman was likely to be better informed because John Gates was not as interested in local gossip as he was in local people, and the day man had been in the Sangerville country almost his entire life. He had only one pet peeve: Mexicans. He did not like them, not even their womenfolk who, while they were young at least, were some of the most completely handsome females on earth.

Later, when the slack time arrived in mid-afternoon, before the evening trade showed up and long after the morning trade had come and gone, the livery barn hostler scuttled to the saloon for a little loafing in the cool, gloomy, old building, and a few drinks. He was not, like most day men, an alcoholic. He just liked a couple of shots in the afternoon to help him keep his good-naturedness until quitting time. After all, he was sixty years old. Men of that age couldn't just keep right on going at top speed all day long the way they once had. His employer had once told him that this was how men became habitual drunks, by nipping a little each afternoon, until eventually they had to have more than just a nip. The day man had gone in worried exasperation to Dr. Ward and had been enormously relieved to be told that it took about fifteen years for a body to become a genuine alcoholic, and, hell, since he was now sixty, the chances of him living long enough to become a social pariah were damned slim.

Up at the saloon he saw Grant Mitchell, his range boss, Cliff Habersham, and Town Marshal Greg Hudson in heated conversation at a table near the far end of the room. Greg looked to be most upset.

There was a little rumor around town that the men who had shot old José Alvarado had perhaps worked for Big M, and that inclined the livery barn hostler to be sympathetic toward the lawman. Grant Mitchell would be a very bad man to tangle with. The hostler threw off his first shot and waited a moment until he began feeling better all over, then called for the second jolt with a grin and a mellow glance.

For John Gates it was a pleasant afternoon exactly as it had been a pleasant morning. Sangerville was not San Francisco, but almost any town was better than being in the saddle day after day. Gates was perfectly content to eat at the hole-in-the-wall café next to the general store, shoot a little pool at the billiard room opposite the gun shop, and engage in friendly conversation with just about anyone around town who was in a mood to sit and talk a little with a stranger.

Gates was one of those men other men instinctively felt comfortable with. He looked perfectly capable of handling himself well in just about any situation. He was clearly a capable fighting man, and yet he also smiled easily and spoke softly, along with a little humor. Other men felt honored for someone like this to approach them; he was a man who would be given respect by the most high and powerful men, which meant that men who were neither high nor powerful were flattered when he chose to sit and listen to them, as he did with the proprietor of the pool room, acquiring local knowledge, a little local history, and a lot of local gossip.

He strolled the roadway until mid-afternoon, visiting the harness works, the gun shop, and down at the lower end of town the blacksmith's forge. He made a number of acquaintances and a few friends, the difference being that among most men there was a distinct reserve toward strangers. It was the Mexicans at the lower end of Sangerville, over behind town on the east side, who lacked that reserve and over there John Gates was able to make friends rather than just acquaintances.

Greg Hudson spoke to the saddle maker just before suppertime, and was told that Gates was a hell of a man; he heard something pretty much like that from the livery barn hostler, too, and over at the stage company's corral yard Hubert wagged his head, looking brightly appreciative.

"Mighty nice feller, Marshal. Considerate of folks. I finally give him that letter and you'd have figured I'd handed him a sackful of greenbacks he was that appreciative. Now, that's the kind of a man folks cotton to."

Hudson stifled a retort and asked a question. "What did he talk about, Hubert?"

"The roads, mostly. Condition of the roads. He's a man as knows what a feller's up to who works for a stage company. The condition of the roads hereabouts is a damned scandal and everyone knows it."

Greg went down to his office and felt the stove to see if it was still hot enough to warrant firing up the coals to make a pot of coffee. It was as lukewarm as a schoolmarm's kiss. He rolled a smoke instead, then went to the barred front wall window nearest his desk, and leaned there gazing out into the settling late afternoon. He never should have weakened, never should have gone along with Grant Mitchell. Somehow or other, this whole damned mess was spreading and growing, like an ink stain. Why it would do this he had no idea, but he could feel within himself the gradually increasing fear that eventually his part would be exposed.

He had argued hard with Mitchell and Habersham, and they had not been the least bit influenced by his urgings that nothing more be done to harass Joe Alvarado. He had warned them that even this stranger named Gates had found out enough to make it look suspiciously as though Big M had deliberately tried to get old Joe assassinated. For all his efforts all he had got from Grant Mitchell had been about what he had got from him that other time he had tried to protest—nothing—just a look of scorn and an airy gesture that no one could do a thing to hurt Mitchell, or whatever scheme Mitchell might have in progress. Maybe that was quite true, but Greg Hudson's worry was not over Grant Mitchell; it was over Greg Hudson, and if people got mad enough—enough of them—and got fired up enough over the loose talk that was going around, there was an excellent chance they wouldn't go after Mitchell—at least not until they had tried their fangs on the town marshal.

He dropped the cigarette, stamped on it, went down into his little separate cell room to look around, making certain the place was empty—sometimes bums slipped into a cell and slept there at night—then he returned to the front office.

Out front, several range men rode past in laughing conversation. They were outward bound from town heading for the south range. He looked indifferently but did not recognize any of them. This time of year there were more strange range riders in the country than there would be at any other time of the year. They came in with the departing blasts of winter, hired on, remained throughout the riding season, and just about the time folks around the countryside were getting to recognize them, and know them, the first frost arrived, the first wind blew down red and golden leaves, and the range men drew their time and headed south for the winter.

VII

For Arthur Ward the walk out to Alvarado's place was briskly refreshing. He owned a fine top buggy and a nice big brown mare he called Daisy, but if it were possible to do so, Dr. Ward walked. He believed in the healthiness of brisk walking. Sometimes he seemed to be the only person in the entire territory who did believe in this. He would walk, and everyone else seemed to try as hard as they could not to walk.

When he arrived shortly before suppertime at the Alvarado place, he discovered that someone else had walked out from town. He was introduced to the handsome, tall, smiling man in black and liked John Gates instantly.

Leona Gomez also obviously liked the quiet man attired in black who had been sitting in the sick room for an hour before Dr. Ward arrived, softly speaking to José Alvarado.

When Gates offered to leave the room, Dr. Ward smiled. "No need. My visits are pretty much routine." He went to work cutting away the bandaging and leaning to examine Alvarado in the poor lamplight. Gates arose, picked up the lamp, and held it closer. Ward murmured—"Thanks."—and leaned over to probe the draining side of his patient. He said no more to anyone until he had redressed the injury, had completed his examination of the older man, and had looked up in appreciation when Leona Gomez appeared with three cups of hot chocolate—her own private remedy for every ailment.

Dr. Ward eyed Joe in the bed. "How do you feel?" he asked.

Alvarado, not as weak as he had been, winked at John Gates. "How do I feel? Doctor, I feel like a man who has been shot and nearly killed. But I also feel as though I am still alive." He allowed Leona to push a pillow behind him and winced only once, then he smiled at her, and she smiled back from the doorway on her way to another part of the house.

Dr. Ward liked chocolate. It was very relaxing this time of evening. He got comfortable, shoved out his legs, and gazed with frank interest at John Gates. "I don't believe I've seen you around town before," he said, and grinned disarmingly.

"I'm new around Sangerville," Gates confessed. "I was here just once before . . . when I was eight years old. I don't remember much from that trip."

Ward sipped more chocolate and turned back to gazing at the old man in the bed. "Joe," he said quietly, "there are rumors all over town concerning those men who shot you."

Alvarado flicked a gray look to John Gates, then said: "The light was very poor, Doctor, but, most of all, I didn't look at them very good because I didn't expect anything to happen. They were strangers. I thought perhaps they were trying to find the town, were lost."

Arthur Ward listened, wrinkled his forehead, and looked steadily at old Alvarado. "You didn't know them?"

Joe shook his head and handed Gates his empty cup. "No, Doctor. I would not know them if they walked into this room right now."

Ward pondered that briefly, then looked relieved. "Good, because I have a hunch that, if they thought otherwise, they might return." He smiled at the old man. "My interest in people is to keep them on their feet as long as I can. It would be hard to do in your case if those men returned. Next time, you wouldn't have a pocket watch to save you."

John Gates spoke up. "Doctor, was there anything unusual about the wound?"

Ward looked perplexed. "Unusual, Mister Gates?"

"Bullet caliber, Doctor, angled to indicate a left- or right-handed gunman?"

Arthur Ward's eyes twinkled. "Mister Gates, it was just a bloody mess. Gunshots all tend to look very much alike. The only difference is that some of them are in living people and some are in dead people. No, I can't say anything about the gunman from what I saw." Ward studied John Gates a moment before also adding: "If Joe can't identify them, I'm sure I can't help, either. Why are you interested?"

"Curious," stated John Gates. "It's natural, I think, for folks to be curious about gunshot wounds. And there is something else. The marshal isn't doing anything."

Dr. Ward nodded. "What can he do? If no one knows who those killers were, no one can identify them. What could the marshal possibly do?"

"Track them," said John Gates. "Send messages in all directions for other lawmen to be alert to those two arriving in their territory . . . and most common of all, Doctor, would be for the town marshal to make up a posse and go do a little manhunting."

Arthur Ward looked back at Joe. He seemed to be wondering what this stranger was doing here at all. "Marshal Hudson is a good lawman," he stated a trifle stiffly.

Alvarado looked a little abashedly back at the doctor from his bed. "I don't know," he murmured. "I can't say."

Dr. Ward looked astonished. "You can't say? Joe, you know perfectly well who brought you in here from the barn and tied off the bleeding, then came running for me. He saved your life."

Alvarado acknowledged his debt. "Doctor, the first face I saw belonged to Greg Hudson. He saved my life, which is true. But he was out here when he should have been riding with a posse."

Ward arose and flapped his arms. "Gentlemen, you are cynics. You are talking about a man who did the right things after Joe was found shot in the barn doorway. You are acting as though Marshal Hudson had a hand in the shooting, and of course that's absurd."

Gates agreed as he arose. "Sure is, Doctor. Almost as absurd as Joe Alvarado being shot in the first place." Gates was smiling as he and the doctor faced one another at the foot of the bed. "I wasn't trying to harm your town peace officer, Doctor, I was simply trying to imagine why this man was shot, and why nothing was done about it afterward."

Arthur Ward pondered a moment, then offered some advice to Gates which was neither original nor novel. He said: "I'm sure there was nothing particularly personal in the shooting. Maybe those men mistook Joe for someone else. But, regardless, Mister Gates, I think you are making a mistake, getting involved."

Gates chuckled. "I've got the same notion, Doctor, but I've got my reasons."

When Dr. Ward picked up his black satchel to depart, John Gates walked out as far as the front verandah with him. Out there, Gates stood gazing around into the soft, bland dusk as he said: "Doctor, you're either very naïve or you prefer to conceal what you know, but in either case let me tell you something. The men who shot Mister Alvarado did not make a mistake. They came over here expressly to do something like that."

"Why?" demanded Ward.

Gates finished his long study of the hushed dusk, and turned as he answered. "Because someone wants the old man's water right."

Arthur Ward stared. He was not a landed man; he had no particular interest in landed things. He was a medical practitioner and was good at his calling. He lacked confidence, but he was beginning to acquire some. Within another couple of years he would be a thoroughly confident and reliable physician, but he would still have almost no concern with the land at all. "His water right?" Ward murmured. "Where did you hear that, Mister Gates?"

"From a bartender in town, Doctor."

Arthur Ward snorted. "From a bartender. You don't look that simple-minded."

Gates grinned. "Thanks. I also heard it from some other men in Sangerville." He kept smiling. "Doctor, take a short walk with me."

"To where?" asked the physician, beginning to eye John Gates warily.

"Out to the creek, where I'd like to show you something," replied Gates, and hooked Arthur Ward's arm as he struck out around the side of the house in the darkness. "It's not just talk about someone being out to take the old man's water away from him, and I don't think that's all they want. They are also after his land. Doctor, a hundred acres like the old man owns is worth ten times that much in regular north-desert grazing land."

Arthur Ward freed his arm and straightened his coat. It was a little late to say he was not going to walk back to the creek. They were half the distance by the time John Gates stopped pulling him along by the arm. He was annoyed, but he was also a little interested in what might lie at the end of their walk.

When they reached the trees, and had to climb a little to get up along the raised, wide, creek-side burn, Arthur Ward shifted his satchel from one hand to the other one. If he had meant to walk out here, he wouldn't have brought the thing.

John Gates knew exactly where he was going, which seemed odd to Dr. Ward. He did not have much of an opportunity to dwell upon this before Gates halted in a twilit, little, compacted clearing and pointed.

A very long while ago, obviously, since the mortar and the stones were worn to a blending similarity, someone had carefully created a stone causeway for water to come through the high creekbank into another, lower ditch, from where it spread in two directions as it was led along to smaller, bleeder irrigation ditches. Someone had rammed that little ancient stone causeway with earth that they had dug from the burn. They had created a very formidable barrier. No water could possibly get through.

Gates watched the doctor's face, then led him farther along to another plugged irrigation outlet. He did this four times, then he leaned under a willow to roll a smoke and tip back his hat as he eyed the medical man.

"Well, Doctor? To tell you the truth, I brought you up here because I got the feeling back at the house that you didn't know any more about irrigating land than I did. But I think you know what you see. These outlets belonging to the old man have been deliberately sealed."

"He can dig them out," said Arthur Ward. "It will be a difficult job, especially for an old man weak from a healing gunshot wound, but he. . . ."

"Doctor, the sequel to the closing off of the old man's taps is this. Unless he uses the water, he forfeits his right to use it. He is shot up and flat on his back. The outlets are plugged."

Dr. Ward put down his satchel and gazed at the surging great roll of water coming overland miles from Blue River.

"Someone is doing this deliberately?" he murmured, turning back very slowly.

John Gates smiled through tobacco smoke. "Yes."

"How do you know for a fact they are deliberately doing this?"

Gates pointed. "Sit down, Doctor, and I'll tell you."

Ward did not sit and he did not take his eyes off the man in the black trousers and coat, until a long way off he picked up a sound of horses. They seemed to be coming along the same riverbank where he and Gates were standing. He turned to speak and John Gates cut him off with a slashing arm gesture, then he unceremoniously grabbed both Dr. Ward and his satchel and shoved them hard into some willows and thorny underbrush, and pushed his own way deeper into the same thicket.

"Not a word," he warned. "Not a blessed sound out of you, Doctor."

Arthur Ward struggled to free himself from the worst of the thorns. He was angry and indignant, but some of that left when he finally got free enough to see the black six-gun in his companion's right fist, and also to see the closed-down look upon his companion's darkened features. He decided to do what he had been told; he even stopped fighting the thicket.

The horses were walking. Dr. Ward knew that much from listening to their approach. He leaned once to try and catch a sighting, but John Gates raised a rigid arm and pushed him back. Gates did not utter a sound as he did this; he turned and warningly shook his head. Then he swung back to keep his vigil again.

The riders were evidently in no hurry at all. It seemed as though an hour had passed before a pair of thick, moving silhouettes showed up where a pair of slouched riders came along the creekbank and halted to look down at the water outlet. One of them said: "Hell, just like the others. I told you back yonder it was a damned wild-goose chase."

VIII

Neither of the riders had shovels with them, the way those earlier riders had had, and it seemed clear that these present men were not here to add more dirt to the sealed outlets. They were here to make an investigation, to ascertain that no one had dug any of the taps out to allow water to flow through again. What interested John Gates was that disgruntled remark one of those men made when they got up close enough to make sure the nearby outlet had not been dug out. He had said this tap, like the others, was still closed, that they were making a useless ride. What that meant to Gates was that someone had sent them over here to make sure no one had opened the outlets. To John Gates's knowledge the only individual who had been told someone might open up the irrigation outlets was Town Marshal Hudson. It had been Gates himself who had told Hudson that in the saloon, after Gates's return from Mex town, and Gates had deliberately done that. He had suspected Greg Hudson's reason for making no effort to run down that pair of assassins went deeper than perhaps individual laziness or indifference because Hudson did not leave that kind of an impression of himself. Gates had deliberately told Hudson that, and then had come out here to the Alvarado place, to wait and see if someone came along to make certain the outlets were not open.

There, sitting their horses not fifty feet distant, was John Gates's answer. Two range men sneaking along the ditch bank at dusk to be sure the old man's taps were not pulling water from the creek. What Gates had to know now was the identity of those two riders, and who had sent them out here. He lifted out his Colt, looked briefly at Dr. Ward—who was staring at him in horror because Ward evidently thought Gates was going to kill those men—then John Gates spoke very softly but very audibly.

"Boys, you move a hand and I'll blow you off those horses!"

Five seconds passed without any of the actors in this drama moving a hand. Gates loosened slightly. "Reach around left-handed, boys, and drop the six-guns. Gents, be careful. Damned awful careful!"

Dr. Ward held his breath until both range men had dropped their belt guns. Part of his interest in the Far West had been the stories of gun duels he had read about back East. He had never seen a gunfight, but just now he had come as close as he decided he ever wanted to come to seeing one.

One of the horsemen turned his head in the twilight, looking through the creekbank willows. Arthur Ward caught his breath. He knew that man. He did not recollect his name, but he had concocted an antidote for the cowboy three months earlier for a scorpion bite. The man rode for Big M.

Gates ordered the riders to dismount, which they both did, then he ordered them to stand at the head of their horses, and they obeyed again. After that, Gates stepped out into the sight of his prisoners, and one of them grunted.

"Mister, I seen you in the pool hall today. I don't know your name, but they'll put it on a headboard for what you done tonight . . . unless you ride out and never look back."

Gates smiled at the speaker. "I'll tell you something about that headboard, friend. You or your partner there just look bad, and neither one of you'll be around to see my headboard." He walked a little closer. "Where are the shovels?"

The other range man glared. "What shovels? We was just ridin' along."

Gates lowered his Colt and eyed this fresh speaker. "I don't want to crack your skull or maybe half tear your ear off. But if you make me do one or the other, I'll do it. Where are the shovels? You were sent over here to make sure no one had dug out old Alvarado's water taps, and, if they had, you were to plug them up again."

"Naw," growled the angry, surly man. "We was sent over to make sure there was no water runnin' out any of his holes in the bank, but no one said anything about us fetching along shovels to plug the holes."

Gates smiled. "You are a sensible man," he told the disagreeable-looking burly cowboy.

The range rider said: "Who in hell wants to get pistol-whipped around the head?"

57

Gates's smile broadened. "True, friend, that is very true. Now, one more question. Who gave you the order to ride over here?"

"Cliff Habersham," retorted the disgruntled cowboy without any hesitation.

Gates leathered his six-gun but kept the coat on that side brushed back and tucked beneath leather while he faced his disarmed captives. "Habersham of Big M," he murmured. "Of course. Gents, there's something else you could help me with. I need to know the whereabouts of those two riders who came over here the other day and shot old Joe Alvarado."

The surly man glowered. "You said just one more question. This makes two questions."

Gates shrugged. "Two questions then, gents." He kept smiling until the surly man and his companion exchanged a look, then Gates reached for his holstered Colt and spoke at the same time. "It was you two, wasn't it?"

The other cowboy spoke up swiftly. "No, sir, it wasn't us."

Gates drew the gun and cocked it. "Alvarado said it was two riders. He also said he thought they came from Big M. There are two of you and. . . ."

"Wait a minute," broke in the less truculent of the pair of horsemen. "No, by God, it wasn't us. It was a couple of fellers named Farrel and Hanson, and they got paid off by Habersham and told to get out of the country that same night we first heard that old greaser'd been shot. Cliff came back to the ranch that night with Mister Mitchell, mad as a coiled snake. He paid them off and sent them packin' that very night." The rider paused to make a quizzical study of Gates. "Mister," he said, "if you're tryin' to make out that Mister Mitchell had anything to do with the old greaser gettin' shot, I think you're on the wrong trail. The way we heard it at the bunkhouse that night, the old greaser done something in town that day those two men didn't like, but it had nothing to do with Big M or Mister Mitchell."

John Gates eased the Colt back into its holster and fished out his makings. He then did something that intrigued Arthur Ward, still invisible in the undergrowth, more than it intrigued the pair of range men who had seen this done before. Gates rolled a cigarette one-handed, using only his left hand, and that left his gun hand free. When he finished and popped the thing between his lips, he gazed at his prisoners with detached coolness before saying: "Gents, it's up to you. You can draw against me, or you can go along as my captives."

The surly man sneered: "How do we draw with our guns lyin' in the dirt?"

Gates smiled and made a hand gesture. "Pick them up."

For a moment neither man obeyed, then only the surly man bent down, palmed his Colt, and arose slowly without taking his eyes off John Gates. When he was fully upright, he eased his weapon back into its holster. Gates kept smiling at him. "I expected you to try a belly shot as you came up off the ground, mister." He waited, eyes slitted against the drift of smoke.

The cowboy also waited. Maybe he was screwing up his nerve, maybe he was beginning to have a bad feeling about the tall, smiling man opposite him, and maybe he was just now arriving at the opinion that this was nothing worth risking his life for. Finally he moved his right hand slowly, and hooked it in the front of his shell belt. He was not going to fight, after all. He said: "The hell with it. I'll let Mister Mitchell handle this."

John Gates seemed to agree. He jerked his head sideways. "Walk southward, gents, lead your horses and keep to the right side of them, so I can see you every foot of the way."

As his prisoners moved, Gates turned in Arthur Ward's direction and called quietly: "It's all right, Tex. They aren't going to make a fight of it. Come on out and let's herd them down to one of the old man's sheds."

Both the astonished cowboys twisted to look back. Gates snarled, and they faced forward again.

Arthur Ward came forth, still clutching his medicine bag. He picked thorns from his clothing and hardly more than glanced at John Gates as he trudged in the wake of the prisoners. He understood, or thought he understood, why John Gates had not addressed him by his correct name, and it was quite all right with him, because Gates had also done something else. He had demonstrated irrefutably that Grant Mitchell and his black-eyed range boss were very much involved in the harassment and persecution of Joe Alvarado, something Dr. Ward had been very skeptical of until the two range men had decided the better part of valor was to tell the truth and to co-operate. Now, as he walked along, Dr. Ward was occupied with his private thoughts and did not see both the captives up ahead sneak swift glances back to verify that there were indeed two men behind them, instead of just John Gates.

The horses were a problem but disposing of their riders was easy. Generations of Alvarados had created a number of outbuildings. There was, for example, a rather large and massively walled adobe structure built around the dug well that furnished water to the ranch. There were perhaps no more than five covered wells in the entire Sangerville countryside. There was also a harness shed, a wagon and buggy shed, a smoke house for curing winter meat, and other sheds. Gates put his captives in the one farthest from the house, which happened to be the curing shed. It had four-foot mud walls and a massive, low roof. It also had something else—a very unique many-layered darkness of wood smoke and curing condiments baked into the walls, something that no amount of scrubbing would ever be able to mitigate. Alvarados had been curing meat in that shed for generations. Anyone spending much time in there was bound to come out blinking at the sunlight—and deliciously redolent of bacon cure.

Gates's advice, before closing the door on his prisoners, was for them not to make noise. "If you yell, no one's going to hear you but me, and, if I have to come back out here, gents, I'm going to make you wish you hadn't yelled. Not a damned sound."

He placed the *tranca*—the big door bar—in its steel hangers out front, then walked with Dr. Ward and the pair of horses in the general southeasterly direction of town. Ward, who was no part of this except as an observer, asked what Gates intended to do with the animals, and, when John Gates looked up ruefully shaking his head, Arthur said: "Suppose they were to be held in town until shortly before sunup, then freed to run back to the ranch?"

Gates shrugged. Unless something like this were permitted to happen, eventually someone was going to accuse him of horse theft, a very serious charge. On the other hand, the moment those horses showed up at the Mitchell cow outfit without their riders. . . . "Maybe," he told Arthur Ward, "they won't get back to the ranch until tomorrow night."

Ward was agreeable. "All right. You need that much time, do you? Give me the reins and I'll lock them in my buggy shed until after supper, then turn loose."

Gates passed over the leathers. "Doctor, you're going to get into this mess if you're not careful."

"Yes, indeed," replied the medical man, "I surely am. Do you have a room, Mister Gates? If not, you could stay at my place. I have an old house with six bedrooms and I live alone in. . . ."

"Just take care of the horses, if you will," replied Gates. "Pretend you never saw me tonight, and forget about being helpful." He smiled and halted as they reached the darkened edge of Sangerville. "Doctor, this isn't like setting a broken leg." He nodded. "Good night."

Arthur Ward turned and headed down the far alleyway, over

on the east side of town. It was midway along that he had his combination office and residence, and it was across this same alley that he had his buggy shed and corrals. He already had one animal there, his big, brown mare. He also had a ton of good, leafy meadow hay.

A dog barked as he walked quietly the length of the alley and took those two Big M horses into the Stygian darkness of his buggy shed to stall them and off-saddle them, then to pitch both their mangers full of hay. They would be contented horses until tomorrow night.

IX

Gates was across the road at the café eating breakfast when he saw Cliff Habersham lope into town and head for the tie rack out front of Hudson's jailhouse office. He sipped coffee, leaned on the counter, and from time to time swung his head to watch the front of the jailhouse. Big M's range boss was in there a long while, and, when he ultimately came forth to the tie rack again, he did not look at all pleased or pleasant.

Gates smiled into his coffee cup, finished breakfast, dumped some coins atop the counter, and strolled forth into the pleasantly chilly very early morning.

Up the road Hubert Townley was stamping irritably around a stagecoach parked beside his plank walk while a Mex yard man hustled around with his grease bucket and his wooden ladle, slathering viscous, black axle grease on the bared hubs. There were two men, apparently traveling salesmen, bundled in coats as though this were the middle of winter, looking sleepily around as they waited for the coach to be ready to roll.

Elsewhere, down by the livery barn two older men were arguing about a sleek chestnut horse one of them had in a halter. They seemed to be discussing the merits, or the demerits, of the horse as though perhaps one was trying to sell the horse to the other one.

Marshal Hudson came out of his office, saw John Gates smoking and idly standing in thin sunshine across in front of the café, and for a moment hesitated, glaring over in that direction as though he would cross the road, but in the end he swung northward, walking briskly.

Gates flipped away his smoke, tipped down his hat brim, and watched until he was certain of Marshal Hudson's direction, then he also started up the roadway, but upon the opposite side of the road. If Hudson walked out to the Alvarado place, then the chances were excellent that, when Cliff Habersham had been in the jailhouse a while back, he had told Greg Hudson about those two riders who had been sent out from Big M and had not returned. Gates was interested. If this were true, then the last shred of doubt would be removed concerning Marshal Hudson's underhanded association with Grant Mitchell in the rich cowman's attempt to get the Alvarado irrigated land.

Habersham would never have told Hudson about two Big M riders being missing unless he also told Hudson where they had been sent, and probably why they had been sent over there. Now Hudson's brisk stride that was carrying him northwest of town in the direction of old Alvarado's house aroused in John Gates a very strong curiosity. He increased his gait until he was up along the north segment of the main thoroughfare, not far from the harness shop. There he could see the lawman out upon the open range, heading arrow-straight for the distant, tree-shaded adobe house of the Alvarado family. Gates tipped back his hat, leaned against an upright, and considered his options, while behind him a large man walked up from the direction of the saloon, and, when he was in front of the harness shop window, he said: "Mister Gates?"

John turned. It was the black-eyed range boss of Big M. Gates nodded and felt the warning in the back of his head.

Habersham stood, legs sprung wide, thumbs in shell belt, gazing bleakly and steadily at the other tall man. "Mister Gates, you been told to keep your nose out of folks' business around here." Habersham paused to allow that to sink in. "Mister Gates, I been told you been all over town askin' questions and makin' statements."

Gates had been through this, in one variation or another, dozens of times. He knew what was coming and he gently turned his body to get squared up as he faced into it. The thing he did not know was the technique Cliff Habersham would use, and for that he was intently watchful, because once an enemy moved in this kind of confrontation, his adversary did not get a second chance.

"I told your friend, the town marshal, I used to be a deputy sheriff over in Arizona, and from that I kept my interest in things outside the law . . . like shooting an old man."

"It ain't none of your concern," murmured Habersham.

Gates did not smile when he made his contradiction, which was unusual for him. "It is my business, cowboy, and it ought to be everyone else's business around here who doesn't believe in bullying and careless gun handling."

Habersham slowly expelled his breath, slowly loosened his stance, and allowed his hands to assume their normal, loose-hanging position down his sides. He did not appear to want to keep this conversation going. Gates allowed the moments to slip past, and, when he was just about certain Habersham was ready, he spoke again. "In case you might be interested, Habersham, you and Grant Mitchell, my interest in Joe Alvarado is reasonable. His daughter was my mother."

The range boss blinked; that was the only indication that he had been astonished. "You are the old man's grandson, then?" he asked, looking very doubtful of this.

Gates smiled, finally. "Yeah. His daughter married a man named Jeremiah Gates who was a journeyman carpenter. He worked around Sangerville for a year or so, and they were married. My mother died in childbirth about thirty years back, Mister Habersham. . . . I came over here to see my grandfather before heading for San Francisco. Now tell me again, Mister Habersham, I don't have any business getting involved in the old man's troubles."

Cliff Habersham said nothing for a long while. He looked up and down the roadway, as though he were expecting to see someone, then he shot a searching glance off in the direction of the Alvarado adobe. Marshal Hudson had already reached the house and was probably inside because there was no sign of him outside in the tree shade. Habersham then swung back and said: "All right. You're the old man's grandson. It don't change anything."

Gates had completed his probe of Cliff Habersham, had completed his thorough assessment, and was sure he knew how Habersham fought. He stepped slowly clear of the upright post and with his back to the roadway and with the sun in Habersham's eyes he said: "Listen to me, you son-of-a-bitch, you came into town this morning because you lost two riders last night. You told Hudson they were supposed to be along the creek above the Alvarado place. Habersham, I was up there too, last night. Do you want your men back?"

The range boss' hard, craggy features closed slowly down into an expression of fierce and uncompromising opposition. He ignored everything Gates had said but one designation. "What did you just call me, Gates?"

The answer was immediately forthcoming, and along with it a little more. "I called you a son-of-a-bitch, Habersham. The reason was because those two men told me last night it was you who sent them over to see if the old man's ditch had been opened again. I'll tell you who told you that was going to happen. Town Marshal Hudson, another son-of-a-bitch."

Habersham's body was completely still, his dark eyes were brilliant but narrowed against sun smash. He started his move without waiting any longer. The saddle maker behind him was watching from his workbench, unable to hear anything that was said or had been said, but perfectly capable of seeing Gates's face and Habersham's back. He saw Habersham go for his gun, but he had a better view of John Gates.

The first shot sounded as loud as a cannon roar. It was followed by two more thunderous explosions equally as loud. All three of those shots came from the same gun. The first impact slammed Habersham back against the building front. The second one broke his right arm and spun him. The third bullet sledged his head back so hard it broke the saddle shop window. Habersham hung half through the casement, then slowly slid out upon the plank walk in a sodden heap. He had been unable to get off a single shot. In fact, when the harness maker finally recovered from his shock and went to the window, he could see the range boss' gun lying just under his right hand and it had not even been cocked.

Someone in front of the general store yelled for the marshal as he ran across to the jailhouse to bang upon the office door.

John Gates kept his back to the morning sun and systematically reloaded his six-gun, then he raised his eyes as he leathered the weapon, caught the harness maker's white look, and said: "Maybe you'd best go for the doctor."

The older man nodded, stepped through his doorway, and for the first time got a good, long look at Cliff Habersham. "He don't need no doctor," the harness maker murmured, and stared. "You never missed, mister," he said, stepped past between the dead man and the man who had killed him, and walked awkwardly southward.

Across the road several men came forth from stores, and down in front of the saloon there were five men standing like stone carvings not speaking, not moving, not even looking away. They were range riders, but they did not belong to Big M, which was perhaps just as well.

Gates heard someone running and turned to look. Greg Hudson was coming fast from the direction of the Alvarado place. Gates moved into the shade, placed his back to the front wall of the shop, and waited.

By the time Dr. Ward got there, satchel in hand, Hudson was crossing the road, breathing hard and looking enormously distressed.

Ward shot Gates a look, then knelt briefly. As Marshal Hudson came over, several sidling men inched in as close as they dared, also to look. Those five range men from down in front of the saloon also came solemnly northward to gawk.

Dr. Ward spoke without raising his eyes: "We'll need a couple of strong men to haul him down to my embalming shed." Ward arose and did not look at Gates at all as he turned toward Greg Hudson. "Once in the heart, once through his gun arm, and once through the head. Those two body shots would have killed him. Either one of them, Greg."

Hudson was struggling to control his breathing when he looked past at Gates and held out his left hand. "Your gun," he said. "You'll be in jail until I get this sorted out. That's the law. We don't have no court in Sangerville so you got no way to post bond."

Gates lifted out the Colt and passed it over. A cowboy standing south of them all said: "Marshal, Cliff made the first move. I was standing down in front of the saloon and seen him do it."

The harness maker shuffled ahead and looked unhappily on as a pair of men stopped to grasp the corpse by the shoulders and ankles to carry it away. "I was inside the shop, lookin' from the window," he said, making room for the corpse carriers. "That's how it happened, Greg. Habersham made the first move. This other feller didn't start until Cliff had his arm half bent. I was right behind them, yonder."

Greg Hudson moved away from the sunlight, although it was not that hot. Not yet, it was still early morning. He looked at the reloaded Colt in his fist. His breathing was easier, finally, and some of the shock had also passed for him, as it had for most of the other onlookers. He raised his impassive face and said: "What happened, Gates?"

The answer he got was perhaps one he did not expect. "I don't think you'd like me to tell you what happened, Marshal, not right here with all these men standing around."

They stared back and forth, then Hudson shoved the pistol into his waistband and jerked his head. "Across the road and southward, down to the jailhouse," he growled.

John Gates moved through the crowd. Men dropped back instantly when he approached them. If it were proved he had murdered Big M's range boss, then he would have a town full of enemies. If it were proved that he had bested Cliff Habersham in a fair gunfight, he would have a town full of admirers, and even those who would disapprove of his gunfighting prowess would strongly respect his courage. Meanwhile, they would yield the right of way to him as Greg Hudson herded him away, and later they would all rush down to the saloon to sidle up to the bar and over several beers retell and reshape and rephrase all their opinions and judgments, along with a lot of eyewitness accounts by people who hadn't even been out in the roadway when the gunfire erupted.

Greg Hudson followed his prisoner into the jailhouse, kicked the door closed after them, and told Gates to sit down. He then went to his desk, tossed down the extra Colt, and thoughtfully eyed Gates with an expression of wary hostility.

"Coffee?" he growled, and walked to the stove to draw off a cup for himself.

Gates declined, crossed his legs to get comfortable, and thoughtfully eyed the lawman. Marshal Hudson's hands were not steady at all.

Gates rolled a smoke, with perfectly steady hands, lit up, and, when the lawman went back to sit at his desk with the cup of coffee, Gates blew smoke and waited for the first question before he let Hudson have it exactly as he had let Cliff Habersham have it.

X

Marshal Hudson did not ask a question; he made a statement. "Grant Mitchell is going to take the killing of his range boss right hard, Gates. Habersham worked for Big M a long while and Mister Mitchell relied a lot on him."

John Gates was sympathetic. "I'd expect it would be about like that. Marshal, it wasn't my idea to fight."

Greg Hudson drank off his coffee, then shoved the cup away to lean and look steadily at Gates. "What is your relationship to old Alvarado?" he asked, showing by the expression on his face that he was convinced this relationship went much deeper than just a stranger's passing interest in justice.

Gates answered shortly: "I'm his grandson."

The marshal slowly raised up off the desk and leaned back, saying: "I knew it. I knew it had to be something."

Gates repeated what he had said before. "Marshal, it shouldn't make any difference who I am. Every person in your territory who believes in justice ought to be concerned about a man being shot down in his own barnyard. An unarmed man, Marshal."

Hudson let that go; it had sounded too much to him like preaching. "Last night, Gates . . . where were you?"

The answer to this was simple, of course, but the moment Gates gave it, he was going to have to reveal what he knew about the town marshal. He sat and considered for a while, then spoke out forthrightly and quietly. "Yesterday I told you some Mexicans were going up along Alvarado's ditch to re-open it so he would be using water again. You already knew that, if that happened, the old man's water right would be in good standing. Marshal, I only told that to one man . . . you. The reason I told you that was because I felt you and Mitchell were in this together. You did what I thought you might do. You went right over and warned Mitchell. He, in turn, had his range boss send a couple of riders along the creekbank behind the Alvarado place to stop anyone from opening those outlets. Do you know who was up there in the darkness waiting for those men, Marshal?"

Greg Hudson did not reply. He was still leaning back at his desk, but his expression was blanked out, his coloring was slowly changing, slowly fading, and the stare he put upon John Gates was glassy. He did not offer any reply to Gates's question.

Gates did not offer the answer without being asked for it, but he went right on with his conversation by saying: "I caught those two men Habersham sent out there. This morning Habersham came riding into town to tell you something was wrong, that his riders hadn't returned, and right away you headed for the Alvarado place to look around along the ditch. Only you never got that far, did you? Habersham called me, up in front of the saddle and harness works, and I killed him, but, before I shot Habersham, I told him who I was and why I was interested. I also called him a son-of-a-bitch, and said you were another one." Gates smiled. "That's the whole story, Marshal. You want to lock me up?" Gates kept smiling while he gently wagged his head. "I don't think so. You're not going to cage me while you ride out to Big M and explain to Grant Mitchell that I know the whole lousy story, and maybe have a bushwhacker ride back to town with you."

Marshal Hudson gently eased forward in his chair. John Gates reached inside his coat and brought forth his cigarette papers. He reached again for his tobacco sack—and pointed the under-and-over Derringer squarely at Marshal Hudson as he cocked it. The thing had two barrels large enough to accommodate the end of a finger. At that range it would tear a hole in a man as large as a .45 Colt slug. "Relax," Gates told Hudson. "Put both hands atop the desk in plain sight."

Hudson obeyed, but he was slow about it. He did not utter a sound. It was not the belly gun or its unexpected appearance that had him half numb; it was the revelation that someone besides he and Mitchell and Habersham knew that he had tacitly allowed everything that had happened up to this point to occur. Gates had read him right a moment earlier when he had slowly leaned forward in the desk chair; he had meant to draw his gun and use it to herd Gates into the cell room. He had not made any hasty attempt to do this because he had not thought he would have to draw fast. He had been wrong. Lately he had been wrong about a lot of things. He sat at the desk now, gazing at the little weapon in Gates's hand, feeling another segment of his world breaking away beneath his feet.

Gates arose, retrieved his own six-gun from atop the desk, holstered it, and said: "Marshal, lift out your Colt." Gates gestured. "Lay it atop the desk." As soon as Hudson had obeyed, Gates picked up the six-gun and very efficiently shucked out every load, then he handed it back with a smile. "Put it back in your holster. Now stand up, Marshal. You and I are going to walk out to the Alvarado place. I can't leave you here to yell your head off the minute I leave, but I've got a couple of prisoners in a shed at Alvarado's ranch that no one knows are out there, and just maybe they would like some company."

71

Gates crossed the room, put the little belly gun somewhere under his coat, and brought forth an empty hand with which he partially opened the door.

"Over here," he said to Greg Hudson. "Now listen to me, Marshal. Nothing is going to happen to you unless you force it." He pulled the door wide. "Walk out, smile, and, as we walk along, look at ease, make this look as natural as you can. All right?"

Hudson did not reply and he did not look very much at ease as he plowed ahead as far as the plank walk, then waited for Gates to close the jailhouse door and walk along beside him.

"You haven't helped me a damned bit," Hudson told Gates. "Maybe I had this coming. But you haven't helped yourself, either. By now someone from town will be riding pell-mell for Big M to tell Grant Mitchell what happened to Cliff."

They walked northward. Gates nodded twice, once at Townley, the stage company representative, and again a little farther up the roadway at the gunsmith, who was just returning from across the road where he had been visiting the saddle and harness maker. There were a number of people abroad, mostly on the opposite side of the roadway, walking toward the general store. There were some riders, too, passing along through town, and Arthur Ward went spinning northward behind his big mare, Daisy, driving his top buggy as though he were on an emergency.

At the upper end of town a bearded man halted them to tell Marshal Hudson someone had raided his hen roost the previous night. Greg Hudson promised to make an investigation as soon as he could, then they left the town's limits and struck out across the open country in the direction of the Alvarado place.

Hudson eyed the shady, old adobe house. "How much does Joe know?" he asked.

"Until yesterday he didn't even know who I was," retorted Gates. "I hadn't been over here since I was eight years old.

That's about all he knows, except that when he was telling me about someone's attempt to steal his water, I said I thought I'd stick around and see him through this trouble. He has no idea I put two Big M riders in one of his outbuildings. About Habersham, he couldn't possibly know yet."

Gates was not surly or vindictive. He was almost amiable in his attitude toward Greg Hudson, and no doubt this went a long way toward influencing Hudson, along with the fact that Hudson was not an outlaw; he had made a bad mistake, and perhaps he was not a man of iron strength, but he was still not an outlaw. Just a fool, perhaps, and a weakling. Gates seemed to accept this judgment of the man he was strolling with because, when they were about midway, he said: "Hell, Hudson, you're older than I am. You darned well knew better than to sell out to a man like Grant Mitchell. Even if you were a young man, you should know better."

Greg walked along, gazing dead ahead saying nothing. When they were close enough to the old house to see beyond the tree shade, Leona Gomez became visible to them both where she was sitting at an ancient table, shelling beans. She had seen them approaching and had watched until she had recognized them both, then she had gone back to her work.

She was not looking out where they were now, as the lawman said: "In a place like this, where one man runs the town and most of the countryside, you don't buck him. Not if you want to keep your job and still live here."

John Gates, eyeing the widow Gomez at her old table under a magnificent old tree, made a wry comment on Hudson's philosophy: "Marshal, I'd guess the world is full of folks who moved to new territory rather than to sell their souls."

Hudson turned slightly. "I'll tell you something you'd ought to be thinking on, instead of me. Grant Mitchell will have you killed for what you did to Cliff. You ought to be thinking of ways of getting beyond his reach."

This was the first candid statement Gates had heard by anyone since the killing of Big M's range boss, concerning Mitchell's reaction to the gunning down of Habersham. Not that Gates required any warnings. He had seen Grant Mitchell, had made his accurate appraisal of the man. He smiled. "I'll be careful, but thanks for the warning," he said, as they covered the last fifty yards.

Leona Gomez raised liquid dark eyes. "He is sleeping now. You cannot see him. He has not been able to sleep well until today, and he should get all the rest he can." She acted as though she expected the pair of stalwart men to oppose this pronouncement, but John Gates smiled down into her lifted face.

"Later, then," he told her in soft Spanish. "The chief and I will go out back and look around."

Leona wrinkled her nose. "So it was you, was it?"

"¿Señora?"

"It was you, then, who locked those two men in the old smoke house."

Hudson looked at Gates, and Gates looked at Leona Gomez. "You found them?" he said. "You didn't let them out, did you?"

She shook her head. "No. That's a good place for animals in need of caging. I didn't let them out but they offered me a hundred dollars if I would. I heard them yelling, which is why I went out there. I also told them that, if they yelled again, I would return with a bucket of scalding water . . . we need peace and quiet around here."

Gates slowly winked. He then jerked his head at Greg Hudson and led the way around back through benevolent tree shade, until they got beyond most of the outbuildings when they also got beyond most of the shade, then, as they walked up to the smoke house, Hudson said: "Hell, it's Mitchell's pair of missing riders."

Gates stopped in front of the oaken door, listened briefly, then said: "Gents, I'm going to open the door now. Get back along the far wall and stay there."

He lifted away the bar and swung back the massive old solid oak panel—and a man hurled himself straight ahead out of the dingy interior of the curing shed. Greg Hudson reacted without thinking, reacted by instinct and perfect co-ordination. His fist blocked the snarling man's forward impetus and violently jarred the man's entire body.

The second man had a steel hook that the prisoners had painstakingly freed from the smoke house ceiling. It had a vicious barb at one end to use in suspending curing hams.

Gates palmed his Colt and cocked it. The lunging man with the meat hook stopped in his tracks, as much from surprise at finding Marshal Hudson there with Gates and having seen Marshal Hudson knock his companion senseless, as at seeing John Gates draw that gun so swiftly. The man dropped his meat hook and took a couple of backward steps.

Gates did not say a word; he holstered his gun and leaned to roll the unconscious range rider back through the doorway inside the shed. Then he and Hudson also walked in, and Gates eased the door partially closed after them, an act that cut off a good bit of the daylight.

The standing Big M rider glowered at Greg Hudson. "What the hell do you think you're doing?" he snarled. "What did you hit Jack for? Whose side you on, anyway?"

Gates interrupted before the lawman could reply. Gates offered no explanation about the lawman's behavior; what he said was dropped upon the snarling range rider for shock effect, and it worked. "Cliff Habersham is dead. Killed in a gunfight in town this morning."

That was all Gates said. He neither prefaced it with anything nor followed it up with anything. The cowboy stared steadily at the pair of men in front of him, but he looked longest and hardest at John Gates. The range boss of any big cow outfit was equally as important as the owner; in many instances he was more important, at least to the men who did the riding.

The cowboy backed up to a bench and sat down. He did not look very defiant now. His friend on the floor groaned, groped along the packed earth for a moment, then unsteadily sat up.

XI

The range man Hudson had knocked flat and senseless pulled himself over to the wall bench beside his companion and eyed both Gates and Hudson as though he made no differentiation, but his friend, who was not as groggy, did make a differentiation. He kept squinting defiantly at Hudson, and eventually he reiterated his earlier, surprised comment, but he worded it differently because now it was fairly obvious, since the lawman had his six-gun in its holster and was obviously on friendly terms with John Gates, that Hudson was not Grant Mitchell's man after all. He said: "Marshal, if Cliff really got himself shot to death this morning and the old man don't know about it, then he's goin' to figure you must have had a hand in it . . . what with you sidin' against him now."

Gates moved across the small room where he could watch all three men. He moved with his customary deceptive looseness. He was smiling when he addressed the clear-headed range man. "About those two fellers who shot Alvarado . . . where are they?"

"Gone," stated the cowboy. "They got paid off that same night. Cliff was mad about that."

Gates continued to smile. "Gone where? Did they say where they would go, or where they had come from, or did they mention having kinfolks somewhere?"

The cowboy stared at Gates, then shook his head with slow

emphasis. "They never give anyone at the Big M bunkhouse any idea about themselves." The cowboy had obviously read Gates's intention correctly. "If you figure to get revenge," he said, "you'll have to find someone other than us fellers to help you."

"But last night along the creekbank," said Gates, "if you'd found some Mexes there trying to open the old man's taps, you'd have done a little shooting, too, eh?"

"Nope," insisted the rider, and this time his friend joined in by saying: "All we was supposed to do was spook them, scare them off. We was told not to use no guns at all, no matter what. And for Mexicans, you usually don't have to use guns. They scare easy."

"Who gave you those orders?" asked Gates. "Habersham or Mitchell?"

"Habersham, but Mitchell was standin' right there in the door of the bunkhouse when Cliff told us what we was to do."

Gates rolled his eyes around to Greg Hudson. For a moment he simply gazed at the marshal, then he said: "Do you want to lock them up in your jailhouse, Marshal, or shall I leave them out here? Thing is, Marshal, if you locked them up and they escaped . . . I'd take it hard."

"Leave them out here," stated the lawman, avoiding Gates's stare.

The groggy cowboy, the one Hudson had knocked senseless, looked balefully at the lawman. He may not have liked Hudson before, but he certainly did not like him now. "I owe you," he muttered. "I sure as hell owe you."

Greg was undisturbed. "Shut up and sit still," he said contemptuously.

The cowboy had one more comment to make. "Mister Mitchell will find out. If he don't find out before we tell him, the minute we get out of here, we'll go tell him ourselves. Mister Mitchell's got less use for double-crossers than he has for Mex raiders or horse thieves."

John Gates seemed to be enjoying this. He rolled a smoke and looked amiably from man to man. When he lit up, the cowboy with the swelling sore jaw had another comment to offer to Greg Hudson: "I wouldn't be in your boots for a herd of fat cattle. It won't just be Mitchell. It'll be everyone who rides for him will want a piece of your scalp. You sure ain't very smart, double-crossing the biggest cowman in the country."

Gates straightened up, gesturing for Hudson to leave the little shed. Gates walked out behind him, and partially turned in the doorway to say: "The lady says she'll fling scalding water on you if you make any more noise. That's down right mild compared to what I'll do."

"Damn it," exclaimed the unharmed rider, "we're hungry! Haven't eaten since last night."

Gates understood that predicament. He said: "Fasting is good for the soul. Ask any priest." He then closed the door, dropped the *tranca* into place, and turned to see Greg Hudson's pale, troubled expression. He said: "Come on, let's see if my grandfather is awake yet."

When they approached the front of the house, Leona Gomez blocked the front doorway with her ample body. She did not speak; she simply shook her head to convey the meaning that Joe Alvarado had not awakened, and she would not allow them to enter the house.

Gates grinned and murmured something in Spanish to which Leona Gomez turned red, then put both hands on her hips and ripped out a staccato retort. Gates laughed, roguishly winked, and, when Greg Hudson was positive *Señora* Gomez would look around for something to swing at Gates, she suddenly dissolved with laughter. Hudson was bewildered and Gates did not enlighten him then, or later.

They went back in the direction of town, crossing the

intervening distance through a hot haze of midday sunshine, and, when they reached the plank walk to start southward, Greg Hudson, who had been seriously considering his personal predicament, said: "Now what? What they said back yonder is true. Grant Mitchell will be arriving in town when he hears what happened to Cliff."

What Hudson meant, of course, was what now was going to happen to him. Gates did not reply. As they walked southward in the direction of the jailhouse and saw Hubert Townley emerge from his stage company office, waving to them, whatever retort Gates might have made died unsaid.

Hubert came over waving a soiled envelope that he handed to Gates exactly as he had handed over that first envelope, down at the livery barn. He also made a similar comment this time. "I don't see how folks know you're here in Sangerville, and get these here messages to you by the stages when only a handful of us even know who you are."

Gates fished for a cartwheel and handed it over with a smile. "I got friends who can read minds," he said, grinning.

Townley made a hard comment about that: "Sure you have, mister. Just like I got harness horses that can read."

Hudson and Gates resumed their way. It was not the same, of course, not after the killing of Big M's foreman. There were people on both sides of the road who looked with particular curiosity at John Gates. Their expressions toward Marshal Hudson showed bafflement. By all rights, Marshal Hudson should have locked Gates into one of the jailhouse cells and here they both were, guns in holsters, strolling around town in broad daylight as though one of them had not very recently shot a man to death.

They were entering the jailhouse when Dr. Ward approached. He looked freshly scrubbed, which was unusual, this being slightly past the middle of the day. He also looked a trifle upset about something as he marched on in and nodded to Gates for holding the door for him.

"It may interest you to know," he said, "that Cliff Habersham had one of those sets of tattooed numbers on his upper arm that they put on some convicts at Eastern prisons."

Gates and Hudson stared. Dr. Ward stepped to the desk and carefully printed five numbers upon a scrap of paper, then tossed down the pencil, and moved clear so the other men could see.

"Habersham certainly spent some time in prison," he stated. "That much is obvious. Otherwise, he would not have had that tattoo on his arm. The question is . . . did he arrive out here and go to work for Grant Mitchell after having been legally released, or did he escape? Was he a fugitive or not?"

Gates straightened back, looking rueful. "It won't make much difference now, Doctor, what he was."

Ward conceded that. "Perhaps not. On the other hand, some effort should be made to find which prison he served in, and let them know he's dead."

Greg Hudson went to his desk and sat down.

Arthur Ward studied his coloring and his expression, then changed the subject. "Greg, you'd better come over and let me have a look at you. You are a mite peaked looking."

Hudson raised his eyes. "I got a right to be, Arthur. I took money from Grant Mitchell to look the other way when he tried to persuade Joe Alvarado to sell Mitchell his irrigated land and move off it."

This admission did not exactly surprise John Gates, but the fact that Hudson had come right out with it, in so many blunt words, surprised him. Hudson had just admitted he was unfit to wear his badge.

Dr. Ward nodded almost as though he were not surprised. As a matter of fact, after what had happened the previous night out at the Alvarado place, Dr. Ward, who was far from being a fool, had fairly well figured out what had been happening, and who, most probably, was likely to be involved in it.

John Gates went to the wall and leaned there, eyeing them both. He and Dr. Ward were well acquainted after last night. They were not friends, particularly, but they knew each other well enough for Gates to say: "Mitchell will be along directly, Doctor, and I expect he'll cause you to have some work to do. My problem isn't really Mitchell so much as it's this damned fool. What to do with him?"

Dr. Ward held up a hand. "No thanks," he said swiftly. "Remember, I still have those two Big M horses cached in my buggy shed, and that's dangerous enough if someone gets to prowling around. I'm not going to take the town marshal down there and lock him up, too."

Hudson looked up. "What Big M horses?"

Ward answered evenly: "The horses those two cowboys were riding last night along the creekbank out behind the Alvarado place."

Hudson was staring. "You were up there with Gates?"

Dr. Ward rolled his eyes. "Yes." He turned on Gates. "Not voluntarily, but I was up there."

Greg Hudson turned to Gates with a sardonic look. He was clearly thinking that Gates was a singularly gifted person when it came to embroiling not just himself but other people as well in troubles of many kinds.

Dr. Ward said he had to go up to Alvarado's place and look in on his patient, and departed.

Gates went to a bench to sit down, opened the note Townley had handed him, and read it while the town marshal went to the stove to see if he could spark it into sufficient life to warm the coffee pot atop it. The fire was dead; there were not even any decent coals left. He closed the cast-iron door and turned just as Gates folded the letter and arose as he pocketed it. Then Gates jerked his head in the direction of the cell-room door. "The choices are lousy," he confided to Hudson. "Let you go wandering around, or I lock you up. Where are the keys?"

Hudson pointed. "On a peg in the cell room. If you think locking me up is going to make anything easier for either of us. . . ."

"Nothing is going to be easy for us," broke in Gates, motioning for the lawman to precede him into the little cell room. "And I don't really believe you'd shoot me in the back if I left you wandering around. But Mitchell might send someone to shoot you in the back, and I'm sure he's going to send someone for my scalp, so I'll get you out of the way where I won't have to wonder about you, and maybe we'll both come out of this yet."

He took the key ring off the peg as Hudson stopped before a door. "You're crazy, Gates. He's got a whole riding crew of damned hard men out there. He doesn't hire any other kind of rider. I don't care how good you might be with a gun, you can't buck those odds. They'll kill you sure as hell."

"Go on in and walk to the back of the cell," ordered John Gates, then he leaned to fumble around at locking the door. When he finished, instead of hanging the keys on the peg on the opposite wall where they usually went, he pocketed them and smiled in at Hudson. "Sure am flattered you are concerned about me surviving," he said. "Incidentally you don't know enough about what's going to happen to pray over me yet."

With that enigmatic remark John Gates walked back to the jailhouse office, stood a moment at a front window studying the roadway, and, when he was satisfied with what he saw out there—or rather, what he did not see, a band of Big M horses tied somewhere along the store fronts—he left the jailhouse, locked the door after himself, and struck out on a diagonal course across the road in the direction of the saloon.

XII

The barman was an older, graying individual, this time, when Gates walked in out of the increasing daytime heat. He glanced up from a face that had been blasted out of a hard and eventful life, studied Gates while the latter walked over and settled against the bar, then raised his eyebrows quizzically instead of opening his mouth to inquire what Gates wanted to drink.

Gates knew the type; that barman had seen it all before, at least once. Much of it he had seen recur time and time again. Gates said—"Beer."—then turned and glanced around.

The room was nearly empty. There were two dusty men in city clothes sharing a pitcher of beer at a window table along the front wall, probably drummers who had recently arrived by stagecoach and had to cut the scorch and dust from their throats before they sought rooms for the night. Three old men were silently concentrating on a pinochle game over near the wood stove, which was their private domain summer or winter. There was a lanky, travel-stained, bronzed man with a hint of gray over his ears at the far north end of the bar, indolently slouching with his glass of beer, gravely studying the hallowed beer company etching called "Custer's Last Stand", which had over the past few years become the epitome of all paintings and drawings representative of that tragic affair and would continue to be this for a full generation yet to come despite a dozen total absurdities. The cowboy, leaning there, gazing at the portrait wore an ivory-stocked Colt tied down, but otherwise his clothing was faded, his boots run-over, his hat sweat-stained and battered, and his appearance was of a hardened, professional range rider—not the kind of man who would own or wear such an expensive six-gun.

The barman went up there, but the cowboy shook his head

without taking his eyes off the portrait on the back wall, so the barman came back down where Gates was drinking and hovered, which was his way of asking whether someone needed a refill. Gates shoved the empty glass forward, then turned slightly as the barman walked toward the beer pump's carved wooden handle, and gazed up toward the far north end of the bar. The lanky man with the tied-down, ivory-handled Colt turned and gazed back. They did not speak or nod or change expression; they simply looked steadily at one another for a few moments, then the cowboy turned back to studying the Custer etching, and Gates faced around when the barman showed up with his fresh glass of beer.

Gates put down a coin, the barman scooped it up, then a couple of perspiring individuals from across at the stage company's yard pushed in out of the sunlight and continued whatever it was they had been discussing outside, while they unerringly approached the bar.

Gates downed his second beer, turned, and walked out. He tugged forth his hat brim as soon as he was in the dazzling sunlight, then began walking down in the direction of the livery barn. People nodded when they strolled past, and they gave John Gates all the plank walk he wanted, but no one offered to stop and talk to him.

At the general store where there were two benches bolted to the front wall on each side of the wide front entrance, several old men, whittling, chewing, or simply leaning torpidly upon their canes, raised shrewd eyes and watched John Gates stroll past, and not a word was said but they all shared their thoughts in that peculiar manner of old men.

Gates crossed over, paused out front of the livery barn in the dark shade of an enormous tree, and scanned the rearward roadway. There were still no Big M horsemen entering town from the northeasterly range, the way they always arrived in

Sangerville. Gates looked elsewhere around the center of town, watched the progress of the weathered and worn cowboy who carried that ivory-gripped Colt for a moment, then went on down the livery barn runway, and leaned on the rearmost exit where the back alley passed. The day man was not around and the proprietor of the barn, who seldom spent much time there any more, was also missing. It was drowsy inside the barn. It was also fragrant and cool. There were two signs nailed upon an overhead baulk. One announced all payments were due in advance and the other one prohibited smoking anywhere on the livery barn grounds and that meant outside by the corrals, too. John Gates did not take out his makings, although the idea had crossed his mind when he came to rest there just inside the long runway, standing in shadows with alleyway sunlight behind him.

When the lanky range rider walked in, tied-down ivory-handled Colt riding easily as he strode through, the day man appeared from a small harness room rubbing his eyes. The cowboy threw him an easy smile and a little wave. "No need to stir yourself, partner. I'm just walkin' on through."

Without a word the hostler turned and went back to his chair and his nap.

When the lanky range man got down where John Gates was waiting, he said: "I figured, when you just stared at me up at the saloon, you were in trouble again, John. What is it this time?"

"Shot some cowman's range boss, Hardy, and now I'm waiting for the whole riding crew to reach town."

The lanky man hooked his thumbs, looked down his nose, and sighed. "You said you were going to stop here to see your grandfather," he said, sounding reproachful.

"I did. I saw him. Two bushwhackers shot the old man in front of his barn, in his own damned yard, and when he didn't have a gun on him. That's only part of it. This big cowman is trying to steal the old man's irrigated land. He's trying to make the old man forfeit his water right from the creek out back of his little ranch."

The lanky man said: "So you shot his range boss. Why in hell didn't you shoot the cowman?"

Gates smiled. "Haven't had the chance yet, Hardy, but he'll be along directly." Gates paused, then said: "Where is Aleck?"

Hardy shrugged. "He'll show up. Did you get the letter from him?"

Gates had. "Yeah. Today. I got your letter last week."

"Did he say when he'd arrive here in Sangerville?"

Gates smiled again. "His aunt is sick over in Albuquerque."

Hardy snorted. "He doesn't have any aunt. He doesn't have any folks at all over in Albuquerque. It'll be that Mex girl from Tucomcori again, sure as hell."

Gates kept smiling. "I figured that, too. And it'll depend how long it takes him to get in the saddle before anyone can guess when he'll show up down here. And that leaves just the two of us."

Hardy faintly frowned. "For what? Wait a minute. You think I'm going to side in with you against some big cow outfit?"

John Gates somberly inclined his head. "I think so, Hardy. Remember that day over at Springer when those beaners jumped you in their *cantina?*"

Hardy glared and pursed his lips and said nothing for a while. He eventually turned at the sound of men out front, then turned back to say: "Hell! How many riders has this old bastard got?"

Gates was not sure. "Four, five, maybe six counting him, too. Just everyday cowboys, I'd guess, Hardy."

The lanky man looked very skeptical. "No cow outfit this close to the border hires just everyday cowboys and you know it. He'll have some good men riding for him." Hardy waggled his head and looked dolorously at John Gates. "Why'n hell is it that the minute you or Aleck get running loose you get into trouble?"

Gates smiled. "I guess we're just lucky."

Hardy drew out his tobacco sack and went to work despite John Gates's pointing to the sign midway in the runway prohibiting smoking. Hardy lit up and turned to watch the hostler stabling the horses of three men who had ridden up out front a few minutes earlier. While he was still facing away from Gates, he said: "I came within an ace of not even coming over here. I was figuring to go right on through and meet you and Aleck in San Francisco. Then I got to thinking. Turning the pair of you loose was like freeing a couple of caged cougars. And sure enough." Hardy faced Gates. "Don't they have any law in this damned place?"

"Yeah. A town marshal. I locked him into one of his cells a while back."

"You locked . . . ?"

"He sold out to the cowman who is trying to break my grandfather."

"You know that to be a fact, John, or are you just jumping to a conclusion?" asked Hardy, and John Gates related how Marshal Hudson had confessed in front of both Gates and Dr. Ward that he had accepted a bribe from Grant Mitchell.

Hardy smoked and considered, and, when the hostler, sniffing smoke, came briskly along looking officious, Hardy turned on him with deadly look, and the hostler, after making his appraisal of the faded cowman wearing the tied-down Colt with the ivory grips, turned abruptly and walked back up toward his harness room without saying a word.

Hardy shook his head, dropped the cigarette to grind it mercilessly underfoot, and straightened up with a loud, noisy sigh. "All right. All right, John, but if this cowman comes to town with his whole riding crew, you sure as hell don't expect to call 'em in the center of the road."

Gates answered in a way that indicated he had either been through this before, or else he had given it a lot of thought this first time. "You walk up past the jailhouse on this side of the road, Hardy. Take a stand somewhere north of there, maybe in the doorway of the gunsmith's shop, which will put you behind them. I'll stand down in front of the jailhouse. They'll see me and come right on down." Gates made a little gesture with both hands. "Beyond that, we have to do things as they fall our way."

"They'll kill you," said Hardy. "Even with me behind them to back you up, if they draw, one of them sure as hell is bound to kill you. Can't the two of us together outshoot five or six men."

Gates was not convinced of this. "I have an idea," he said, then did not elaborate on it. "You just go on up there and get into place."

Hardy looked less resigned than disgusted. "Then what, assuming you walk out of the smoke, then what?"

"We head for San Francisco like we said we'd do. I told you last winter, I had to go see the old man. Maybe I'll never see him again, and he's the only kin I've got left."

Hardy was agreeable, finally. "All right. But if you don't stay here permanent, so's the old man can go every Sunday and put flowers on your grave, I'll sure be surprised."

Hardy turned to walk back up through the livery barn in the direction of the front roadway, his tall, lean silhouette moving with lithe grace.

The hostler looked from the harness room doorway, watched him walk past, then hastened down where John Gates was standing. "Who'n hell is that feller, Mister Gates? He looks like a bad feller to cross."

Gates smiled, clapped the hostler on the back, and also started on up through as he said: "He is a bad man to cross. Next to that feller, Billy the Kid, Jesse James, Bill Hickok, and

Johnny Ringo are beginners."

Gates reached the roadway, stopped to scan it for sign of Big M, and all he saw was a couple more horses at the tie rack in front of the saloon than had been there a half hour earlier when he and Hardy had left that place. He was not deluded. Grant Mitchell would arrive. Whatever was delaying this event would be unable totally to prevent Mitchell from coming to Sangerville to avenge the killing of his range boss.

Gates rolled and lit a smoke, then began slowly strolling up in the direction of the jailhouse. The reason he had chosen this to be his place of confrontation was because he did not want anyone going inside and finding the town marshal locked in one of his own cells, and, although Gates had the jailhouse keys in his pocket, he was not convinced someone like Grant Mitchell, arriving in town for blood, would not shoot open the cell door. For a while yet, he did not want it widely known that Town Marshal Greg Hudson was a prisoner, a discredited lawman, and a cohort of Grant Mitchell in another of Mitchell's land-grabbing enterprises.

XIII

John Gates entered the jailhouse and was seen doing this by a number of people who observed that he had first to unlock the jailhouse door, and that inevitably caused talk and speculation. He was not the local lawman; he had no business locking and unlocking the local jailhouse. There was something more than surprise to prevent anyone from walking over there, demanding to know who he thought he was.

Gates went to the wall rack, removed two shotguns, made certain both were loaded, then left them leaning upon the wall beside the roadway door when he went down to the cell where Greg Hudson was sitting disconsolately upon a wall bunk.

Greg looked up and said: "I didn't hear any shooting, so I

89

didn't figure they'd shot you, but I'm surprised to see you anyway."

"Tell me that in a couple of hours," retorted Gates, and shoved a hand through the bars. "Give me that badge off your shirt."

Hudson made no move to comply; he simply sat staring out.

Gates withdrew his hand and reached in his pocket for the cell keys. "All right," he mumbled, "you want to bait me into coming inside to get it, I'll do that, too." He swung back the door and Greg Hudson unwound up off his bunk, turning fully and bracing him. He was ready. He did not have the appearance of a man who wanted to fight, but he did have the look of a man who would fight.

Gates paused in the doorway. Hudson was a thickly put-together, powerful man. Gates had, during his law-enforcement years, tangled with many men. He had long ago decided that the least likely men to be defeated in a brawl were men built the way Marshal Hudson was built. Gates sighed and held out his hand again. "Big M will be showing up directly, Marshal. We can shoot it out or I can try for a legal arrest. With the badge I might bring the thing off. Without it, there are going to be some dead men in the roadway before suppertime."

Hudson was not convinced. "They won't pay any attention to you wearing my badge. They know who is town marshal here-abouts."

Gates dropped his hand to his side. "Then let me put it to you differently. You keep the badge, and come out front into the roadway with me. Two men, two shotguns, one badge . . . and one ace in the hole."

"What ace in the hole?"

"A partner of mine is in town. He's going to back me from a doorway on this side of the road. He'll be behind Mitchell when Big M rides down here."

"To shoot someone in the back?" asked Hudson.

Gates cocked his head a little when he replied: "You've got ethics all of a sudden, Marshal? You, who teamed up with a son-of-a-bitch like Mitchell to rob a helpless old man?" Gates shook his head at the lawman. "You coming out with me or not?"

"No."

"Then toss over the badge." This time Gates drew his Colt and slowly tipped it and just as slowly cocked it. For Greg Hudson there really was not much of a choice. He knew John Gates had killed one man today and that influenced him to believe Gates would kill again. He could not quite make up his mind as to whether John Gates would shoot him down in cold blood or not. He decided not to take the chance, unpinned the badge, and pitched it over for Gates to catch one-handed. Gates put up the gun and smiled.

Outside, someone called a greeting and someone else answered it in a gruff, flat-sounding voice. Greg Hudson thought he recognized that voice, and looked worried.

"Don't go out there and buck him," he said to Gates. "You don't know Mitchell. He'll send his whole damned crew to ride you down, and, if you shot them all, he'd just go and hire more, and send them after you, too."

John Gates accepted this. "Just tell me one more thing about Mitchell," he said. "Is that how he got to be the biggest cowman hereabouts . . . by riding folks down and hiring them shot?"

Hudson squirmed, did not answer, and went across to the narrow, high little window in the three-foot-thick adobe wall to stand on his toes and peer out into the roadway. Gates closed the door and was locking it when Hudson turned from the window. "What the hell are people going to think . . . you out there wearing my badge, doing my job?"

Gates smiled. "Darned if I know. Maybe they'll commence to

think the truth about you, Marshal."

Hudson swore. "Truth! God dammit, what truth? The first time in my life I ever took money from anyone. . . ."

Gates believed this. He had made up his mind about this days ago. Hudson was weak, and maybe he'd been a damned idiot, but he was not an outlaw, a coward, or a renegade lawman. Gates leaned on the door, looking in. Most men, sometime during their lives, do things that are out of character, and usually they get away with it and never do anything like that again. Lawmen were different; they couldn't do what Hudson had done; by avocation they were exposed to every suspicion and every degree of taxpayer curiosity.

Gates pulled back. "Did you see Mitchell out there?"

Hudson hadn't. "No. But I saw two men he hired on a month back. They aren't range riders any more than I'm the man in the moon. Gates, I'll give you odds he didn't come to town, didn't figure he had to take care of someone like you. He sent those two."

Gates was relieved. If this estimate were true, then there would not be five or six men to be faced; there would only be two of them. That made everything seem very different. Gates smiled. He and Greg Hudson stood gazing at one another with the cell bars between them. Gates wished he dared allow the lawman to leave his cell. If Hudson had agreed to go out there with Gates, he would have freed him. Now he turned, and walked on up into the office, closed the cell-room door, reluctantly pinned on the badge, and went over to pick up the pair of scatter-guns and stand a moment weighing what had to be done against what he thought might turn out to be the crux of all this trouble. In the end he did not take the shotguns outside with him but left them leaning against the wall. Nor did he lock the jailhouse door from the outside as he had done earlier. He simply closed the door, and stood a moment to allow his eyes to become fully adjusted, then he looked up the road in the direction of the saloon, and made out the Big M brand on two horses at the rack up there.

He crossed to the front of the general store. There were still some of the old men sitting there on those wall benches despite the fact that the sun had finally got around to where it could throw its direct rays under the overhang and reach the benches. Not a word was said, as before, when John Gates strolled past, but all those old men saw Hudson's badge on Gates, saw that the tie down was hanging loose on Gates's six-gun, and that he had brushed back his coat so that the big black six-gun was fully exposed. The old men had lived through many of these episodes and knew every indication. They still did not turn to talk among themselves, though. They sat and leaned on their canes and watched Gates's steady progress like vultures watching the death throes of a dying victim.

There were other people who saw Gates and the badge, too, and, generally the word had already passed around among the stores that Big M had sent in two men, so the plank walks were anything but crowded with people. In fact, John Gates had the plank walk between the general store and the saloon entirely to himself. The only pedestrian was a loafer from the corral yard, and, when he saw Gates coming, he flung half around and walked faster across the road than most men could trot, and disappeared inside the corral yard's big log fence in record time.

A skinny range man idling out front of the harness shop turned and ambled to the doors of the saloon, looked once again to be certain of the identity of the man wearing the badge, then he pushed on inside with an exaggerated air of total indifference. He did not fool anyone who saw him; he had rushed to warn the pair of Big M riders at the bar.

John Gates paused to glance across in the direction of the

gunsmith's shop. Things were different; there was to be no band of mounted riders armed to the teeth and conditioned to kill, backing up an old bleak and bitter-eyed cowman. The confrontation would not come down in front of the jailhouse now, either. If Hardy was in the gun shop across from the saloon and slightly north of it, he would not be behind the men from Mitchell's cow outfit as much as he would be nearly opposite them when they emerged from the bar.

Gates considered all the aspects. He could not afford to do otherwise. If he made one serious miscalculation, Marshal Hudson's prediction would very probably come true—his grandfather would take flowers to a grave out back of town every Sunday. A lanky, faded silhouette came to the door of the gun shop and hovered a moment, then retreated back deeper into the shop. Gates smiled and began moving again.

Gates dried his palm down the outside of a trouser leg, walked slowly but purposefully until he was under the overhang of the apothecary's shop, which stood just south of the saloon, then he heard sounds from within the saloon, so he halted. That skinny cowboy who had made the exaggerated entrance moments earlier pushed out upon the plank walk and gazed insolently at John Gates before turning his back and walking up to the front of the saddle and harness works. There, in roughly the same place he had been standing in earlier to keep his vigil, he settled again with his back to the rough boards.

Gates waited. He expected the Big M gunmen either to come out slowly, spread wide to catch him in a cross-fire, or to come out fast and shooting. He was wrong on both counts. Only one of them walked out. Gates thought he had seen this man before, either in the roadway or at the saloon. The rough-looking dark man sneered and faced Gates. Behind him that skinny jackal kept his gun hand high, away from his hip holster, but Gates was not fooled. If he missed or if the Big M beat him to the first shot, the jackal would buy in. In every gunfight there was at least one glory hunter.

The gunman said: "You didn't give Cliff a chance. Let's see how good you are when you're facing someone who's ready for you."

Gates said nothing. There was no time to deny that charge. He gently nodded. One second later a rifle exploded from across the road. Its flat, reverberating sound caught Gates totally unprepared. He knew where Hardy was and he knew Hardy did not have a rifle. The gunman up in front of the saloon was also thrown off balance, but that explosion triggered him. He reacted by streaking for his holster, but he had partially twisted at the sound of the rifle. Now he had to twist back. He was still moving when Gates's thumb slid off the cocked hammer. The second explosion was louder, more thunderous. Big M's gunman looked amazed as he completed his draw one second ahead of the second shot Gates got off. The gunman dropped to both knees, trying to cock his Colt. He fell forward and the Colt skittered from the plank walk into the dusty roadway.

With a clear sighting past the downed man Gates cocked his weapon for the final shot. That skinny man up there was ramrod erect, his eyes bulging in disbelief. Then he decided he had to try, but he was much too slow and far too late. Gates let the hammer drop one more time. The skinny cowboy screamed as the bullet broke his leg and dumped him, sprawling, in the dirt. He did not try to draw; he simply rolled and screamed and used both hands to try and stop the gushing blood from his broken leg. His outcries were the only sounds, when the last gunshot echo faded, and, when he was able, finally, to grit his teeth and stifle the sobs, there was no sound at all until Hardy walked forth but without the rifle from the gunsmith's rack, and hooked his thumbs in his shell belt, gazing southward.

There was a spread-eagled dead man fifty yards southward.

He had fallen from the roof top where he had been maneuvering to get a shoulder shot at John Gates from behind, when Hardy had shot him through the head. It was an extraordinary shot. In years to come men would argue about whether Hardy had actually been that accomplished a marksman, or whether he had taken a long chance by aiming at the head, and had been exceptionally lucky. The reason the argument would never be resolved was that no one ever knew Hardy, ever saw him again after he rode out of Sangerville, and all the searching the world over never turned up anything about him again. Right at the moment, though, he was no mystery at all as he stepped forth to walk over and gaze downward at the Big M gunman Gates had killed. Neither he nor Gates acted as though they knew that pain-wracked jackal was wallowing in the hot dust out in front of the saddle and harness works.

They picked up the six-gun of the dark dead man in front of the saloon, then walked down the road to retrieve the smashed carbine of the second Big M gunman, then they walked on down to the jailhouse without a soul coming forth to speak to either of them. The roadway and both plank walks were totally empty.

XIV

At the jailhouse the conversation was to the point. Hardy had seen the man on the roof top stealthily making his way along until he could see Gates near the edge of the plank walk, partially protected by the wooden overhang in front of the apothecary's shop. If Hardy hadn't been situated exactly right, the man with the carbine would probably have killed Gates. Otherwise, the man who came out of the saloon was an ordinary range man who thought he was much better as a gunman than he actually was. There was nothing unusual about this attitude at all. Every town west of the Missouri had headboards in its cemetery attesting to other range men who had made this same mistake.

This was not simply a gunfight. While he was making a fresh pot of coffee in Greg Hudson's office, John Gates emphasized this by saying: "Now the old man will come to town. This time, when someone rushes out there and tells him what happened, he'll saddle up. We just stopped his attempt to organize one murder. The old bastard will try again."

Hardy stood leaning in a roadside window, gazing out. "The town's taking it well," he reported. "Some men are loading them into a handcart and wheeling them southward. Otherwise, folks don't look like they'd want to hang us."

"It's a fair town," said John Gates. "They don't know what this is all about, but the impression I get is that they're willing to hold back judgments as long as these fights are plumb fair."

Hardy ignored this estimation to say: "They've got that feller with the busted leg between two fellers." Hardy was interested. "Who the hell was he? I thought it was supposed to be just two gunmen."

Gates did not know who he was. "Some damned two-legged coyote," he said, listening to see if the coffee pot was simmering yet. "Are they taking him southward, too?"

"Yeah."

"Doctor Ward's diggings are down there."

Hardy continued to lean, watching the roadway. He may have thought the townsmen would become hostile, or he may simply have been intrigued by the fact that they did not become irate, after all, but in either case he continued to lean there, looking out, and, when John Gates handed him a cup of fresh coffee, he took that to the window with him and raised his sights a little to scan the roof line across the roadway. It was not altogether unusual for a man to climb atop roofs in time of trouble, but it was not considered fair fighting to do it the way that dead man had done it. Maybe the townsmen were also aware of that.

Gates took a cup of black coffee down to the cell where Hudson was standing. He had heard the shooting and had to be enormously curious. When he saw who was bringing him coffee, he slumped slightly and shook his head. "I didn't expect you," he said, emphasizing the last word. He accepted the coffee through bars. "What happened?"

Gates told him. "One of them was atop a roof to shoot me in the back. My partner nailed him. The other one came out of the saloon like he was a whole lot faster than he was, and I got that one." Gates loosened the badge and flung it through the bars upon the bunk. "Never got a chance to try and make a decent arrest," he explained, "and I figure it'll be the same way when old Mitchell rides in. I won't get the chance then, either."

Hudson said: "Let me out."

Gates stood in the dingy, little, narrow corridor gazing through the bars. "Fifteen minutes ago I would have," he stated. "Now . . . I don't think so." He turned on his heel.

"Listen," exclaimed Greg Hudson, "what you did out there washed me up! Folks won't just wonder why I wasn't out there. They'll wonder about you using my badge, and they'll wonder about some other things . . . mostly when Grant Mitchell gets here, he's going to tell them I took his money. He'll do that for revenge."

Gates was not convinced. "How would Mitchell even know you're not still on his side?"

"Because I didn't ride out and tell him about Cliff . . . about you. After those riders tried to kill your grandfather, I argued hard with Mitchell and Habersham about killings, and about them riding roughshod over folks when they didn't have to. We were about to break off even before you showed up. He'll know how I felt then, and he'll figure I still feel the same way. He'll think I sold him out, and, by God, it sure looks like I did."

Gates considered, and finally made his decision. "Marshal, if he's that fired up against you, I think the best place for you is right where you are." Gates turned, hung the jail cell keys on the peg across from the cell, and walked on up to the office doorway with Greg Hudson's pleas ringing in his ears. He closed the door, returned Hardy's quizzical look with a shrug, and went to draw off another cup of coffee as he explained: "The town marshal wants out. He figures he's washed up anyway, so he might as well help us against Grant Mitchell."

Hardy scowled. "You going to let him out?"

"Nope." Gates turned, cup in hand. "I feel sorry for him. He's not bad. He's just weak enough to take a bribe. All the same, when we're in this kind of trouble, I'll be damned if I want someone like that behind me, with a gun in his hand."

Hardy agreed and left his window to refill his coffee cup. Someone was walking up the plank walk outside with a solid tread. Gates went to the vacated window to look out. It was the bearded stage company representative, Hubert Townley. He did not look exactly resolute but he seemed to be compelling himself to act that way.

Gates stepped over and yanked the door inward. Townley halted in his tracks, then he turned in, and, as he passed John Gates, he said: "Folks are afraid of what's going to happen next." He eyed Hardy askance and got back an equally sidelong look as the other stranger turned from the stove with a cup in his hand. But Hardy's glance was also skeptical.

"Mitchell will come to town," stated Gates. "That's what'll happen next, *amigo.*"

Townley bobbed his head. "Yeah. That's what folks are figuring. And they don't want him here with you fellers still around. We never had a big battle and we don't want one." Townley looked around, then back at Gates. "Where's Greg Hudson?"

"Not available," grunted Gates, and turned the topic back to its original theme. "What do folks figure we'd ought to do, then?"

"Leave," blurted out the stage company agent. "Leave Sangerville right away. They've even went so far as to send some men down to the livery barn to saddle your horses and lead 'em up here for you."

Hardy strolled to the window, looked out, then turned and spoke for the first time since Townley's arrival: "Trouble is, friend, by now Mitchell will be on his way, and, if we run, he's going to take up the chase."

"We'll keep him here as long as we can," stated Townley. "I told 'em that when they first said you fellers had ought to ride on out. I told 'em he'd run you down and outnumber you all at the same time."

Gates smiled. "You're a thoughtful man, friend, and you're plumb right. If we run, Mitchell will catch us out on the range away from shelter, and under those circumstances we won't stand too good a chance, so maybe you'd best go on back and tell your friends we're staying."

Townley licked his lips, glanced around again, then turned back toward the door. As a sort of afterthought he put his earlier question to John Gates again: "Where is Marshal Hudson?" Someone yelled from across the road over in front of the general store and Townley pulled back the door to crane out and around. As he straightened up, he looked accusingly at Gates and said: "Too late to run now."

Townley stepped through onto the plank walk and pulled the jailhouse door closed after him. He moved swiftly, as though he wanted to be well away from the jailhouse when the Big M riders rode down the main thoroughfare. He did not want anyone mistakenly to assume he was friendly with the men forted up in there.

Hardy strolled over, looked out, looked northward where the

riders would be appearing, then drained the last of his coffee, put the cup aside, and said: "Where's the back door out of this place?"

They left the jailhouse without a sound.

The west side alleyway was deserted from one end to the other end. Even down by the livery barn where there usually was activity, the alley was empty. It was, Hardy muttered, like walking through a ghost town. After that one shout of warning from out front of the general store there was not another sound. Evidently the town knew it was no longer possible to avert trouble, and was now holing up to the best of its ability in anticipation of a savage gunfight.

Gates said: "He'll be coming from the north."

Hardy did not wait. He jerked his head and started up the northward alleyway. Gates was hurrying along beside him when they both heard a familiar sound, distant but clear and recognizable. There was a stagecoach coming from the northeast.

Gates decided this might create a slight diversion. He beckoned Hardy to follow him down between two buildings where they would have a fair view of the wide and empty main roadway, while the sounds of that oncoming vehicle grew louder. When they could look up and down the roadway from their secret place between the buildings, all they saw was a cowboy hastily untying three horses from a tie rack as though he wanted to get those animals out of harm's way if a gunfight erupted in the roadway.

There was no sign of a band of armed, mounted men. Hardy, scratching the side of his head with the barrel of his Colt, looked doubtful. "Where is this ring-tailed roarer? I don't see anyone."

The coach bore down into town, dropped from a flinging gallop to a jangling trot, and held to this gait to minimize the dust—according to city ordinances—and that was all anyone could see, so Gates pulled back a little, shaking his head. "I don't know where the old bastard is," he complained. "Sure as hell that's what they yelled about before we left the jailhouse."

Hardy, watching the coach halt in front of the way station, suddenly sucked back his breath. The sound was so sharp it brought Gates around. Hardy used his six-gun as a pointer when he said: "Look! Look yonder getting off the blasted coach!"

Gates turned back. The man alighting from the stage, apparently the only passenger, was dark-headed, dark-eyed, well-built, handsome, when he turned his head, and was wearing an elaborately tailored brocade vest under his rumpled, dusty, buckskin coat.

"Aleck," said Gates, "the damned fool."

Hardy pushed his hat back, using the tip of his gun barrel. "How do we get him out of the road without letting everyone know we're not still in the jailhouse?"

Gates said: "We don't. Look yonder, out behind the coach northward."

There was a bunched-up band of range men out there, to the north, walking their horses steadily toward town without any attempt at haste. If this was what the man had seen earlier, when he had yelled, then he must have seen them while they were still a mile out because it had taken them this long to reach the outskirts of Sangerville.

"How many?" asked Hardy, craning past to try and make a count.

Gates had no idea. "They're bunched up too close to make a count, but there are more of them than there are of us, I can tell you that." Gates swore. "Look at Aleck."

The handsome man had accepted a carpetbag from the coach driver and was now standing in the center of the roadway, gazing out where Big M was approaching. It was easy to tell from Aleck's stance that he recognized those horsemen as being trouble-bound. While Hardy and Gates watched, their partner very slowly turned and looked down the empty roadway. Gates risked a frantic gesture, but apparently Aleck didn't notice because when he had completed his study of the empty southward roadway, he casually faced the oncoming men again. About this time Hubert Townley scuttled out, ordered the driver to put his rig and hitch inside the corral yard, and grabbed Aleck's sleeve to tug as he anxiously explained those oncoming horsemen were arriving in town for a fight.

Aleck allowed himself to be half dragged into the stage company's office. Up the road, Hardy and John Gates sighed disgustedly, then Gates turned quickly and gestured. "Go on back to the alley. We can still make it up to the corral yard before Mitchell gets here."

Hardy hastened to obey.

XV

To reach the corral yard they had to hurry along the alleyway for another hundred yards. There was a log gate there, kept closed most of the time because the alley was rarely used by the rigs and men inside the stage company's yard. It was a heavy gate and it sagged. Hardy cursed and grunted until he had it dragged free far enough to admit a body, then he and John Gates eased through. There were four men standing by the stage that had just arrived. One of them, in the act of pulling off a pair of gaudy-beaded gauntlets, saw Gates and Hardy and paid them no attention as he went on with his glove-removing routine while the other three men talked and did not glance toward the back of the yard at all.

It was a large yard. There was ample room for several rigs at the same time, and along with a jacked-up coach, lacking both rear wheels there were long pole racks for harness, some corrals out back, and even several box stalls. Where the small combination cook shack and bunkhouse stood, an old Mexican was painstakingly stacking lengths of firewood cut for a cook stove. He saw the pair of men crossing on an angle from the rear gate in the direction of the front office and recognized them both because he had been witness to the recent gun battle in the roadway. He went right on slowly racking up the wood from his ancient wagon, but never once took his eyes off the two men, and, when they finally got over to the open door of the office, the old Mexican paused to remove his hat and mop perspiration from his leathery face. He made no move toward the other men in the yard. He was old and he was peaceful, and he had lived to be this way because of his outstanding characteristic of minding his own business. If *Señor* Satan himself had levered himself up through a crack in the parched earth, the old *mestizo* would have pretended not to have seen anything.

Hubert Townley was inside his office, going through a thick sifting of papers atop the litter on his battered desk, and did not raise his eyes when the door was pulled silently back and a man beckoned to the handsome stranger wearing that elegant brocade vest from out in the corral yard. The stranger did not say a word. He picked up his carpetbag and followed the beckoning man out of the office. Hubert, with his back to the door, did not know his passenger had departed.

Out back, Gates and Hardy did not allow the man with the fancy vest to say a word to them. They walked briskly in the direction of the back wall gate and he followed. Again, the coach driver, with his splendid pair of gauntlets tucked under his gun belt, looked up, then turned indifferently to join in the conversation of the other men, the yard attendants and hostlers who were still breathless over the dual killings that had occurred shortly before the coach had reached town.

The Mexican, though, saw those three men as Gates

contrived to use that jacked-up coach as a shield while he and his companions headed back toward the rear gate. The Mexican watched. When Hardy turned in his direction, the Mexican resumed his wood stacking as though he had never for a moment considered anything else, and he did not risk another look until the three men had whisked out of the yard, leaving that rear gate partially open. Then he rolled up his eyes, breathed a short prayer, and went back to work. Whatever happened now, there were three of those gunfighting strangers in town, not just one or two of them.

Gates paused to run a sleeve across his shiny face and Hardy eyed Aleck's carpetbag skeptically. "You won't need that thing," he told Aleck. "Unless you got a dismembered Gatling gun in it."

Aleck looked from one to the other of them. "You get running free and right away you get into trouble. A man can't leave fellers like you for a minute before. . . ."

"Hey, damn it," croaked Gates, "we didn't ask for this trouble. And if you'd showed up a couple of days ago, we could have cleaned out the whole. . . ."

"My aunt was ailin' down in Albuquerque," stated Aleck, and, when he saw the silent, long stares of total disbelief he was getting for that remark, he rushed on to change the subject. "What the hell is going on? That feller who runs the stage office said something about two men having been shot."

Gates looked up and down the alleyway, then led the way back toward that dogtrot between two buildings where he and Hardy had first seen the stagecoach arrive. When they were safely hidden from searching eyes, he explained as much as he felt he had the time to explain. When he finished, Aleck looked irritably at them both, but he made no comment; he simply turned and leaned to look up and down the back alley, then he pulled back, speaking quietly. "Couple of horsemen coming down this way from up north. Would they be some of your Big M friends?"

Gates edged past for a look. He did not recognize either rider but he did not have to recognize them. Both range men were walking their horses quietly, and both men had carbines balanced across their laps. They were Big M riders without a doubt, and they were now flanking the jailhouse, obviously because they had been told to do this in order to prevent the men who were supposedly forted up in the jailhouse from escaping out the back way.

Gates pulled back cautiously, palmed his six-gun, and, when his partners saw this happen, they did the same. Nothing was said until Hardy, who was in the poorest position to see out into the back alley, grumbled at Aleck for usurping his position, and Aleck growled back for Hardy to be quiet, and, when he raised his gun to be certain, he raised it high enough so as to avoid hitting either Aleck or Gates. Hardy swore.

John Gates sank to one knee, eased his face half around until he could watch the progress of those cowboys, then he sighed and spoke softly without taking his eyes off the armed horsemen. "I'll call 'em, and you fellers let them see guns. No point in cutting loose unless they do."

Hardy muttered about that: "With us squeezed into this narrow damned slot, if they shoot blind, they're going to get all three of us like shooting quail on a tree limb."

The horsemen paused. One leaned, staring intently at the back wall of the jailhouse, and said: "Suppose they ain't still in there, Jerry?"

Jerry did not answer; John Gates did. He raised the gun in his fist and said: "They ain't in there, gents. Don't raise a hand."

The riders looked, saw three six-guns aimed in their direction, and froze.

Gates gave the orders. "Get down, gents, and let those Winchesters fall. Good. Now turn your backs to us and stand right still."

One of them, evidently certain of what was now to ensue—being knocked over the head from behind—suddenly said: "Listen, fellers, we just ride for the old man. We don't hold with all his fights with folks. We just hired on to ride and. . . ."

"Shut up," growled Hardy, pushing out of the dogtrot with his friends. "I never could stand a whinin' bastard."

The pair of cowboys stood like stone, awkwardly stiff and obviously full of foreboding. Gates and Aleck hung back a little while Hardy stalked out there to complete the disarming of their captives. He flung down their six-guns and roughly manhandled each man for a belly gun or a boot knife, neither of which he found. Then he overhanded them both as impersonally as though he had been pole-axing beeves. Gates winced and Aleck made a little clucking sound, but neither man had a word to say as Hardy leaned to drag his unconscious victims out of the center of the alleyway.

They clucked up the loose horses and allowed them to go meandering in the direction of the southward livery barn.

Gates smiled at his companions. "By my count, we've just about evened the numbers of old Mitchell. In fact, we might even have the edge on him by one man . . . unless he's rounded up more men than he's supposed to have riding for him."

Out front, a man whistled loudly. Gates looked wry about that. "Whistle back," he told Aleck. "That'll be the old bastard's signal that him and the rest of his crew are in place."

Aleck used two fingers in his mouth to return the whistle, then the three of them ducked back into their dogtrot and headed for the main roadway out front.

Big M was not in sight, but over at the tie rack in front of the saloon there were five horses. Aleck looked, then scowled. "What was that you said about us being evened up with these fellers?

107

Are those their horses? You've mentioned Big M, Gates. That's the mark on those critters."

Hardy swore again, which seemed characteristic of him when he was exasperated or troubled. He did not say whatever it was that annoyed him; he just swore about it.

Gates could only offer a guess. "He's rounded up some other range riders sure as hell. Maybe he's borrowed some men from another cow outfit."

"Counting those two in the alley, he reached town with seven men," stated Hardy.

Aleck took that up, sounding a lot less perturbed. "All right. And already we whittled it down to five. That's not too bad, Hardy. Five to three, and the three are right handy fellers, not to mention being handsome in the trade, and elegant, and. . . ."

"You numbskull," growled Hardy. "There's five men over yonder who'll kill us on sight. You pick some awful times to make jokes."

Gates studied the saloon, then reached his decision. "Gents, Mitchell figures to block us from escaping out the back of the jailhouse, and about now he or at least one or two of his men are watching the front of the jailhouse from the saloon's windows. Well, Hardy, you slip around to the north end of town, cross over and come down that east side back alley and get into position out back of the saloon. Aleck and I'll wait for someone to come out of the saloon. Only Aleck's going to stroll back up to the corral yard. So far, he's a plumb stranger in town." Gates turned. "All right?"

Aleck shrugged his indifference to the plan, and Hardy turned without a word and ducked back toward the rear alley.

When Gates was alone in the dogtrot, he took time to examine his six-gun, to squint a brief glance skyward to estimate the time of day, then he settled forward as far as he dared move and looked up and down the completely empty and silent roadway. Sangerville was as hushed and empty-seeming as though it did not have a single living resident. The sun was overhead, the sky was azure, there were a few skimpy, light clouds edging down from the north, and from a very great distance came the short, grunting, high bellow of a range bull.

Up the road and roughly opposite the saloon was the stage company's roadway office, depot, and corral yard. From up there came sounds of someone beating steel on an anvil. Evidently the repairs to that jacked-up coach were in progress despite the fact that all the rest of the town was holding its breath.

Two Mexican cowboys approaching from the east paused to look and listen, and afterward to alter their course so as to reach Mex town at the southern end of Sangerville without entering the main business sector. Men had an almost unfailing ability for sensing this kind of trouble whether their hide was pale or dark.

John Gates removed his hat, mopped sweat, dropped the hat back down, and felt thirsty without being in a position to do anything about it.

Across the road a man strolled indifferently from the saloon, paused under the wooden overhang to gaze thoughtfully down in the direction of the jailhouse, then he moved ahead to untie all those Big M saddle animals and move them farther away up the roadway to another tie rack. Following this, a pair of riders walked out, untied, clambered across leather, and booted out their horses in a lope northward. They did not slacken pace or glance back until they were a half mile north of the town.

Gates waited, mopped sweat, and became irritable over the delay. He guessed what Grant Mitchell was doing—letting the men he thought were forted up in the jailhouse see his horses, realize his numbers, and slowly dissolve in their own sweat inside the jailhouse. Gates's disapproval of a man like Grant

Mitchell was strong from the very beginning. Now, it was almost overpoweringly antagonistic, and the longer he stood there sweltering in his airless little gloomy narrow place between two buildings, the more overpoweringly antagonistic it became.

Finally the cowboy who had moved the horses ducked abruptly to the far side of the roadway—the same side Gates and Aleck were upon—evidently as part of some pre-arranged strategy, and because he could not now be seen by anyone inside the jailhouse, when he began his southward stalk, although he palmed his six-gun, he was not very cautious as he walked along.

XVI

Aleck saw the man. So did John Gates. So, presumably, did a great many secret and silent other observers up and down the roadway, but only Gates and Aleck were vitally interested, and Aleck allowed the range rider to pass the corral yard where he was secreted and get two-thirds of the way along toward the dogtrot where John Gates was waiting, before he moved toward the front gate of the corral yard and took up his position there, watching—not the armed range rider walking toward the jail-house—but the batwing door across the road. He expected someone to come forth from the saloon in support of the range man.

John Gates watched with his face half in dark shadows until the cowboy was almost close enough, then he raised his handgun. The cowboy was close, no more than fifty or sixty feet, when he either saw movement in the dogtrot, or felt an instinctive alarm. He turned his head and John Gates aimed the cocked Colt.

The cowboy missed a step and almost staggered, but recovered quickly enough to lurch toward the edge of the roadway as Gates called softly to him: "Drop the gun and stand still."

The cowboy gave a tremendous leap and tried desperately to spring past the dogtrot. He was swinging his handgun to bear as he made this frantic effort. Gates, who had expected almost anything but a tremendous bound like the cowboy gave, twisted his body sideways just as the cowboy fired. Gates fired back and the mid-air figure lost its soaring equilibrium and struck the edge of the plank walk, then fell and rolled.

Across the road three men burst from the saloon, firing in the direction of the dogtrot. One of those bullets caught the folds of Gates's coat and rammed him hard against the nearest wooden wall. He stumbled and almost went down to one knee. The other two slugs did not enter the narrow place but splintered the wooden siding out front.

Gates struggled to regain his stance. The cowboy he had shot flopped but made no real effort to reach the gun that had fallen from his hand, and, as the fighting became more violently intense, the cowboy ceased to move altogether.

Aleck sang out a profane challenge to the gunmen opposite in front of the saloon, and shot the legs out from under one of them. The other two, astonished at this fresh attack from so unexpected a place, broke away to the right and left and ran for cover. Aleck followed one of them, the man fleeing northward, and one of Aleck's bullets blew the harness shop window to pieces. It had only been painstakingly taped together within the past couple of hours after the killing of Cliff Habersham.

Gates got back to his feet. One of those startled range riders was opposite him across the road, running southward as hard as his legs would pump. Gates aimed and fired, and effected a clean miss. The fleeing cowboy did not even wince, did not even turn his head or fire back.

Across the road a sudden fresh burst of gunfire erupted. This time it sounded as though Grant Mitchell and his remaining riders had sought stealthily to leave the saloon by the back alley, perhaps with some thought in mind of infiltrating the dogtrots on their side of the roadway, which would have been an excellent tactic except that Hardy Campbell was out there, behind a rotting old tumbledown wooden fence, and, when the first man rushed forth gun in hand, Hardy fired.

Gates and Aleck, both trying to track their fleeing range men out front, were abruptly relegated to a minor rôle as the brunt of the gunfight shifted completely, and most of the deafening gunfire now came from the alley out behind the saloon. A unique event suddenly took place out front, and for a while only John Gates knew it had happened. That fleeing range man across on the west plank walk came abreast of the jailhouse, still fleeing as swiftly as he could, still not looking left or right, when the jailhouse door suddenly was punched open and a man loomed up over there with a shotgun in both hands. Gates did not see him, at the moment, did not even know he was down there when Gates leaned, a little recklessly, to look down and see where that fleeing cowboy had gone. Gates heard the roared challenge, heard and recognized the town marshal's voice as Greg Hudson yelled for the fleeing cowboy to halt. The cowboy finally looked over his shoulder. He saw Hudson, saw the shotgun, changed leads in mid-stride, flung up his six-gun, and thumbed off two rapid shots. Gates heard the shotgun roar. It sounded as though someone had fired a mountain Howitzer. Gates saw that fleeing range rider suddenly lifted bodily from his boots and hurled through a window of the general store from the full charge of that shotgun. Gates also saw the man holding the shotgun step out, start to take an onward step, then drop like stone. That was all Gates had time to see for a while. The fight around back in the alleyway was spilling over into the front roadway.

He heard Hardy's bull-bass roar of defiance as the fighters gave away before his blazing weapon and tried to make a rush northward where that man had taken the Big M horses. Aleck was yelling through the gun thunder for the men across the road to stop it, to throw down their guns, to stop firing. No one heeded him, but one of the men who had been driven down the side of the saloon toward the front roadway, crouched and fired twice in the direction of Aleck's shouting.

Gates sucked far back in his dogtrot, plugged in fresh loads with fingers that were slippery with sweat, then closed the loading gate, and took a forward step just in time to see a grizzled, fierce-faced man jump into plain sight with a blazing six-gun in his right hand.

Gates yelled—"Mitchell! You son-of-a-bitch!"—and fired. Mitchell swung toward the dogtrot, accepting Gates's challenge. He fired. Wood splintered overhead, making Gates wince when slivers cascaded downward, then Mitchell fired again, grinning from ear to ear. Gates steadied his right wrist, aimed, and squeezed off the shot. Mitchell was in the act of firing again. He tugged off the shot and hung his thumb pad over the hammer to draw it back again, and without a word or any change of expression he dropped. Gates was in the act of firing. It was too late to stop it, so he tugged off the round, but it struck wood where Grant Mitchell had been. Mitchell was face down, still holding his gun, unmoving in the dust.

Aleck bellowed again for them to stop fighting. Hardy called out his ultimatum the same way, but with Hardy Campbell it was a challenge; he was willing to pursue this battle down to the last lone survivor.

John Gates shook off blinding perspiration and did not fire again. There was still fighting, but it had dwindled now to only three or four guns. When Aleck called out for the firing to stop, it did in fact dwindle, then Hardy cut loose again, and someone returned his fire, backed up by another man.

Gates called out: "Hardy! Damn it, let 'em stop!"

Finally the last reverberation sounded, the last echo dwindled. The bad scent of burned black powder lingered, and would continue to linger for several hours to come. The brilliant sun hung high over Sangerville. There was a light haze, perhaps from dust or heat or maybe even from gunsmoke, and there was a silence that filled the void after all that devastating and deafening gunfire, with a solid barrier of hush that no one seemed able or willing to break.

John Gates looked out from his hiding place, then took a tentative forward step, and eventually emerged entirely. He was wringing wet with sweat. Partly from the gunfight, mostly from that breathless, hot, little dark place where he had been confined. He squeezed off perspiration with a soiled sleeve and let the cocked six-gun dangle at his side as two Big M cowboys, standing like wilted silhouettes gazing at the facedown form of their employer, raised their faces a little. Gates called over to them without having really to raise his voice at all: "Drop those damned guns!"

The cowboys obeyed. Hardy came up behind them, gun in hand. They turned and paled at the look on Hardy's face. But he only snarled at them: "Head for the jailhouse."

Aleck walked out of the corral yard with his hat far back, reloading his Colt, still looking elegant in that brocade vest, except that now, with dead men lying in plain sight here and there, the brocade vest looked more nearly obscene than elegant. Aleck looked over his shoulder where some men in the corral yard were staring back at him. One of them was the bearded and frog-built Hubert Townley. Hubert still had no idea there was any connection between Aleck and John Gates. All he and the other men back there with him knew was that Aleck had downed at least two men in the wild gunfight, and that was enough to know for the time being.

They waited without moving until Aleck turned to stroll down and join Gates, before even speaking. Hardy called from the jailhouse steps: "How did the lawman get out?"

Gates did not answer. He turned and, with Aleck, walked down there. Gates had seen Hudson cut that Big M rider into mincemeat with the scatter-gun from no greater distance than the width of the roadway, and he had seen the range rider cut Hudson down with two fast shots from the same deadly distance, but until he got down there and saw Hardy rolling Hudson out of the doorway, he had not been sure Hudson had been killed. He had.

Gates and Hardy exchanged a look. Hardy shrugged. "Well, I wouldn't have wished it on him, John, but, for a fact now he won't have to pull out, will he? He can be buried a local hero. Would you tell his story?"

Gates shook his head. "Of course not."

Hardy jutted his jaw northward up the roadway. "Neither will Mitchell. Neither will I, and who else knows it?"

Dr. Ward emerged into the sunshine and ignored the men over in front of the jailhouse to hasten up the roadway where a Big M range rider was awkwardly supporting that cowboy Aleck had shot the legs out from under, up in front of the saddle and harness works.

Gates said: "I'm thirsty enough to drink a river dry." He stepped past to enter the jailhouse office, and ignored the pair of cowed range riders standing there as he went to the water bucket and dipped up a dipper full of tepid water. As he did this, his eyes fell upon the open cell-room door. Down there, he saw a long wooden handle of some kind, off a mop or perhaps a broom. Where it had come from he had no idea, but the way it was lying left no doubt as to how those keys he had draped from the peg on the opposite wall from Hudson's cell had gotten down from there, and how Hudson had managed to get out of that cell.

Gates hung the dipper from its nail and pointed. Both the surviving Big M riders turned without a word and hiked into the cell room. Gates locked them in the same cell, and this time, when he returned to the office, he had the brass key ring with him. He flung it atop the desk and went back out front.

Dr. Ward had organized several teams of townsmen to help him with the wounded and the slain. When he got down where Greg Hudson was lying, he looked from Hardy to Aleck, then back to Gates who was leaning wearily in the jailhouse doorway. Then he knelt down to examine the town marshal. He glanced up: "I suppose, if a lawman had to make this kind of a decision, this would be how he would prefer to die."

Gates said: "I suppose so, Doctor. Doing his duty." Gates did not take his eyes off Arthur Ward. "Mitchell . . . ?"

"Twice through the chest," replied Ward. "Either one of them would have done it."

Hardy turned to Aleck. "Where's your carpetbag?"

"Out in the back alley. I'd better go and fetch it, too. I don't want someone running off with the only clean shirt I own."

Hardy nodded and walked away with Aleck. There were two more men, still unconscious, in the back alley that they'd also have to fetch.

Arthur Ward looked at Gates. "Have you fed those two captives out in Joe Alvarado's smoke house?"

Gates smiled. "No, sir, and I'm not going to, either. The folks in town saddled our horses a while back, and I expect they're still tied down at the livery barn . . . except for Aleck. He doesn't have a horse. Anyway, we're leaving. You can turn those men loose if you care to. Doctor, about the extra horse we'll be needing . . . ?"

Ward said: "They're both still in my shed, and Grant Mitchell isn't going to say a thing if you borrow one of them. The other one I'll turn loose this evening."

Gates nodded.

XVII

Leona Gomez hastened to close and bar the door when she saw three horsemen, one with a carpetbag tied to his saddle, riding in the direction of the adobe from town. She, like everyone else within several miles, had heard that savage gun battle in the center of town. She went to Joe Alvarado's bedroom to get his rifle, dusty and uselessly leaning behind a door. Joe watched, then demanded to know what she was doing.

Her answer was grim. "No one enters this house until we know what all that shooting was about down in the village, *patrón.*" She hastened to the parlor where she pushed the barrel through an ancient slot in the door.

Those three riders halted in the yard, solemnly gazing at that rifle barrel. Gates called softly in Spanish: "*Señora,* be tranquil. Look closer and recognize the grandson of José Alvarado. These are my companions. Open the door then that we can see my grandfather. We are leaving the country."

Leona Gomez left the rifle plugged into the door hole and tiptoed to a window carefully to peer out. When she recognized John Gates, she went back, pulled the rifle from the door hole, leaned it against the wall, and opened the door part way as she looked intently at Hardy and Aleck. She was not in the least impressed by Hardy—few women ever had been—but she admired the brocade vest and the amiable look on Aleck's darkly handsome face—as other women had invariably done.

Gates swung off, tied his horse in tree shade, and walked over into the house followed by his friends. Leona Gomez stood aside. Unfortunately she had recently managed to marry off her last handsome daughter; otherwise the exciting-looking, dark-eyed, very handsome man with that magnificent vest. . . .

"Can we see the *patrón?*" asked Gates, smiling at Leona.

117

She did not answer, but she led the way, and, when those three stalwart men filed into the dingy, little room, she retreated—just as far as the yonder shadowy hallway, and there she heard Gates say: "Grandfather, this is Aleck, and this is Hardy. My partners."

The old man made the customary stately acknowledgment of an introduction and, although neither of the men he spoke to understood that much Spanish, the meaning was abundantly clear. "My home is your home, gentlemen." Then the old man straightened up a little in the bed. His color was good and obviously he was in no pain. "The gunfire in town, then, friends . . . ?"

Gates pushed back his hat. "Mitchell is dead. His foreman, Cliff Habersham, is also dead. I think he lost about four men, too, but I'm not sure they were all Big M riders. Grandfather, Town Marshal Hudson is also dead. You have your water right back."

For a moment the old man sat erectly against his pillows looking at his grandson as though he were in deep shock, which he probably was, then he wanly shook his head. "Why, Juan, why has this been necessary for some water? There has always been enough for everyone."

Hardy and Aleck exchanged a look and said nothing. From the doorway a strong, female voice said: "Because, *patrón*, it was Grant Mitchell, that's why. And you know it. You've seen him do this same thing to other people over the past thirty years. When he couldn't steal their water and their land, he hired them shot or burned out or whipped off their land."

Joe Alvarado listened, but not with true appreciation; he belonged to the generation that did not believe in assertive females speaking out even when they were correct. He fixed Leona Gomez with a dark look, then turned again to his grandson. "And you . . . ? Tell me, Juan, who killed Grant Mitchell?"

Before Gates could speak the truth, Aleck spoke up, looking the old man directly in the eye. "I killed him, *viejo.* What difference does that make?" Aleck spread his hands wide. "I can't even take pride in killing a snake like that."

The old man considered Aleck, considered the brocade vest, then neither looked at Aleck again nor spoke to him. He smiled at his grandson and offered a dark hand. "You go now," he said. "Well, of course, when a man is young, he must always be moving. Juan, someday, come back."

Gates shook the old man's hand and smiled, then he led the way back out of the room to the parlor where he felt in a pocket for some folded greenbacks and offered half of them to Leona Gomez.

"To make certain he has whatever he needs until he can leave that bed," Gates told her.

She straightened up and glared. "If I needed money to perform my duty, I wouldn't stay in Sangerville. I would go to a big town."

She did not relent so Gates shoved the offending greenbacks into his pocket, and swiftly leaned to kiss her cheek. She would have recoiled from that, too, but he was too fast, and the kiss was too unexpected, but afterward she smiled when they went to the door, and she was still smiling when those three stalwart men mounted their horses in the shade and turned to ride southwesterly out into the afternoon sunlight.

Down in town a dozen watchers saw the three horsemen depart from the Alvarado place, heading away from Sangerville, and sang out so that other people who were interested could also observe the departure from New Mexico Territory of the three strangers who had left their town a shambles and who had broken the spine of the Big M cow outfit that had dominated the entire countryside for a full generation.

★ ★ ★ ★ ★

KANSAS KID

★ ★ ★ ★ ★

I

"It was the fastest I ever saw a man come to trouble," related Jared Plummer, "and the fastest I ever saw a man killed."

Race Dunphy beat summer dust off himself with his hat. He was, for a saloon man, in remarkably good shape. He was tall and lean, hard-muscled and supple. Furthermore he was layered over with sun scorch, which made him appear to be anything but a bar owner. There was a little sprinkling of gray over Race Dunphy's ears, and to complement this there were shrewd little lines at the outer corners of his deep blue eyes.

Jared Plummer, on the other hand, would have passed for a store owner anywhere, even without the apron, the sleeve garters, and the necktie. He was paunchy, pudgy, and soft. His skin was pale, his hands fat, and his jowls quivered when he spoke.

"You should've been in town to see it," he went on. "Race, that young feller rode in, got down, tied up, an' was leanin' there in front of your saloon rolling a smoke. I was standing right here, leanin' on my broom looking over there." Jared paused, squinted, and waited.

Race looked up. "Well," he said, "go on."

"Yes. Well, that cowboy came out of your place, startin' around to his horse."

"What cowboy?"

"One of those Bear Trap riders," said Jared irritably. "How would I know which one? He started around where his horse

123

was tied, you see, and he was drunk. Well, he wasn't walking very straight anyway, I can tell you that. Now then, when he came even with this young stranger . . . who was mindin' his own business, just standin' there smokin' his cigarette . . . and this cowboy stopped, looked the stranger up and down, and said, real loud . . . 'Hey, sonny, how'd you like to dance a jig out in the center of the roadway?' "

"That's all he said?"

"That's every word. But you see, Race, he went for his gun. He had a silly grin on his face and there he stood with his hand on his holstered gun. Well, sir, that stranger dropped his cigarette, but he didn't even straighten up. He just said . . . 'Mister, you've got a load on. You better go on home and sleep it off.' "

"And . . . ?"

"That Bear Trap cowboy quit grinning, Race. I could see his face plain as I can see yours right now. He looked the stranger up and down again, then he called him a fightin' name . . . called it real loud, too, so a dozen men standin' over there heard it." Jared folded both hands over his paunch and mournfully wagged his head. "That young stranger said . . . 'Now!' He barked it out. . . ." Jared wagged his head again. "Damnedest thing I ever saw, Race. I'm tellin' you I was standin' right here watchin' them. That Bear Trap man had his hand already on his gun."

"You already said that."

"All right. And I'm sayin' it again. He had his hand plumb on his gun." Jared put a significant stare upon Dunphy. "But when that stranger said . . . 'Now!' . . . that cowboy didn't even get his gun out. Mind you, Race, I was watching him like a hawk, because you know the reputation those Bear Trappers have, but so help me, his gun wasn't clear of its holster before that stranger had shot him square through the brisket. That fool drunk cowboy was dead as a post before he hit the roadway."

Race Dunphy removed his hat, shaped it, and put it back on. He stood there, gazing across the roadway at his saloon. A number of men were standing over there under the wooden awning, conversing. Sheriff Tim Wade was among them, his broad back toward Race and Jared Plummer. Race considered those broad shoulders.

"And Tim came," he said, filling in the part Jared had thus far left out. "Arrested the stranger, took his gun, marched him down to his building, and locked him up."

"Yup, that's exactly what happened. Tim came runnin' up almost before the echoes had died out. But, Race, I'm here to tell you I never saw a man get into trouble so fast, nor another man die so quickly. It plumb left me breathless."

Dunphy looked strained. He stood there obviously deep in private thought for a moment longer, then stepped away, took the reins of his horse, and walked up the road to the livery barn, handed the animal to a hostler, and struck out across the way to his saloon. He knew Tim Wade would hail him, and he was correct in this. When the lawman saw him approaching, he left the idlers in front of the saloon, walked over, and intercepted Race fifty feet north of the doorway.

"Been a killin'," said big Tim Wade, his voice as blunt and forthright as always. "Some two-bit stranger with a fast gun killed Gus Meadows of the Bear Trap."

"So I just heard," said Race, eyeing Tim Wade blankly. There was no love lost between these two, but the reasons for this mutual antipathy were vague and stretched back over a number of years, a lot of little things that had pyramided one atop the other until these two tough men tolerated one another with a cold civility.

"Franklyn won't like it, Race. Meadows got tanked in your place. He was killed at your hitch rack."

Race nodded. Earnest Franklyn, the wealthy owner of Bear Trap Ranch, was not only a grim, taciturn man, he was also a teetotaler with no use for saloons or saloon men. It was not difficult to see what was in Tim Wade's mind; Franklyn would explode over this killing, the manner in which it occurred, and the fact that Dunphy's Saloon was involved.

"The way I heard it," said Race, "Meadows was at fault."

Wade's light gray eyes turned sardonic. "Franklyn won't believe that."

Irritability reddened Race Dunphy's face. "I can't help what he believes or doesn't believe," he said, and started past the sheriff.

"Race, you been out at your ranch?"

"Yes. What about it?"

"Nothing. Just wondered where you went this morning is all."

Inside the saloon a few loiterers sat sprawled. Their conversation dwindled as Race entered, looked out over the low-ceilinged long room, then cut on across to the bar where his day bartender, Jack Pritchett, was absently washing glasses.

Jack was a roly-poly man of indeterminate age. He'd been with Race since the saloon had opened seven years before. Jack was a raffish man full of earthy humor; he was popular with the range men, and was known as a man who kept his mouth closed. He saw Race coming across toward him, straightened fully around, and leaned upon the bar, waiting. He knew Race Dunphy as well as anyone living, and, when he saw that look of narrow-eyed concentration upon his boss' face, he never said anything until Race had spoken first.

"Reckon I shouldn't have left town," explained Dunphy, hooking both elbows over the bar and leaning there, regarding Pritchett.

"It wouldn't have made any difference," said Jack. "You

wouldn't have known it was going to happen."

"How about Meadows . . . just how drunk was he?"

Jack looked over at the tables, and back again. He minutely shook his head and lowered his voice. "That's the strange part of it, Race. He wasn't drunk. Oh, he was talkin' loud and flingin' himself around all right, but I'm the feller who set 'em up, and Meadows only had two short shots."

Race's face faintly clouded, then cleared almost at once. "Only two here, Jack, and five somewhere else."

Pritchett shook his head. "They came directly here from the ranch. I heard 'em talking about how fast they rode."

A little interval of silence settled between these two. Race looked straight at Jack and Pritchett returned this look with grave conviction, then moved, brought forth a sour rag, and mechanically swiped off the bar top.

"He wasn't drunk at all, Race, take my word for it. I've seen more drunks in my time than most men, and Gus Meadows was putting it on."

Race went back in his mind to resurrect an image of Gus Meadows. He recalled him as an arrogant man, big and rough and conceited. Earnest Franklyn used him every spring as Bear Trap's rep at the roundups; sometimes, when Frank Andrews, Bear Trap's range boss, was not around, Meadows had substituted as ranch foreman. There'd been a rumor that Meadows was sweet on Franklyn's daughter Eleanor, but that was purest rumor as far as Race Dunphy was concerned. He'd seen Eleanor Franklyn twice since she'd returned from school in the East and he could not believe she would be interested in a man like Meadows. They were poles apart.

"If you asked me," put in Jack Pritchett, scattering Race's reflections, "that there was a deliberate thing. Only it didn't come off like it was supposed to."

Race considered Jack's face. His heavy dark brows rolled

together. "What do you mean?"

Jack's voice dropped still lower. "Now think back. How often has old Franklyn sent men to town in the morning? In seven years I can count the times on the fingers of one hand, that's how many times. Yet Meadows and two other Bear Trappers rode like hell to get to town. They come in here, had a couple of drinks, kept goin' to the door to look out, and, when that stranger rode in all covered with dust, they come together at the far end of the bar. They talked a minute among themselves, then Meadows left. The next thing any of us knew . . . he was dead out by the hitch rack."

"What about the other two Bear Trap men?"

"They rushed outside with the rest of us at the sound of the gunshot. They stood there like a pair of idiots, starin' at one another. You could tell by the look on their faces they were plumb flabbergasted."

Race's frown faded and his irritability returned. "You were flabbergasted, too, Jack. So was Jared. He saw the whole thing from across the road." Race shoved up off the bar. "You're reading something into this that's melodramatic, but not likely."

"What am I reading into it?" challenged Pritchett, faintly coloring, his voice sharpening toward Dunphy.

"You're saying Bear Trap knew this stranger was coming, sent three men to Lone Pine to watch for him, and, when he showed up, Meadows or someone was supposed to force him into a fight."

Pritchett emphatically nodded. "All right," he said flatly. "That's exactly the way it looked to me, Race, and, if you talked to Jared, then you heard how pointless the thing was."

"Jared thought Meadows was drunk."

"And I know a damned sight better."

Race braced into the anger coming at him from across the bar. He'd known Jack Pritchett too long to believe Jack exaggerated or embroidered things. Pritchett was a shrewdly observant man, level-headed and as solid as rock.

Race sighed, leaned forward again, pushed back his hat, and kept gazing over at Jack. He slowly began to look perplexed. "Why?" he said. "What would be the reason, Jack? Someone Gus Meadows didn't like, some old enemy out of Meadows's past?"

Jack lifted his shoulders and let them drop. This was beyond his knowledge and he would not therefore comment on it. He swung his head as a cowman rattled a coin southward. He looked briefly at Race before starting toward this customer, and said: "Go see the stranger. He might tell you something. Tim's got him at the jailhouse."

But Race did not do this at once. He went instead to his cubicle office that opened off the end of the northward bar, tossed his hat aside, and sat down at his desk.

It was gloomy and cool in here. Race brought a bottle out of a drawer, poured himself a stiff drink, and downed it. He propped his feet upon the desk, leaned far back, and for the time being forgot the killing of Gus Meadows.

His father had left Race Dunphy six sections of range northwest of Lone Pine. He'd also left him a herd of cattle, but the cows were beginning to lose their teeth now and Race, with his one hired hand, had been culling for the last ten days. It was a kind of work he thoroughly enjoyed; it kept him out of town and away from the saloon. The longer he stayed away, the less he wanted to return. Then this.

But Jack had to be wrong; at least he had to be wrong about his innuendo that Earnest Franklyn had anything to do with sending Meadows to town to force a fight. If a fight had been forced, then Meadows probably had done it by himself.

Little annoying, jangling inconsistencies kept bobbing up, though, to trouble Race's reasoning. For instance, did the Bear

Trap men really know the stranger was coming? If, as Jack had said, they kept watching for him, then they somehow knew he was on his way all right. And that other thing Jack had said was true enough—Franklyn did not permit his men to ride to town on ranch time, that was a long-established and commonly known Bear Trap regulation. And, finally, why would Meadows pretend to be drunk?

II

Tim Wade offered no objections when Race Dunphy appeared at his office with a request to see the killer of Gus Meadows. He wordlessly guided Race back into the little cell-block, separated from the sheriff's office by a massive, bolt-studded oaken door, and left him standing in shadows facing a strap-steel cage.

Gus Meadows's killer sat propped on a wall bunk idly smoking and idly kicking one dangling leg back and forth. He returned Race's curious stare with a look just as ironically interested.

He did not appear to be over twenty-one or -two years of age. His features were good, his build was sinewy rather than stocky, and his bearing was that of a capable, confident man. He had light blue eyes, nostrils that slightly flared, and a good square jaw.

Race had, over the past twenty years, encountered his share of fighting range men. Usually they had been wary and cold-eyed and wire-tight; there was something about killers that sang out across a room full of people to touch a man's nerves. It was something that unmistakably set them apart. The man looking out of that steel cage had it, and yet he did not entirely look the part, either. It was a little confusing.

He struck Race Dunphy as a perfectly co-ordinated human being, as a man capable of blinding speed when he wished to move fast. But the cold, hard look was not there at all. Race told himself this was perhaps because of the killer's youth. His own experience instantly contradicted this, though; very few gunmen were older than this youth. Very few lived to be much older, and those he'd seen who had also been youthful had possessed that unmistakable look this man totally lacked.

"Well," said the killer, "we ought to know each other the next time we meet."

Race put up a hand to lean upon the bars. "I guess you've told the sheriff your version," he said as an opener.

The prisoner nodded and smoked his cigarette and looked brightly at Race without speaking.

"You probably wouldn't want to tell it again."

The prisoner's gaze hardened just the slightest bit, resisting Dunphy's steady regard and his quiet tone. "You some relation to that cowboy?" he asked.

Race shook his head. "I'm Dunphy. I own the saloon where it happened."

"What's your interest, Dunphy?"

"I guess you could say it was curiosity, stranger."

"Why? You own a saloon. A feller gets killed out front of it. It's happened before. What's worrying you about it?"

This one, thought Race, *is cool and smart.* "Where did you know Gus Meadows?" he asked, side-stepping that other question. "How did he know you were on your way to Lone Pine?"

The killer punched out his smoke, shook his head at Race, and said: "I never saw that Meadows feller before in my life."

"How about the rest of it? Why would he be interested in knowing you were coming to Lone Pine?"

The prisoner stood up. He was as tall as Dunphy but not as broad. When he moved, it was with a loose, easy grace. "Listen, Dunphy," he said, his tone becoming quietly menacing, "go tend your bar and keep your nose out of places where it doesn't belong."

131

Race continued to lean upon the bars. He told himself that Jack Pritchett had been right, after all. There was something here, something perhaps only three or four men knew, and one of those men was now dead.

For a moment longer he studied the prisoner. Out in the front office Tim Wade's chair creaked. In the alleyway behind the jailhouse two boys ran past excitedly calling back and forth. Race turned and walked out of the cell-block.

Sheriff Wade's heavy-featured, tough face was expressionless as he considered Dunphy, passing across the room toward him. If someone had asked him to define his antagonism toward the saloon man, Tim Wade could not have done it, at least not without taking a moment to gather the loose strands together and weave them into a logical sequence, but notwithstanding Wade and Dunphy grated like flint grates on steel.

"Well," said Wade, "did he let his hair down for you?" He said this with thinly veiled sarcasm and Race heard it that way. He went as far as the front wall beside Wade's desk and leaned there, looking coolly downward.

"It's what he didn't say, Tim."

"What does that mean?"

Race let this go past unanswered. "Do you know who he is?"

Wade looked at a paper lying under his arm and looked up. "Sure I know who he is." Wade picked up the paper and held it out. "Here, stuff this in your pipe and smoke it."

The thing was a Wanted flyer of the kind sent out all over the West by law agencies. It had a fair likeness of Meadows's killer's face sketched upon it and beneath this was a legend: *The Kansas Kid.*

Race read the description, the notice of reward for information leading to apprehension and conviction, then read the crime: murder. He lowered the poster, gazed down at Wade, and said: "Something eludes me here. Why Meadows?"

Wade shrugged. "Look at the date," he said. "That's an old flyer. The Kid says he served his time for that killing. I've telegraphed Kansas for verification."

Race had overlooked the date but he glanced at it now. "He was only fifteen years old when he did this, Wade."

Another shrug from the lawman. "One thing about a gun's handle. When you're big enough to get your fingers around it, you're old enough to shoot it." He held up his hand, Race put the flyer in it, and Wade dropped the thing. He looked sardonically at that likeness of the Kid's boyish face. "Meadows was a damned fool. He never was real bright but he thought he was. Look at that picture . . . The Kansas Kid. Hell, anyone with an ounce of sense could have smelled gunman from as far off as they could see that feller. Anyone but drunk Gus Meadows."

Race straightened off the wall. "Meadows wasn't drunk, Tim," he said, and turned toward the door.

"You could get pretty odds on that!" called Wade, his gray eyes brightening, hardening toward Dunphy. "Old Franklyn'll give you even bigger odds."

Race turned with one hand on the door latch. "Someday you're going to think with your head instead of your gun barrel," he said softly, "and, when you do, you're going to get a helluva surprise, Tim."

Wade sat there after Race Dunphy had left. He looked a little angered and he was. He scowled at the old Wanted poster for a moment, then shoved up out of his chair, and went lumbering to his cell-block.

Race Dunphy, after he left Wade's jailhouse, encountered the cowboy who worked for him out at his ranch. This was Curt Lake, a quiet, capable man near Race's own age who had once worked for Race's father.

"Came in for some rope," Lake explained when he bumped into his employer. "The whole town's talkin' about what happened to Meadows over at the saloon."

"If they're talking about that," growled Race, "then they're not talking about you or me." He started past.

Lake said: "Wait a minute. We had a couple of visitors out at the ranch about sunup."

Race stopped and turned and waited.

"Couple of strangers. Said they were lookin' for work. I gave 'em coffee, we talked for a while, then they rode on."

"All right," said Race a little impatiently. "Drifters come and drifters go."

"Naw, you don't brush these two off that easy, Race." Curt's gaze thinned out, turned shrewd and knowing. "These two were gunmen."

Race stood there with sunlight burning against him and the ebb and flow of pedestrian traffic breaking around him, considering Curt Lake solemnly. "How do you know that?" he asked.

Curt said: "Now that's a foolish question. I knew they were gunmen the same way you'd have known if you'd been there to see 'em."

In Race's mind a number of irrelevant things clashed and ricocheted and bounced around making no sense at all, yet seeming to have some kind of an affinity. "Tell Jack I said to stand you to a drink, Curt. Get your rope then and head for home."

"Yeah," retorted the cowboy, his tone turning slightly acid. "Maybe you'd like to know a question them two asked."

"I would."

"They wanted to know where the Bear Trap outfit had its headquarters."

Race fitted this fragment of information into the puzzle in his head. "Anything else?"

"No, just general talk. They asked about the country, the

wages, roundups, stuff like that. The usual guff a feller hears over a cup of coffee . . . except for that one question."

"Looking for work, maybe," suggested Race, not believing it himself.

Curt snorted. "Sure," he said very dryly. "Only their kind of work's got damned little to do with cows."

"You told them how to find Bear Trap?"

"Yup, told 'em Franklyn's range adjoins ours to the north an' east, and, if they ride that way, they'll see the buildings after a while."

Curt watched his employer's face turn puzzled and troubled. He muttered something finally, and walked on around Race heading for the saloon and the drink Jack Pritchett was going to give him.

Foster Dunlop, the expansive blacksmith whose shop was between Dewey's saddle and harness shop and Hank Henrickson's livery barn sauntered out to expectorate lustily into the roadway and afterward turned to face Race, who was standing nearby, and said: "You missed the shootin', Race. It's been dull enough around Lone Pine this summer. That sort of breaks the monotony."

Race turned, looked squarely at the beaming blacksmith, said nothing back to him, and walked away. Dunlop stared and scratched his head in bewilderment at this rough treatment, then ambled back into his shop thinking uncharitable things of Dunphy. To his grimy helper he growled: "That cussed Race Dunphy gettin' so serious a feller can't even josh with him no more."

Jack Pritchett watched Race come in. Jack was beginning to get the pre-evening customers along the bar and had only time to notice that Race went directly to his office and closed the door, his expression troubled and thoughtful.

Outside, the afternoon wore along, the sun began to drop

away, riders passed back and forth upon the roadway, and women with shopping baskets came and went. Except for the killing of Gus Meadows the town of Lone Pine seemed as normal this day as it did any other time. But along Jack's bar the day-to-day topics of conversation concerning weather, beef prices, a little sly, salacious gossip were quite lacking; everyone was discussing the gunfight, the incarcerated killer, and the probable reaction of Bear Trap's grim and rugged owner to the loss of one of his top hands.

After hours Jared Plummer came in for his usual nightcap. He and liveryman Hank Henrickson, both having been eyewitnesses, were offered drinks. Jared enjoyed this sudden celebrity status but Henrickson, a gaunt, tall old man with a perpetually jaundiced expression, grew less and less talkative as time—and the drinks—wore along. He had been sitting tilted back in the doorway of his barn when he'd witnessed the gunfight. Hank had seen plenty of men killed in his long lifetime and he had a theory about witnessing those killings. The best way in the world to get involved was to let your tongue wag. He sat there at a poker table with his jaundiced gaze fully upon perspiring Jared Plummer, his long legs thrust out to their full length, and his bleak old face looking scornful. Jared not only talked too much; he talked too loud. He was giving his views of why Meadows never got his gun out, and he was making both Gus and his killer look pretty bad. Hank stood it as long as he could, then downed his drink, wiped his mouth, got up, and stalked out of Dunphy's Saloon.

III

It was near 7:00 with the last faint light of day fading out in a lingering way when six bunched-up riders came walking their horses down Main Street from the darkening north country.

This was supper hour and mostly Lone Pine's boardwalks

were empty. But the few idlers who saw those six horsemen pacing quietly along all in a group had little difficulty recognizing Earnest Franklyn and five of his Bear Trap riders, including his range boss, Frank Andrews. These idlers drifted off to spread the word of Bear Trap's arrival in Lone Pine, and it was from Jack Pritchett at the bar, who heard it from someone else, that Race Dunphy learned of Franklyn's arrival. He walked out onto the plank walk in front of his saloon to watch those six men get down and tie up over in front of Dewey's saddle and harness shop.

The light was not good; Race recognized Franklyn by his size, his stoop, and his width, but he did not see Frank Andrews until the range boss stepped away from his animal, stepped out into plain sight in the roadway's center, and looked squarely over at the saloon hitch rack, laden now with tied horses, where Gus Meadows had died.

Race was speculating on Franklyn's intentions, when the familiar hulk of Sheriff Tim Wade drifted southward from the entrance to Henrickson's livery barn, came in behind those six men, and halted.

"If you came for Meadows," said Wade, bringing those six men twisting around toward him, "he's in Doc Cooper's embalmin' shed."

Speaking the same way Wade had, offering no customary good evening, his voice blunt and roughened, Earnest Franklyn said: "The wagon's coming for Gus. It'll be along directly, Wade. What I want is the man who killed him."

"Do you?" said Wade coolly. "There'll be an inquest. If he's acquitted, he'll be turned loose. After that, what happens to him is his business, not mine."

"When'll you hold this inquest?"

"Not until Doc Cooper gets back to town. He's got to certify the cause o' death and sign the burial certificate."

137

Big Earnest Franklyn's stooped shoulders jerked; his voice, when next he spoke, was a clue to the look in his eyes. "The cause o' death was a gunshot. You don't need Cooper to tell you that."

"The law says I do, Mister Franklyn."

"Then the law's asinine."

"It may be," shot back Sheriff Wade, "an' maybe you can change it. But I can't. My job is to enforce it, asinine or not. That's what I'm paid for an' that's what I do."

Bear Trap's range boss leaned over, said something to Franklyn, and the cowman swung his head to look over through dusk where Race Dunphy was standing. Race could almost feel the malevolence of that glare. He braced into it, not offering to speak or lower his own eyes from the dimly discernible rugged old face across the road from him.

"Another thing, Sheriff," growled Franklyn, not taking his eyes off Race. "I want that saloon closed."

Tim Wade crossed both arms over his thick chest. He stood sardonically gazing over where Race stood. Without looking at Franklyn, he said: "There's a way to do that, if you want it done badly enough, Mister Franklyn. Buy Dunphy out, then padlock the building."

Franklyn swung around. "Don't get funny with me!" he exclaimed. "I want that place closed as a den of vice and a detriment to this town."

Wade said nothing; he simply looked at Franklyn with a saturnine expression. Frank Andrews slowly pulled off his riding gloves, slowly pushed them into his shell belt. The other Bear Trap riders stood still, looking and listening and saying nothing. Andrews once more leaned over to speak indistinguishably to his employer. Franklyn listened and nodded and said to Sheriff Wade: "Where is that killer? I want to talk to him."

"He's in my jailhouse," replied Wade, then he did a strange

thing. He raised his head and called over to Race Dunphy. "Come along. You'll want to be in on this, too."

Race was surprised. He tried to read Tim's face through the intervening darkness and could not. The others started walking southward, Wade still upon the plank walk, the Bear Trap men out in the dusty roadway. None of them looked back to see whether or not Race was coming.

There were little cliques of men standing silently, motionlessly along the roadway, watching all this, townsmen and range men, all solemn and closed-faced and cautious.

Race stepped out into the roadway, went on over to the yonder plank walk, and swung left to trail along behind Tim Wade. He still had not figured out the lawman's invitation to come along.

At the jailhouse Tim let Franklyn, Andrews, and their riders enter first. As Race came up, Tim put a dour look upon him. "If you're wonderin'," he said, "I asked you along because whether you know it or not . . . or like it . . . you're up to your ears in this thing. Franklyn's got it in for you as much as he has for Meadows's killer. Don't you ever think otherwise."

All eight of them crowded the narrow alleyway running along in front of the sheriff's strap-steel cages. There were four of these little square cells, but only one was occupied.

Dunphy watched Earnest Franklyn move heavily over to halt directly in front of the Kansas Kid. He stood for a long time looking in, exchanging stares with the prisoner and neither speaking nor moving. Then, when Race and the others were positive the old cattleman would explode, would denounce and threaten the Kid, all old Franklyn did was peer intently and say in a voice so soft the others barely heard: "You."

The Kansas Kid's face looked shadowed and yellow beneath pale lantern light. He was without any expression at all that Race could make out, and he stood in the middle of his cage, returning old Franklyn's stare with a look equally as uncompromising and knowing.

"Who'd you think it'd be?" he asked thinly. "Mort and Pete?"

Wade, looking swiftly from one of those men to the other, shouldered past Frank Andrews to Franklyn's side. When he spoke, Race heard the surprise, the chagrin, in his voice. "Mister Franklyn, you know this feller?"

Franklyn drew upright, tore his gaze off the prisoner, and turned away, brushing past Tim Wade making for the separating doorway. He said nothing. His men moved back and the old cowman came face to face with Race Dunphy at the exit. He looked through Race and pushed right on by, but for a moment Dunphy got a good long look at Earnest Franklyn's face—it was slack-muscled, gray, and stricken-looking.

Tim Wade called out: "Mister Franklyn . . . !"

But Bear Trap's wealthy owner had passed over into the office and his men went trooping after him, cutting off the sheriff's outcry and his thrusting stride until, at the doorway, Frank Andrews turned, fixed Wade with a cold look, and said: "Slack off, Sheriff. You said your job was enforcing the law. Do it, but outside of that keep your beak out of Mister Franklyn's business."

Andrews turned and followed the others on out of the jailhouse into the lowering night.

Sheriff Wade would have flung after those six men but Race caught him by the elbow, swung him around, and shook his head. "Let 'em go. You'll never find out anything that way. Maybe you never will anyway, Tim. Like I told you earlier . . . until you start usin' your head instead of your gun barrel you're going to run into a lot of surprises."

Wade, if he heard any of this, did not heed it. He said: "By golly, old Franklyn knows the Kid."

"Well, it's a pretty small world, Tim, and Franklyn goes out with his drives every now and then. He probably knows a lot of folks."

Wade looked over at the open door where the Bear Trap men had exited. He stood like a statue for a while, turning things over in his mind, then he went to his desk, dropped down upon an edge of it, and fixed his belligerent gaze upon Race.

"There's something goin' on here I don't know about. That Meadows killing didn't just up an' happen. Gus had a reason for chousing the Kid."

Race went as far as the door. "Thanks for inviting me in," he said.

"Wait a minute. Where do you think you're going? What took place in there didn't surprise you, Race. What d'you know about this that I don't know?"

"Not a whole lot, Tim. Nothing, in fact, that you can't piece together for yourself."

"You knew those two knew cach other, didn't you?"

Race shook his head. "No, Franklyn surprised me just as much as he surprised you, but I never believed Gus Meadows just picked the Kansas Kid out of the clear blue sky to push into a gunfight. Gus was a lot of things, mostly stupid, but he wasn't a raw killer."

"Why? What's behind all this?"

Race slowly shook his head. "Damned if I know, but I'll tell you this much . . . whatever it is, it's only just beginning." He left Sheriff Wade perched upon the edge of his desk looking baffled. He started northward toward his saloon and hadn't progressed more than a hundred feet when Frank Andrews stepped out of a doorway. Frank had his riding gloves on and he was alone.

Race knew Bear Trap's range boss as well as he knew most of the range men in the Lone Pine country. If he hadn't met them in his saloon, he'd met them at the roundups or out on the range. He'd always rather liked Andrews, who was a thoroughly reliable, thoroughly loyal man.

"I got a message for you," Frank said now, keeping his voice low and his face blank. "Mister Franklyn says you either close up your saloon or we'll close it for you."

Frank was Race's size and heft. He wore his holstered gun lashed down and there was no hint of fear anywhere around him.

Race considered the expressionless lips, the steady eyes, and the wire-tight stance. "What's it all about, Frank?" he asked, choosing for the moment to ignore Franklyn's relayed ultimatum. "For now forget that your boss hates saloons and saloon men, and give me some idea of what Meadows's killing is all about."

Andrews shook his head slightly and brusquely. "I only waited to deliver the message, Race. That's what Mister Franklyn told me to tell you, and that's all I'm going to say." Andrews turned and started off.

"Frank," Race called softly, "I don't like being on the other side from you. But as for old Franklyn, tell him I'm not closing and I doubt if he's big enough to do the job."

Andrews stood looking back and gently tugging at his doeskin gloves. He seemed very close to saying more, but in the end he simply turned and walked on northward where a dark clutch of mounted men were waiting. Race watched the others impatiently waiting, and afterward he watched all six of them break away, heading northward out of town in a long lope.

He strolled thoughtfully toward the saloon, but at the last minute, because the place was packed with hell-raising cowboys in off the ranges, hooting and hollering, he swung off the plank walk toward Henrickson's livery barn, his destination no place in particular but somewhere there would be quiet enough for a man to hear his thoughts. He scuffed along through roadway dust, stepped up across the way, and walked northward toward the quieter residential section of Lone Pine. He did not see the gaunt, raw-boned man standing still in formless gloom whittling idly with a pocket knife until the man snapped the blade closed with a sharp, small sound, drew up off the livery barn's front wall, and said quietly: "If you let him close you down, next month it'll be someone else."

Race turned. Hank Henrickson moved out of the gloom. He pocketed his knife, shoved both bony fists deep into his trousers, and rocked back and forth upon his booted feet.

"That's the way it goes, Race. First they run one out, then another, and another, until nothing's left they don't own or control. I never before seen one attempt it against a town, but I've seen range hogs gobble up hundreds of thousands of acres. That's how they get big and rich and powerful." Henrickson continued to stand with both fisted big hands plunged to the depths of his pockets, looking doggedly at the younger man. "You goin' to let him do it, let him close you up?"

"Of course not," answered Race irritably.

"Good. Now then, if the going gets real rough, you let me know."

"He didn't mean that, Hank. He had something else on his mind. I don't believe he even cared too much about Meadows."

Henrickson's brows climbed a little. He turned, spat, and turned back. "Race, you're a pretty good man. Your paw before you was a pretty good man. But your paw was a pretty wise man, too. Maybe you just ain't lived long enough to know about Earnest Franklyn. Your paw knew and I know. We been around a long time."

"Knew what?"

Henrickson considered this over an interval of strong silence. He removed one hand from a trouser pocket, ran it over his lined face kneading the loose, tough hide there. "Franklyn's got ice water for blood, and he's got a chunk of granite the size of your fist for a heart. An' if them things don't mean anything to you, boy, then take my word for this. He's got reason to hate saloon men. Now then, you knot them three things together and they can spell another killing . . . yours."

IV

Race would have asked Hank Henrickson what he meant by stating that Earnest Franklyn had reason to hate saloon men, but the gaunt old liveryman didn't give him a chance. He turned and walked northward, swung left, and disappeared into the dinginess of his barn.

For a little while Race drifted aimlessly over town, rummaging for some key to what hung over the Lone Pine country, and, when he ultimately failed, he decided to ride out to the ranch. All the noise and forced gaiety at the saloon held no allure for him at all.

He got his horse, rode out of town through the back alley, swung west for a while, slouching along with nighttime's pleasant quietude around him, then angled northward until the solitary light from his bunkhouse showed through the dimensional dark. By the time he got to the barn he'd been heard and Curt Lake was standing quietly with a Winchester waiting to see who it was. As Race rode up, Curt slid the gun behind him and strolled forth.

"Just makin' a fresh pot o' coffee," he said, trailing Race into the barn, leaning there while he watched the off-saddling and unbridling process. "Got a few fried spuds left, too, if you're hungry."

Race hung his rigging, turned his horse into a corral, and went along with Lake into the bunkhouse. Here, in a building built to accommodate ten riders, one man rattled around like a pea in a pod. Once, before Race's father had died, this ranch had run a thousand cows, but Race's interests had, until now, centered pretty much in town. He had therefore let the cattle dwindle, and used the ranch as a sort of hobby. But of late, for the past year or so, he had been turning more to the ranch and less to the saloon. He couldn't explain this in definite terms, but the saloon lacked something a man needed that the outdoors possessed in abundance. He had, in fact, only recently been considering selling his saloon and moving back to the ranch.

Now, he accepted Curt's offer of coffee, sat at the bunkhouse table, pushed back his hat, and sipped.

"Hot," the cowboy said, smiling. "I never make very good coffee, but I sure make it hot."

Race eased back, lifted his eyes, and regarded Curt's seamed, knowledgeable face. He'd often thought that cowboys were like poets; they were sometimes wise, very understanding men, rollicking at times, hard as iron at other times, a cut above average in intelligence, and yet because they worked at what they wanted to work at instead of what would make them rich, none of them was ever wealthy in the accepted sense.

He swished the coffee, emptied the cup, and set it down. Well, if you measured wealth in personal satisfaction, then Curt Lake was a heap happier and contented than his boss was.

"How about some potatoes, Race?"

"No, thanks. You been out to look at the critters?"

"Yeah, they're fine." Curt rinsed out some tin plates and cups. "They sent you their regards," he said, eyes faintly twinkling.

Race put down his hat, leaned far back, and propped himself against the wall. "Old Franklyn came to town tonight."

"I thought he might. Over Meadows's killing, wasn't it?"

"Yeah. Y'know, Curt, I've lived all my life in the Lone Pine country and I don't think I've talked to that old bull a half dozen times. Hell, I was eighteen before I even knew he'd been married and had a daughter."

Curt swung shaded eyes, considered Race interestedly, then swung back to his work at cleaning up supper utensils. "I ain't seen him to talk to in a couple of years, but when your paw was alive, he used to ride over every once in a while. As for the girl, he sent her off East to a bunch of fancy schools before she even learned to ride good. I recollect seein' her a few times, but if she was to hit me in the face with a shovel today, I wouldn't know her."

Curt finished, hung up a ragged dish towel, took out his tobacco sack, and sank down across from Race, sitting upon his made-up bunk. He worked up a smoke, lit it, leaned back, and watched smoke rise straight up and mushroom outward under the ceiling.

"Old Franklyn's always been pretty much of a loner. I reckon when a man's got all that stuff on his mind . . . you know, runnin' the biggest ranch, herdin' the crew Bear Trap keeps around, makin' up drives and all . . . why he just don't have no time for other things."

"That's what folks have always said," mused Race. "But an idea's beginning to firm up in my mind, Curt. It's not that Franklyn's ranch takes up all his time. He's got some other reason for losing himself in his work."

Curt kept right on watching that straight-standing smoke. His face was elaborately blank. He said—"You don't say."—and took a deep drag of his cigarette. "Well, it may be, Race, it may be. But I'll tell you somethin' your paw an' me always figured was a pretty good rule of thumb. Leave another man to his own problems an' just sort of worry about your own."

Race got up, stretched, and faintly smiled over at his range rider. "All right," he said. "I'm rebuked, Curt. I know what you're trying to tell me. That I'm stickin' my nose where it hadn't ought to be. You're probably right, too, but I'll tell you one thing. Franklyn sent me a message tonight by Frank Andrews, that if I didn't close up my saloon, his Bear Trap outfit would close it for me."

Curt did not show surprise at this. He simply said— "*Ahhh.*"—stood up, squinted at the flaky tip of his cigarette, and spoke without raising his head. "It's been a long time coming, an' I expect he'd have tried it before if you hadn't been your paw's son. Earnest and your paw was real close once, Race. Real close. You was just a button then, so you wouldn't remember, but they was mighty good friends once."

Race crossed over to the bunkhouse door, opened it, and said dryly: "I'm glad he waited. It was mighty considerate of him, Curt. Mighty considerate." He nodded and passed on out into the night, bound for the main ranch house.

Curt shuffled over to stand in the doorway, looking up where Race moved through faint light. His face was quietly composed and quietly sad. Even after Race had disappeared inside, the old cowboy stood there, smoking and squinting outward and running a number of private thoughts through his head. Ordinarily things that occurred fifteen, twenty years before dwindled from the lack of the interest it took to keep events alive, but not always. Sometimes there were exceptions; sometimes, too, there were men who would not let past events quietly turn to dust. Curt killed his smoke, wagged his head, and shuffled back into the bunkhouse. He blew down the lamp mantle, sat in darkness to kick off his boots, and eventually to turn in.

Up at the main house Race also turned in, but it took him longer because he could not clear his mind or compose his body for rest, and even after he finally did get to sleep he was wide awake again by sunup. He arose and dressed, thinking affectionately of his range rider; it was so typical, the way Curt

147

had gently chided him last night about taking so much interest in the affairs of Earnest Franklyn. Range law prohibited gossip, personal questions, and prying into other folks' affairs.

He went out into the large kitchen, started breakfast, and afterward stepped outside to strike the old triangle hanging there, traditional means for summoning all hands to meals. He returned to the kitchen, finished preparing food, waited a little, then went out through his house to the front door. There, he bellowed for Curt. Only his own echo came back. He frowned, walked over the yard, swung up onto the bunkhouse porch, and looked in. Curt was gone. For a moment Race stood there considering this, then he shrugged, returned to the main house, ate alone, and afterward went down to the barn after his own animal. He thought it likely that Curt was watching some particular little bunch of first-calf heifers; sometimes there was trouble; sometimes a feller had to use his lariat, his saddle horse, and pull first calves. It could be a nightmare of a job alone. Race rode out into the night-hazed, still morning, intending to seek Curt and, if need be, help him.

The land lay quiet and still and cool. Far out where night shadows had not entirely faded out lay a band of broad sootiness. The sun had not yet been able to erase all of night's heavy imprint. There were tiny, perfectly shaped drops of dew on the ground, each one reflecting some different shading of daylight. The day was brand new; it had the requisite magic to go down into a man and touch something latent, something mysterious, bringing his soul and his conscience to an attuned rapport with everything around him.

A little band of his cattle threw up horned heads at sight of his horse plodding along. They turned with all their attention upon man and horse, watching for as long as Race was within the range of their wariness.

A mile farther along, near the unmarked boundary between

Race's land and Bear Trap range, a rider was distantly visible. Because there was nothing else moving, Race watched this horseman, saw him rein over toward some broken country, drop from sight in a wide arroyo, rise up, and drop down in another one. If that was Curt, he told himself, he was riding as though he had a specific destination in mind.

There was a spring and a pool in the bottom of one of those breaks, Race knew, because as a boy he'd often ridden over there during the height of summer to swim and lie in the lacy shade of wild plum thickets.

It was entirely possible that some calving heifer, seeking the solitude all cows sought at birthing, had made for that cool, lonely place, and Curt either knew this or suspected it. It did not occur to Race the rider he'd seen heading for the pool might not be Curt.

He did not hasten; there was no real need. Besides, it was deucedly pleasant just riding along through this warming, empty world, breathing air as heady as wine, astride a sound horse whose every footfall struck down upon his own land. For this little while his saloon back in Lone Pine was a thousand miles away and forgotten. He was doing the thing for which both his nature and his early environment had fitted him.

The land began to buckle, to break sharply where winter winds and spring freshets had cut wide gulches over the centuries, making this area where his land bordered Franklyn's Bear Trap a series of cutbanks, arroyos, little lonely pinnacles, and broad, deep gashes. There were a number of converging, meandering cow trails winding down here, for this was a haven in hot summertime and also a protective place in the blustery winters. There were a number of ancient buffalo wallows, too, but the bison had been gone a long time now and their dusting sites were little more than gentle depressions overgrown with grass.

When he'd been younger, there had still been a few stone teepee rings where Indians had pitched their camps, but rubbing cattle had pretty well scattered those stone rings.

He took a cow trail down off the plain, felt his horse tip, his cantle tilt up gently to strike his back, then he was down where sunlight had not yet reached, riding northerly through a maze of arroyos. For a little while there was no sign of that other rider. He startled a brush rabbit whose ears were ridiculously short, undoubtedly the result of having been frozen some previous winter, and he heard a pheasant drum on a log ahead, warning all wild things something alien was down in this secret place.

Where an intersecting cow trail angled down, he cut fresh sign of that onward rider. After this he allowed his horse to follow the trail without additional guidance, confident the scent of that forward animal would hold his animal's curiosity and interest, which it did. His beast ambled patiently along, skirting sage and buckbrush and some sapling cottonwoods that were having a hard time surviving the bark hunger of small game.

He was entirely relaxed and unprepared when the gunshot came, its slamming echo bouncing off arroyo walls back down toward him in a dull, fierce way. Even his horse started, whipping half around as it shied.

Race caught himself, regained his balance, and lithely stepped down. The shot had not been meant for him, he was certain, and yet because whoever had fired that shot probably had no inkling he was in the same arroyo, they might accidentally fire again, and this time in his direction.

He led his horse in behind a sod wall where the arroyo swirled westerly, left him there, and eased forward on foot. His initial thought, after recovering from surprise, was that Curt had found a heifer beyond saving and had ended her suffering.

He still thought this likely when he stepped around the barranca where he'd left his horse and saw, not a hundred yards ahead, a big, shiny sorrel mare tied to a red-barked manzanita. The sorrel had her head up, her little ears nervously pointing ahead, and her attention so fully forward she neither heard nor saw Race until he came almost even with her. Then she swung, side-stepped, and snorted. He said—"Easy, girl, easy."—and glided past.

He did not recognize this animal, but knew it was not one of his. The saddle was an expensive hand-carved rig; it was recently new and the headstall matched it. The bit was a solidly overlaid silver half-breed with Santa Cruz cheek pieces. Whoever owned this horse and outfit had a lot of money tied up in both.

Race stepped over into some brush on his far right to see ahead. Somewhere up there was the rider of the sorrel mare. He saw nothing until a scarlet blouse stepped up. It was a girl and she had a nickel-plated six-shooter in her right hand.

V

The girl was no less astonished when Race stepped forward out of the underbrush than he was at seeing her in this distant and lonely place with a gun in her hand. They exchanged a long stare before Race, moving in closer, spoke his name, explained why he was here, and asked what she had been firing at.

The girl was tall and slim and carried the unmistakable poise of full and knowing womanhood. Beneath strong brows was the inquiring line of direct blue eyes. She had a long composed mouth, full at the centers, and a willful jaw that showed a temper capable of charming a man or chilling him to the bone. Her scarlet riding blouse had a fullness that sang over the little intervening distance to Race, and her rusty-colored riding skirt fell from a tiny waist the full length to her ankles. But it was her face, her expression, which most strongly held his attention. Her skin was smooth and fair, and flushed now from heat, from exertion and surprise. It was a strikingly handsome face with something about it Race could not define, as though this beautiful girl were lonely or sad or wistfully wishing, wistfully reaching for something just beyond her fingertips. It was an expression to haunt a man, to recur to him in the watch hours of the night with its riddle and its promise.

She told him her name was Eleanor Franklyn and that a friend in the East had recently sent her that nickel-plated pistol, and that she'd ridden over into the rough country to practice with it.

He smiled at that, his face turning soft and his eyes showing candid admiration. "I was poking along half asleep," he said, "and that shot near turned my hair white."

She was apologetic and murmured something to this effect, but her dead-level violet gaze did not leave his face; it was as though she were saying one thing and thinking another.

He stepped closer, moved into barranca shade, and dropped his gaze to the pistol. It was one of those gambler models with a stubby barrel and a flip-down hammer that would not become caught in a sleeve or a shirt front. It would be deadly enough at a hundred feet but beyond that, unless it was in the hands of a competent gunman, its noise would be worse than its sting.

Eleanor Franklyn saw his interest and offered him the weapon. He smilingly shook his head, turned a little, and looked across where moist earth showed a bullet had recently struck near a large white stone. He suspected she'd been aiming at the stone.

"Try again," he said. "Hold a little more to the south."

She turned, sunlight struck the mass of burnished copper that was her hair, and Race looked at her profile, forgetting the stone altogether. Side view she was like an old cameo carving he'd seen as a boy upon his grandmother's throat. He sought flaws and found none at all. He was dumbfounded that this utterly lovely creature could be the daughter of grim, slovenly old

Earnest Franklyn.

She fired, earth flew, and the white stone remained serenely unharmed. Race looked over and looked back. She was smiling at him, near to laughing.

"I imagine if women'd had to win the West, Mister Dunphy, it would still be owned by Indians."

She held the gun out to him. It sparkled like new silver in her small, square, tanned hand.

"You try it. Maybe it's the sights."

He took the gun, let it lie loosely, closed his fist slowly, and tugged off a shot. The white stone disintegrated. He smiled into her twinkling eyes. "It's the sights all right," he drawled, and they both laughed.

She took the gun back, dropped it into her waist holster, and raised her eyes to him, saying: "To tell you the truth it's the noise. I brace myself for that awful explosion just before I pull the trigger, and afterward I'm a little breathless."

He nodded. "When I was a kid, I had the same trouble. I couldn't see the slug so it wasn't immediately important, but that racket sounded like the world had blown apart."

He tried to find something of old Earnest in her and failed, unless it was in the squareness of her jaw and perhaps a little in the brooding look around the eyes.

"It's odd we've never met before," he went on, turning to a fresh topic. "I was born about three miles south of here and you were raised over at Bear Trap."

She looked away from him, but just ahead of this he'd seen a darkening of her eyes. "I went East to school," she solemnly said. "I've been away most of my life."

"Then I reckon you never missed the Lone Pine country."

"You're wrong, Mister Dunphy. There have been a thousand times when I missed it." She turned back to him. "There is something born into people . . . some part of their environment . . . that never lets them forget. In me I believe it's quite strong. Much stronger than in most people."

He tried to remember her mother and could not. Could not in fact recall ever hearing anything about old Franklyn's wife except a guarded word here and there; he had always assumed she'd died, the time or two he'd thought of her at all. Now, he wondered about her anew; this beautiful, tall girl did not resemble her father scarcely at all. She must, therefore, have taken after her mother, and, if that was so, then her mother must have been a startlingly beautiful woman.

"Well," he quietly said, "it's a good land. It offers a good way of life for folks."

"Have you ever been out of it, Mister Dunphy?"

"Yes, many times."

"In the East, perhaps?"

He shook his head, making a small, slow smile over at her. "No farther east than the Missouri settlements, and to you that wouldn't be East at all, would it?"

She matched his grin. "It would be a start, though. I've been largely in upstate New York and New England, places such as Massachusetts and Maine and New Hampshire. Girls' schools in those places. It's quite different. Everything there is on a much smaller scale than out here."

"Are you going to stay?"

She looked over where that shattered white stone lay. All the relaxed faint humor died out of her eyes. "I suppose so," she murmured. "I'm finished with school now."

"You don't sound very enthusiastic about staying."

She put her back to an earthen bank and was silent for a time. "There are other things, Mister Dunphy. . . ." She stopped, shot him a quick sidelong look, and briskly changed the subject, pushing her voice at him and running the words together in a hurried way. "I'm sorry for startling you with my shooting and I think I should be getting back to the ranch now. I'm glad I met you."

He went with her to the sorrel mare, untied the reins, swung them up, and half turned to hold the stirrup for her. She was standing slightly behind him, her body rigid, her head tilted, and her gaze rising up over his head to the earthen bank above them that formed the brink of their arroyo. Something in her face struck a sudden warning through him, but he did not whip around to follow out her line of vision; instead he turned quite slowly, quite carefully.

Two men on foot were standing up there, looking down at them. Both men had six-guns in their hands. Race could not recall ever seeing this pair before, but, even as he considered them, a sudden, jarring thought flashed through his awareness—this must be the pair Curt had spoken of, the two gunmen who had been seeking Franklyn's ranch.

"Just drop the pistol, mister," said one of those tough, warylooking strangers. "And you too, lady. Do it nice an' easy now, or you'll spend eternity down in that gulch."

Race did not immediately obey. He stood like a statue trying to imagine who these men were, what they wanted. There were renegades in the land, there always were, but these two, if they were the same pair Curt had spoken to, would not be simply itinerant outlaws. They had some reason for being here. That reason, he told himself, had something to do with the Kansas Kid, dead Gus Meadows, and Eleanor Franklyn's father.

"Mister," spoke up the youngest of those two standing above them upon the arroyo's crumbly lip, "you keep horsin' us around and you're goin' to get yourself killed. Now shuck that gun."

Race obeyed; he lifted his gun clear of its holster, dropped it, and turned to watch Eleanor do the same. Her face was white from throat to hairline; her violet eyes were dark and wide.

"What was the shootin' about?" asked the older, unshaven, and least presentable of those two gunmen up there.

"Target practicing with that nickel-plated gun," replied Race. "Who are you two? What do you want?"

"Target shootin', huh," said the older gunman, ignoring Race's questions. "Sounded like a regular war. We followed the sound of it, left our horses back a ways, and crept up here, figurin' to find a whole pile of dead men." This stranger made a thin, long-lipped smile at his own mirthless humor. "Mister, who are you? What's your name an' all?"

"My name's Race Dunphy. I own the range where you're standing and southwesterly behind you." Race paused, phrased a fresh statement, and tried it. "I own the ranch where you had breakfast coffee yesterday morning, south of here."

Although neither gunman said anything about this, neither did they show ignorance of what Race had meant. He knew then these were the same men Curt had told him about. He also knew something else; Curt had been correct; this pair were professional gunmen, professional killers. As Curt had said, Race knew this by the look of his captors.

Going back a little further in memory, recalling something Franklyn had said to the Kansas Kid in Tim Wade's jailhouse, and the Kid's reply—two names—Race thought he'd try for another bull's-eye. He said: "Which one of you is Mort and which one is Pete."

The gunmen stared at Race, looked at one another, and back again at Race. The older one, a man in his late thirties, puckered his forehead, pursed his lips, and studied Race for a long time before he answered.

"What difference does it make?" he demanded.

"None," said Race, satisfied he had scored again. "I just wondered is all."

"Wondered what? Who you been talkin' to, Dunphy?"

"The Kansas Kid."

Those two men put up their guns. They stood for a while frowning down at Race, saying nothing. The older man ultimately hunkered down, thumbed back his hat, and dredged up a tobacco sack. The young one did not become this careless; it was almost as though these two had done this same thing many times before: one gave the impression of relaxed indifference while the other one stood there ready to draw and willing to kill.

The older man finished making his smoke. He leaned a little to offer the sack downward. When Race shook his head, the gunman shrugged, pocketed his tobacco, and lit up. Through smoke his perpetually squinted eyes raked up Race and down him. Neither of those men seemed at all interested in Eleanor Franklyn now; their whole attention was focused upon Race.

"Tell me somethin'," drawled the older man. "How is the Kid?"

Race was only half listening. He was controlled now by the avenues of fresh speculation opened up by his recent discoveries.

"Mister, I'm talkin' to you . . . or don't you hear good?"

"The Kid? He's all right. At least he was last night."

"In jail, ain't he?"

"Yes."

"Well then, mister, he ain't all right."

Race looked from the older man's unshaven, hawk-like expressionless face with its drooping cigarette, its narrowed eyes, to the more open, smooth countenance of the younger gunman. That peculiar aura this breed of killer emanated was identical with these two. The younger man's eyes strayed every once in a while to Eleanor's full scarlet blouse and otherwise desirable figure, but never for long; this one might have his powerful hungers but he also had his inherent wariness. He viewed Race Dunphy as an enemy and therefore he came first in the gunman's view.

"The Kid's all right," Race said again. "They won't hold him."

"Why won't they, mister?" drawled the older man. "He downed one of Franklyn's hands, didn't he?"

"It was a fair fight. There were a half dozen witnesses."

"I see," mused the older man. "And this Franklyn feller . . . he's heard about it by now . . . how's he feel about the Kid gettin' released?"

Race had no difficulty at all recalling Franklyn's threats of the night before but he had no intention of repeating them now to these two, who obviously were friends of the Kansas Kid.

"How should he feel? He won't like it, I suppose, but he won't buck the law. When the law says you're justified in a killing, that's the end of it."

"Sometimes," drawled the older man. "Sometimes it's the end of it." He straightened up again, dropped his cigarette, and tromped on it. "Tell me something, mister. How come you to talk to the Kid? You two know each other, maybe?"

Race was being hemmed in by that older man's shrewdness and knew it. He would have to be very careful here. Maybe it would be to his advantage to say he knew the Kansas Kid, and maybe it wouldn't. He tried being evasive.

"What difference does it make?"

Now the younger gunman spoke up for the first time. "Who's she?" he demanded, bobbing his head at Eleanor, his dull, lusterless eyes showing banked fires in their deepest depths.

"I'm Earnest Franklyn's daughter," said Eleanor sharply.

VI

Race knew instinctively, and at once, Eleanor had said the wrong thing. Those two men upon the arroyo's earthen lip turned to stone while they put their attention over to Franklyn's daughter. Race could almost hear their forming thoughts. He rummaged swiftly for something to alleviate the congealing atmosphere, something that would draw that cold, thoughtful consideration away from Eleanor back to him. He could think of nothing, and in fact there was nothing he could have said, although at the time he only had very recently come to suspect this.

"Well, well," drawled the older gunman, his squinted, sunk-set eyes turning slowly pleased and exultant. "We got old Franklyn's girl right here before us neat as a greased pig. Now, Mort, you couldn't ask for anything neater'n this, could you?"

Mort did not answer; he was keeping his hot and hungry gaze upon Eleanor with obvious thoughts.

The older man turned slightly, to smile downward. "Mister, you could've saved a heap of time in the first place by tellin' us who this fine-lookin' heifer was."

"Knowing who she is," said Race, "isn't going to make any difference."

"Isn't it, now? Well, I got a hunch it sure enough is, because, you see, I don't exactly hold with your good faith in the law hereabouts, or any other place for that matter."

"What are you talking about?"

"The Kansas Kid, mister, the Kansas Kid. This here heifer's going to make it damned certain the Kansas Kid gets out of that Lone Pine jail." The gunman began to smile widely; clearly something relative to this idea in his mind had just come to him. "An' that's goin' to be a real belly laugh, mister. I'll tell you why. Franklyn's goin' to not only help the Kid get out, he's goin' to guarantee him safe passage out o' Lone Pine . . . or else he gets back his long-legged girl wrapped in blankets, two blankets, mister, each one separate from the other one."

"The Kid will be released," assured Race, turning cold in the stomach. "I've already told you that. He killed Gus Meadows in a fair fight."

"Maybe," said the older gunman. "And maybe not, like I already said. But this way, mister, we make plumb certain that he not only gets loose, but that he gets clear of old man Franklyn and that town o' yours, too." The older man stopped smiling; his narrowed eyes swung. "Mort," he ordered, "go fetch our horses. I'll get these two astride."

Mort scowled and ran pale eyes over the empty landscape. "You figurin' on holdin' 'em?" he asked.

"Yep, the girl at least. We'll let Dunphy go give our terms to Franklyn."

"Where, Pete? There ain't a cave nor a. . . ."

"Why, boy," said the man called Pete in his drawling, almost chuckling tone, "we got a ready-made place to keep her. At Dunphy's ranch south o' here."

Mort's thin, hatchet features expanded into a slow smile. Without another word he turned and started off away from the arroyo's lip.

Race felt Eleanor's eyes upon him. He did not look around; instead he dropped his gaze to the ground where those two pistols lay.

"Don't try it," warned Pete from up above. "Mister, you'd never make it in a million years."

Race looked up again. Pete had his handgun out again, one thumb pad lying ready upon the hammer. There was no hope at all and Race recognized this.

"Start walkin' folks, slow now. Head for your horses, untie 'em, and lead 'em up out o' there. Don't mount 'em . . . lead 'em."

Finally Race looked at Eleanor. Her expression made him inwardly wince; she was so frightened when she started along toward her sorrel mare the elasticity was entirely gone from her movements and she moved jerkily, as a sleepwalker moves.

Farther along, when they came to Race's patiently waiting horse, the man called Pete who paced them upon higher ground, watched Race closely. Afterward, as they were trudging along ahead of their animals, Eleanor in front, Race behind, the young gunman came up with two saddled horses. He tossed Pete his reins, drew his gun, and covered the prisoners while his companion got gruntingly astride. After that it was a comparatively short walk to the first upward cow trail. Here, Pete directed Eleanor to lead up out of the arroyo. Race was still obediently following after.

Upon the plain, with two guns covering them, Eleanor and Race mounted, reined southerly, and started off. Mort rode on one side, Pete on the other. Pete put his gun up now, turned bullyingly genial again, and said: "Tell you what you're goin' to do, mister. You're goin' to ride into Lone Pine, hunt up this Franklyn feller, tell him to get the Kid released today, then you an' Franklyn and the Kid are coming back out here to your ranch."

Race, who was watching Mort as Pete gave these instructions, saw a quick clearing of the younger gunman's troubled face. It was like a signal to Race; these two did not only want the Kansas Kid safely away from Lone Pine, they also wanted Eleanor's father. To affirm this suspicion Race said: "I'll fetch the Kid back and take Eleanor to her father."

"Nope," contradicted Pete, turning crafty now. "Nope, mister, you'll fetch her pappy back to the ranch with you."

"Why him? Hell, I'll get the Kid for you."

Mort said: "Dammit, Dunphy, you sure like to argue. I got a notion to blow you out of that saddle here and now."

Eleanor swung an anguished look around, beseeching Race in powerful silence not to antagonize those two further. He didn't; he had what he wanted to know anyway, so he rode along quietly, watching the land smooth out, become gently rolling again, free of arroyos and erosion washes.

The sun stood higher in the sky, near its meridian. Sunlight burnished the world to a high, dazzling polish; it struck sharply off an old tin roof at his ranch and it also struck down noticeably upon a converging speck far out where a solitary rider was jogging toward the ranch out of the golden east.

Race's heart sank; he recognized Curt even at that considerable distance. He'd only just begun to hope this coincidental meeting would not take place, that somehow his cowboy might happen in behind them, spy Mort's palmed gun, surmise what was going on, and somehow interrupt it. As soon as Pete, squinting ahead, said—"There's a rider yonder, Mort."—Race knew this last hope was dead.

"Hey, Dunphy!" called the younger man. "Who is that headin' for your barn?"

There was no way out now, and in order to protect Curt from the cold-bloodedness of these two, Race said: "That's my rider, the feller who gave you two coffee yesterday. He's heading home after riding the range looking at cattle."

"Oh, yeah," said Mort, his voice rising a little. "Real helpful feller. His name's Curt, ain't it?"

Race nodded, looking from beneath his hat brim out where Lake was riding.

"Watch 'em," said Mort, putting up his gun and lifting his reins. "I'll mosey on ahead and get the cowboy's gun, Pete."

The three of them watched Mort lope onward, angling so as to intercept Curt Lake. When it happened, when those two horsemen came together down in the Dunphy ranch yard, the others were close enough to see Curt's shoulders jerk up, stiff, and his head swing. He had just lost his six-gun; they could all of them see its black brightness where sunlight struck down in Mort's right hand.

At the barn Mort and Curt were waiting afoot. When Race

passed by, Curt looked up mournfully at him, dolorously wagged his head, and looked down. This silent, abject apology did not pass the gunman called Pete. He laughed and said to Curt: "Cheer up, cowboy, you're not the first feller ever had someone get the drop on him."

Curt put an expressionless, bright stare upon Pete, followed the others inside the barn where they all dismounted, and stood there all loose and dispirited.

"I'm hungrier'n a bitch wolf," said Pete, still half smiling over the ease with which Race's cowboy had been taken. "How about it, mister, you got plenty o' grub over at the house?"

Race nodded.

"Then come along, let's eat up hearty," ordered Pete, walking toward the barn's front entrance. "Stay behind 'em, Mort, just in case."

"In case of what?" grumbled the younger man. "What're they goin' to try . . . sprout wings and fly off? Sometimes you get on my nerves, Pete."

If this admonition was intended to raise Pete's hackles, it failed. He marched across the yard to the house, kicked open the door, poked his head in to look around, then stamped on in. He was grinning again, his spirits undiminished by Mort's sullenness.

In the kitchen Race said to Curt: "Put the coffee on. I'll fry up some meat and potatoes." He turned, saw that Eleanor was standing over beside Pete and keeping a goodly distance from Mort, and said to the older man: "Unless you don't like fried meat and spuds."

Pete chuckled. "You sure got your nose out o' joint, mister. Be damned if I know exactly why though. We ain't hurt you nor your girlfriend here. Be a little cheerful, mister, it could be a heap worse . . . I could let Mort shoot you."

They ate, the five of them, in an atmosphere made tense and

hushed by their individual thoughts. Eleanor only toyed with her food but the pair of gunmen did not stop stuffing themselves until there was no food left. They then smoked and relaxed, with the older man, as usual, doing the talking. To Race he said: "You remember all I told you, mister? Find Franklyn, get him to release the Kid, then fetch the brace of 'em out here to your ranch."

"I remember," retorted Race. "But I want to be plumb certain Eleanor and Curt will be safe until I get back."

"Safe." The older man chuckled, his voice coming on again in the sly drawl. "Why they never been safer in their damned lives." He looked from Race to Eleanor, on over at Curt, and back again. "You got nothin' to worry about there, mister."

"I think I have," said Race, arising from the table. "I'd like to hear Mort say Eleanor will be safe, too."

The younger gunman's face flooded with rusty color. His sullen, smoky eyes erupted with a savage blaze and he sprang up across the table from Race. He called Race a vile name, saying: "You got nothin' to say, Dunphy. Nothin' to say at all. In fact, if I had my way, I'd kill you. I'd have killed you back there in that damned gulch. We don't need you." He flung around to include his partner in that fiery stare. "We don't need any of 'em. We can catch some dumb damned cowboy, give him the girl's dress, and let him take that to her old man. What the hell do we need Dunphy and this cowboy for, anyway? I say shoot. . . ."

"You said enough," snapped Pete, his face changed completely, his little pouched-up eyes like wet stone. "You said more'n enough an' now you better sit down an' shut up."

Mort stepped back one step and Race, seeing the expression he wore, gathered his legs under him. He'd seen that look on men before; the slightest movement, the faintest jangling wrong word, and all hell was going to break loose there at the kitchen table. Mort was keyed to kill.

Pete could not have but seen his partner's stance, his putty stare and his lock-jawed pose, yet he went right on raking the younger man with his biting words, went on giving Mort stare for stare.

"You damned pup. The only way Franklyn's goin' to be got out here where we can do what we rode seven hundred miles to do . . . before we can ride back and collect our money . . . is when someone he knows brings him out here. The Kid couldn't do it alone, not now, not with half the lousy territory up in arms about him shootin' that lousy cowpuncher Franklyn sent after him. So we send this Dunphy feller in an' he brings the Kid back safe and old Franklyn, too. There ain't no other way, not that we can be plumb certain of."

Mort heard his companion out but he did not immediately ease off from that gunfighting stance. Pete, though, evidently knew that he would ease off; he sat there, staring the younger man down.

Finally Mort moved, pushed out his hand, grasped the back of a chair, drew it out, and dropped down upon it. He swung his hating eyes to Race and said bitterly and coldly: "All right, Dunphy. But God help her if you fail. If you try anything cute like maybe fetchin' back some posse men or something, or if you don't fetch the Kid back." Mort's teeth shone cruelly past his thin and bloodless lips. "God help her . . . you better remember that."

Race got up and moved off a short distance. This was the best he could hope for. He knew now that of those two the younger gunman was by far the most vicious and deadly. If he tried for any additional assurance again, there was little doubt about it; the next time Pete would not be able to talk down his partner.

He looked at Curt, over at Eleanor Franklyn, looked longest into her frightened, deep violet eyes, then swung his head toward the gunman named Pete.

Pete inclined his head. He was not smiling at all now: "Go on, mister, saddle up and head out . . . and if you think I'm kiddin' or Mort's kiddin' . . . you just fail to come back, or try and bring in the law, or return without the Kid and old Franklyn. You just try it. Now go on."

VII

Race rode into Lone Pine with strong daylight making the town look cleaner than it actually was. He left his horse at the livery barn, went along to the saloon, and asked Jack Pritchett if any Bear Trap men had been in.

Jack shook his head. "After what happened yesterday mornin' I got a feeling old Franklyn'll lay down the law about this place."

"That suits me," said Race. "Let him keep them out of here if he wants to, but right now I've got to find Franklyn or one of his men."

Jack shook his head. "Can't help you, Race. There may be a rider or two in after sundown, but I doubt if there'll be any in earlier. You know how the old man is about that."

"Well, have you seen Tim Wade?"

"Yeah. He was in here a while back. I expect he'll be at the jailhouse."

Race walked back out to the roadway. He stepped forth into dust, pacing along, bound for Wade's office. Around him Lone Pine was bustling with activity. There were supply wagons in from outlying ranches, a few riders after the mail, a lot of shopping townswomen passing back and forth. Everything seemed normal. Race hiked southward feeling like some kind of a conspirator; he entered Sheriff Wade's office with that feeling strong in him, and also with a sensation of urgency driving him physically and mentally.

Wade was there, pawing through a pile of unkempt papers on

his desk. He cocked an eye at Race's entrance, eased back, and kept looking up, saying nothing, just waiting.

"Tim, you've got to release the Kansas Kid."

Wade continued to look upward at Race in the doorway. He began to frown faintly. "You heard what I told Franklyn. When Doc Cooper gets back to town and certifies the killing of Meadows so we can bury him, there'll be an official inquest. After that, the Kid'll be turned loose."

Race reached for a wired-together old chair, drew it up close, and sat down upon it. "Listen to me," he said, speaking crisply, forcefully. "If you don't let the Kid out right now, you'll be responsible for two more deaths." He told Sheriff Wade everything that had happened since he'd ridden out of town the evening before. Wade's relaxed position at his desk gradually fell away. By the time Race was through speaking, Wade was sitting upright with every bit of his earlier lethargy gone.

"But what's it all about?" he asked.

Race shook his head. "I don't know. Up to a point I understand it, I think, but the real basic fact still escapes me. But right now that's not important. Eleanor and Curt are what matter now." Race sprang up, walked to the door, turned, and walked back. "It's not quite noon, Tim. We've got about five hours left. After that . . . ?"

Wade got up heavily from his chair. He puckered his face into a troubled expression and said: "Wait here. I'll send a rider out to fetch Franklyn in."

"Tim, dammit, there's not time for that. Bear Trap is. . . ."

"Franklyn's not at his ranch. He was in town this morning. He told Jared over at the store he was goin' over to the Spannaus place to identify some strayed Bear Trap bulls they're holdin' for him." Wade moved past. "Wait here, Race."

With Wade's departure the jailhouse was suddenly a lonely, hushed place. Race looked around; his gaze halted upon the bolt-studded oaken door across the room. He visualized the Kansas Kid in that cool and musty other room and crossed over, flung back the door, and turned sharply left, hiked along until he saw the Kid sitting loosely upon his bunk braiding some leather scraps into a watch fob. The Kid had a cigarette hanging from his lips. It was unlit. He stopped what he was doing, raised cool, steady eyes, and put them upon Race.

"You look like you been ridin' hard," he said. "You look sort of upset, Mister Dunphy? What's the trouble out in the yonder world? Somebody stub their toe on a bullet maybe?"

"I reckon you know you're going to get out of here," retorted Race, "don't you?"

"Sure. Sure I'll get out. But that stupid sheriff's got to play his little game, got to hold me as long as he can to satisfy some sadistic streak he's got."

"No, it's not that at all," said Race. "He's got to wait for the doctor to get back to town before Meadows can be legally written off."

The Kid tossed aside his plaiting work. He dug out a match, struck it, and lit his dead cigarette. He squared around on the bunk, looking steadily out at Race.

"I already heard all this," he said. "You didn't come in here to tell it to me again, Mister Saloonkeeper. Why did you come in here?"

"Because of Mort and Pete."

The Kid's brows went up a little. He sat on, waiting for more.

"They're out at my ranch, Kid, waiting for you."

"Is that so?" The Kid's voice got very soft, very cautious-sounding. "Why your ranch, Dunphy? What's your part in this?"

"Until this morning I had no part in it. Now I have a big part."

"Oh?" murmured the Kid. He rose up off the bunk, stepped

close to the bars, and said: "How come Mort and Pete to go to you?"

"We met by accident," Race said truthfully. "We talked and went down to my ranch. Like I said, they're waiting for you there right now."

The Kid dropped his smoke, ground it out underfoot, looked sideways and upward at Race, giving an impression of conspiracy. "I get it," he said, speaking very softly. "You want old Franklyn dead, too." He pulled his lips down in a cruel expression. "All right, Dunphy . . . it'll sure make it a heap easier havin' someone local helpin' us."

Race had not entirely come upon this admission of the Kansas Kid's purpose for being in Lone Pine by accident. He'd had several strong clues concerning some plot against Franklyn right from the start. But this was the first time he knew without reservation that his suspicions were correct.

He tried now to figure some way this information could be used to save Eleanor and Curt. Perhaps if he knew why Earnest Franklyn was to die it would help.

"Listen," he said to the Kid. "I got rid of the sheriff but he'll be back. Whatever we say has got to be said quickly. Mort and Pete aim to break you out of here today."

"They're crazy," growled the Kid. "You tell 'em to hang and rattle. I'll get released in another few days. If they try breakin' me out of here in the middle of town, we'll likely all get killed. That's the trouble with those two . . . no brains, no sense at all. I wish I'd tackled this job alone."

"I'll tell them," said Race, forcing this conversation because he knew Tim Wade would be back any moment now. "I don't know that they'll change their minds, but I'll tell them. The trouble is . . . I can get you out of here the back way without any trouble at all, right now . . . but those two might ride to town anyway."

The Kid shook his head. "No hurry," he said, smiling at Race. "The three of you just relax. I'll be out when that sawbones rides back to town."

"That's not the point," said Race. "Sure you'll get out, but Franklyn's got men stationed in town and out on the range with orders to kill you on sight."

The Kid's smile faded. "How many men, Dunphy?"

Race shrugged. "I don't know exactly, but I've recognized nine Bear Trap riders here in town, just loafing. There are probably another five or six outside of town covering all the trails."

The Kid turned, paced to the thick back wall of his cage, paced back, and said: "That damned old whelp. I should have killed him ten years back." He shot Race a frosty look. "Dunphy, I think you might be right. Maybe I'd better not wait for the law to turn me loose. Those are damned big odds out there. All right, how can you get me out of here?"

"Easy. The sheriff trusts me. I can send him off like I did this time, get the keys, unlock the doors, and take you out of town through the back alleyway."

"At night," put in the Kid. "At night, Dunphy, when we can't be recognized."

Race nodded at this, but he was beginning to draw back a little; the conversation had progressed about as far as he dared let it, at least for the time being, at least until he worked out in his mind how the Kid's confidence could be best exploited.

"All right," he said, also speaking in a low, conspiratorial tone of voice. "I'll make the arrangements." He affected to turn away, then turned back again. "One thing interests me," he said directly to the Kid. "Why? What's between you and old Franklyn? Why did you and Mort and Pete ride so far for this job?"

The Kansas Kid stood looking straight out at Race, his face blank, his eyes unblinking. It was almost as though Race had

170

said the wrong thing, had undone all that he'd just accomplished. Then the Kid dispelled this thought with his next words.

"It's a long story, Dunphy. It goes back to the time I was born." The Kid's lips parted in a wolfish smile. "You see, Earnest Franklyn is my uncle."

Race froze. The Kid saw this, broadened that cruel smile, and went right on speaking, obviously enjoying the shock he'd caused.

"His brother owned a big combination dance hall and saloon over at Salina, down in Kansas Territory. His brother was my paw, Dunphy, and old man Franklyn's wife run off from him and went to live with his brother. I guess they'd had somethin' goin' between 'em long before I was born, but that's not important. Anyway, my maw had me. When Franklyn learned where she was, what she'd done, he sent a gunman after his brother. They fought it out in the roadway of Salina. The gunfighter got killed but my paw was so bad off he died a month later." The Kid's eyes were darker now than they'd been earlier, his nostrils flared, and his expression was vicious.

Race leaned upon the wall, looking into the shadowy face of that youthful gunman feeling dirty and cheap and a little sick to his stomach.

"Pretty isn't it?" said the Kid. "Dunphy, you look like you just seen a ghost."

Race pulled himself together. "So you're over here to avenge your pa, is that it?"

The Kid shook his head. "Naw, to hell with my paw. He and my maw are both dead. Been dead near ten years now. Naw, I'm here to kill Franklyn and inherit his Bear Trap cattle spread."

"You couldn't inherit it, Kid. Franklyn's got a daughter."

"I know that, dammit. She won't give me any trouble, Dunphy. Women are weak. I won't have to do much to get her to step out."

Race had his lips parted to speak when out in the front office a man's heavy footsteps sounded. The Kid threw up a finger over his mouth and jerked his head. Race wheeled and walked out of the cell-block, closed the massive oaken door behind him.

He walked over where Tim Wade was standing, looking at him, felt for the chair he'd previously occupied, and sank down upon it.

"What's the matter with you?" inquired the sheriff. "You look like you got a bellyache."

Race said nothing for a while. He shook himself slightly, brought his head up, and said: "Did you send for Franklyn?"

"Yeah, he ought to be along in an hour or so." Wade put aside his hat, eased down at the desk, and watched Race's color gradually come normal again. He made a mistaken analysis and said quietly: "I know how you feel, but we'll get 'em. We'll work something out so the girl and Lake don't get hurt."

"There's only one way, Tim. Release the Kansas Kid."

Wade promptly inclined his head. "I'll do that, don't sweat over it. He's not worth anyone gettin' killed over."

"I've been talking to him."

"Find out anything?"

"Enough," said Race. "Enough, Tim. Let's wait until Franklyn gets here before we talk about it."

Wade eased forward in his chair, scenting something. "You found out what it's all about?"

Race inclined his head but did not speak.

Wade sat forward for a moment, considering Dunphy's features, then he gradually relaxed again, leaning far back. He was a rough, rude man, but he was not without patience. "We'll wait," he intoned, and said no more.

Race got up, crossed to the doorway, and leaned there, looking out into Lone Pine's solitary, wide, and dusty main thoroughfare. He saw Jack come out onto the plank walk up at the saloon, wiping his hands upon his soiled white apron, stand briefly in sunlight, then turn and reënter the building.

Jared Plummer and gaunt Hank Henrickson were in deep conversation in front of Jared's store. Hank, as usual, was mostly listening. Obadiah Dewey, who owned the saddle and harness shop, was earnestly talking to several cowboys in front of his shop, and three riders came jangling into town from the north, riding abreast. They turned in at the hitch rack in front of his saloon, got dustily down, tied up, and trooped on inside.

Very gradually Race recovered from what the Kansas Kid had told him. Gradually, too, he began fitting all the fragments he'd been assimilating lately into a solid pattern. No wonder old man Franklyn could not stand the sight of saloons or saloon men; no wonder he had sent someone to head off the Kansas Kid—the trouble was, he sent Gus Meadows, a man whose pride and arrogance made Gus and nearly everyone else think Meadows was a lot better man with weapons than he actually was.

He recalled the way Curt had looked at him the night before in the bunkhouse. Curt had known; he could see that now. Curt, his own father, and probably half the other old-timers in the Lone Pine country had known about Franklyn's wife, his brother over in Kansas, and everything sordid that had come out of this relationship.

He dwelt for a time upon these unpleasant, converging facts, then remembered that peculiar, wistful look he'd seen in Eleanor Franklyn's eyes. He now wondered if that haunted look was because she also knew, or whether it was simply because of the monumental bitterness in her father that had turned him harsh and grim and taciturn. Of one thing he felt quite sure: the relationship between Earnest Franklyn and his daughter was not the normal relationship between father and daughter.

From behind him Tim Wade said quietly: "Whatever the Kid told you, Race, must have been the tale to end all tales."

Wade did not sound particularly curious. When Race turned to face back into the room, Sheriff Wade was making a cigarette, concentrating wholly upon this and seemingly interested in nothing else. When he lit up, though, he raised his eyes and said: "The only thing I care about right now is getting Curt and that girl out of there alive." He puffed and looked straight at Race. "The rest of it, right now, doesn't amount to a hill of beans to me."

Race wondered if Earnest Franklyn would feel the same way.

VIII

Old Franklyn came jogging into town at high noon with the roadway nearly empty and the cafés doing their rush-hour business. He had with him his range boss, Frank Andrews. These two didn't look right or left until they swung down in front of Wade's jailhouse, tied up, and paused to run their grave glances northward and southward. They then stepped up onto the plank walk, crossed over, and entered the sheriff's office.

Race was standing over by a front window. He did not turn at once, although he heard Franklyn and Andrews enter. Tim Wade stood up, nodded at Franklyn, and began his solemn recital of Eleanor Franklyn's predicament. Neither Bear Trap's owner nor its foreman moved or said a word until Wade was finished, and even then the pair of them stood like stone, looking from Wade to Race Dunphy and back again to Wade. Finally the older man reached for that wired-together chair Race had earlier vacated, sprung his knees outward, and sank down upon it.

"Dunphy," he said huskily, "is all this true?"

Race turned away from the window, saw Franklyn's gray lips and faintly quaking hands, and nodded. "Every bit of it. I met your daughter in those badlands near our range boundary. She was practicing with a nickel-plated pistol. It was the gunfire that drew me over. The same gunfire also drew those two who are now with her out at my place."

Frank Andrews started to say something. Franklyn lifted a hand, silencing Frank. He kept staring over at Race. "Will they keep their word?" he softly asked. "Will they let her go if I ride out there with the Kansas Kid?"

"I think so, Mister Franklyn. At least as far as Eleanor is concerned they probably will. It's not your daughter they want. It's you."

Franklyn dropped his head. "I know," he murmured. "I know what they want, even though I've never seen either of them before I know who they are, what they want."

Race took a big breath. "They were hired by the Kansas Kid," he said quietly. "They came here, Mister Franklyn, to help your nephew."

Old Franklyn's shaggy head shot up. He fastened a bleak look upon Race. "So you know," he said.

Now Tim Wade broke in. He looked over at Race, frowning. "You mean to say that two-bit gunman in my cell is Mister Franklyn's nephew?"

Race nodded. "That's what he told me while you were gone, Tim."

Wade swung forward. He glowered at Franklyn as though to speak, but he didn't say a word. Frank Andrews did, though; Frank hooked both thumbs in his gun belt and looked dead ahead at Sheriff Wade.

"I guess it all happened before any of us were around, Wade. I've known it for about five years, but most folks, if they ever knew, have let it lie. The Kansas Kid is the son of Mister

Franklyn's brother and Mister Franklyn's wife. She ran off, got divorced, and married the brother down in Kansas Territory. The Kansas Kid is their child."

Tim went to his desk and perched upon the edge of it, looking steadily at old Franklyn. "An' he wants to kill you," he said directly to Franklyn. "Why? What did you do to him?"

"Not to him," muttered the stricken, older man. "To his father . . . to my brother. I hired a gun, sent him to Salina to kill . . . my brother."

"I see. And this gunman . . . he killed him?"

Franklyn nodded. He kept his face averted, his head lowered. Both his work-swollen, big old hands lay dead upon his legs.

Wade twisted, looked helplessly over at Race, and said softly: "I'll be double damned. Now the Kid's back to do a little killin' of his own."

"Not for the reason you think, though," said Race. "Or at least he says that's not the reason. He wants Mister Franklyn dead so he can inherit the Bear Trap."

Both Franklyn and Andrews started at this statement. Both of them stared hard at Race. "He couldn't inherit it," said the older man hoarsely. "There's Eleanor. She was born to my wife an' me before my wife run off with my brother."

Race pushed clear of the window. He walked softly around the room. "I know that and so does the Kid. But he's got plans for Eleanor."

Franklyn's anguished gaze followed Race's steps. "I see. I understand how it is now. His hired guns have my girl. When I ride out to your place with you an' the Kid . . . they make a clean sweep . . . they kill us all."

Race stopped, turned, and said: "I don't know. I've got a feeling about the Kansas Kid. Tell me something, Mister Franklyn. How did you know he was going to show up here in Lone Pine the day that he did?"

"I told him," said Frank Andrews. "I figured a long time ago that damned killer would try something like this someday. I paid an old ridin' pardner of mine who lives down in Salina to let me know the minute the Kansas Kid left town, riding west."

"And Meadows," said Race, pushing this line of inquiry. "Why did you send Meadows to kill him?"

Old Franklyn wagged his shaggy head back and forth. "No, not to kill him, Dunphy . . . only to force him to keep on going." He raised agonized eyes. "I hope none of you is ever in the position I've been in these past few days. Listen to me. Whatever that boy is, he's still my wife's son. My brother's son. What they did to me isn't his guilt." Franklyn clenched a big fist and struck his leg with it. He moved both lips but no more words came out for a moment. "You know what tears the guts out of a man? Not the infidelity. A man can get over that, bad as it is. It's the knowledge that all these people are your own flesh, your own blood."

Tim Wade surprised Race. He said gently: "Don't talk about it any more, Mister Franklyn. We understand."

But the old man shook his head and squeezed his eyes nearly closed. "You don't understand, any of you, and I hope to God you never have to understand. It's living with a curse eating out your insides twenty-four hours a day, three hundred and sixty-five days a year, for so many years you don't know anything but torment."

Race, watching Eleanor's father through the breathless hush that followed his last words, understood at last what it was that had kept those two apart all these years. Understood, too, the reason for that tragic wistfulness in her face, just below the surface, like a marring, faint shadow.

The old man got up. He said: "I'll go. Sheriff, turn the Kid out. I'll ride out there with him."

But Wade shook his head and Frank Andrews spoke up

quickly: "It won't solve anything, boss. They want to kill both of you. You ridin' into Dunphy's yard will guarantee that they'll do just exactly that."

Franklyn shook his head in an exasperated, almost bewildered or confused manner. "I think I can get them to let my girl go," he muttered.

Race spoke out ahead of either Wade or Andrews. "You can't. Take my word for it, Mister Franklyn, you not only can't bargain with them . . . but as Frank says, the second they see you ride in, they'll no longer have any reason for keeping Eleanor alive. You won't be her father then. You'll be her death warrant."

"Then what?" demanded Franklyn, raising his voice. "Then what can be done? They'll kill her anyway, won't they?"

Race said: "No. As long as you and the Kansas Kid and I are away from my ranch, they'll do nothing. At least not until after dark anyway."

Andrews drew those doeskin roping gloves he wore absently off his hands and twisted them. "We could get up a posse and make a surround," he said, not sounding very convincing about this. "But the trouble is, as I see it, we still couldn't get them until after they'd . . . done what they're here to do, at least to Miss Eleanor."

"No posses," growled Tim Wade. "No posses and no talk about this to anyone outside this room." He began unconsciously to wag one leg back and forth while he sifted through a dozen possibilities, none of which was feasible as long as the Kid's hired killers had Eleanor Franklyn.

"It's a damned riddle," Wade said after a while. "It all hinges on getting the girl out of there some way." He looked at the others. "But how?"

Race had been thinking. He now spoke forth, giving them an idea of how the Kid had jumped to some incorrect conclusions and had come to believe Race was also an enemy of Earnest

Franklyn's. When he finished speaking, the faces of Wade and Andrews showed a forming germ of an idea. Earnest Franklyn, unable to shake out of his gloom, only listened and looked and sat there, ageing before the eyes of the others.

After an interval of thought Frank Andrews said: "As soon as you ride in, this Mort and this Pete will tell the Kid who you really are, Race. You'll be a dead duck."

"But I don't aim to ride in, Frank. All I figure to do is get the Kid out there where they can hear him and maybe see him."

Tim Wade's face lit up. "Sure," he boomed. "Why in hell didn't I think of that?" He began to look less and less distressed.

Frank Andrews, still perplexed, looked at Wade, looked at Race, then rocked his head back and forth. "I guess I'm too dense. What's so clear, Sheriff?"

"Race takes the Kid out to his ranch. The Kid will believe Race is spiriting him away to save his life an' because he hates Mister Franklyn. As soon as Race has the Kid close enough to beller, he'll have him yell at his pardners. They'll come out."

"So far so good," muttered Andrews. "Then what? That's the part that's got me guessing."

"We step in, Frank," said Wade, and swung for confirmation of this toward Race. "We let 'em get out in plain sight, then it's up to them. If we can get between those two and the house where they're holding Curt and Mister Franklyn's girl, they're finished, either way. Frank, it's sort of like playin' checkers. We move, they move, and somebody gets outmaneuvered."

Andrews's brows drew inward and downward as he ran all this through his mind. Beside Andrews, his facial expression beginning to clear, to turn resolute and tough again, Earnest Franklyn drew in a large breath and slowly let it out.

"They'll smell something wrong," he said, speaking once more in his normal, bitter voice. "You're supposed to have me along. They'll likely yell to the Kid something's wrong. It'd only take one yell to spoil the thing. To make sure it'll work, I'll have to be there in plain sight, too."

Race looked at Franklyn, thinking privately that he could scotch the older man's reasoning very easily. It wouldn't make any difference whether Franklyn was along or not, because, although Mort and Pete had Eleanor, he would have the Kid as his prisoner. So, in the end, Mort and Pete would have either to kill Eleanor and Curt or trade them for the Kid, if Race laid down those terms, and this was in the back of his mind. But, gazing upon old Franklyn now, it came to him also that Eleanor's father—and the Kansas Kid's uncle—had some other reason, some powerfully motivating urge, to run this risk. Whatever it was—and Race thought he knew—he did not now try to spike it. All he said was: "Mister Franklyn may be right. One thing I'm sure of. With him along, those two out at my place will come outside a lot quicker than they will if he's not with me when I ride in with the Kansas Kid."

Wade nodded and Frank Andrews, looking strongly of dark misgivings about the entire venture, did not dispute this. They waited in long silence for Franklyn to speak.

He said: "Dunphy, your life won't be worth a plugged nickel once you get into Winchester range out there."

Race said nothing at all to this. He instead swung his attention to Sheriff Wade. "Give me your cell keys, Tim, then the three of you head out. Whatever you do, don't come anywhere near the Kid or me. He's got to believe he's being busted out of here."

"It'd work a lot better after nightfall," muttered Wade.

"That's out," contradicted Race. "Those men out there are going on nerve alone about now. Don't push it, Tim, or they might start shooting."

Andrews agreed with this by strongly, but glumly nodding his head up and down. Old Franklyn kept watching Race. When another interlude of thoughtful quiet filled the office, he spoke up again.

"I owe you an apology, Dunphy," he rumbled. "I never liked you, and it makes me feel pretty mean now . . . what you're doin' for me."

"I'm not doing anything at all for you," Race said evenly, "and I'm not sure I would, either. But your daughter and my cowboy . . . they've got this much coming from me or any other man."

Franklyn looked away from Race, ran his eyes around the wall and back again. "I deserved that," he said, pushing upright and standing there, big and rough-looking and craggy. "But I want to tell the three of you this. Whatever happens, whatever it takes afterward to make things right, I'll do. If it takes money, you will have it."

Tim Wade looked embarrassed, so did Frank Andrews.

Race looked straight at Franklyn and said: "Tim, the cell keys." He had not yet sorted this thing out sufficiently in his mind to make his judgment of Earnest Franklyn's part in it, and he did not propose now to attempt this. "Come on, Tim, the keys. Then the three of you head out. And Mister Franklyn. You join the Kid and me on the trail after we're clear of town."

IX

Race waited a while after Sheriff Wade and the two cattlemen had left. He killed more time by going along to the livery barn, hiring two fresh horses, and returning by way of the back alley to the rear of the jailhouse. He estimated the time lapse, the route the others would take, and the gait they would use in getting out to his ranch, then went inside, passed into the cellblock, and made a quick, warning gesture at the Kansas Kid.

He held up Tim Wade's ring of cell-block keys, glided forward, and began trying them in the Kid's door. By the time he'd found which key would open the cell, the Kid was straining forward with both hands wrapped strongly around the bars.

"Dunphy, dammit, not in broad daylight," the Kid hissed.

Race had to improvise. He straightened back, flung open the door, and said swiftly, forcefully: "It's got to be right now. Franklyn's men are drifting into town. It looks like maybe the townsmen might join them. Kid, it smells like a lynching to me. Come on, I've got horses out back. We can make it if we're careful."

Race started away, then swung back. The Kid was standing in his cell doorway, looking undecided and troubled. "I need a gun," he muttered.

Race drew indignantly upright. He lashed the Kid with quick anger. "Gun be damned. Listen, I got the sheriff to go on a wild-goose chase, but he'll be back any minute. Do you want to stay here and maybe do a rope dance tonight, or not? If not, then shake a leg. I don't want to be caught doing this. I stand to lose more than you do. Come on, dammit!"

The Kid made his decision; he passed fully out of the steel cage, began to move with increasing swiftness until he was close to Race over near the second bolt-studded oaken door, this one leading from Tim Wade's cell-block out into the alleyway.

"Take a good look first," he hissed at Race, as that seldom-used alleyway door groaned open. "How is it? All clear?"

Race looked and nodded, and stepped through. The Kid did the same. They hastened across where Race had left the livery horses, scrambled swiftly astride, and the Kid would have flung away in a wild run except for Race's restraining hand.

"Slow now. Slow and easy. Don't make a break for it or folks'll notice."

"Damn the folks," gritted the Kid, but he obediently eased out beside Race, riding with a slowness that made him look agonized. There was perspiration on his forehead and upper lip when they finally eased off westerly breaking clear of Lone Pine, beginning their long ride toward the Dunphy place.

They had been gone from town nearly an hour before the Kansas Kid turned loose in his saddle, stopped riding sideways watching their back trail, and made a flinty little grin at Race.

"Feel better if I had a gun," he said.

"What for?" asked Race. "No one's following, no one even knows you're gone yet. By the time they do. . . ." Race didn't finish this; he simply lifted his shoulders and let them slump. He then put a close look on the Kid and said: "Now that you're clear, how do you aim to get Franklyn?"

A quick, faint shadow passed over the Kid's face. "I'll get him, don't you worry your head none about that." He looked bleakly over at Race. "I like 'em to sweat a while first, before I really go after 'em."

"He's been sweatin' for as many years as you are old," retorted Race. "That's long enough for any man to lose his sleep and miss his meals."

"Naw," argued the Kansas Kid. "It's nowhere nearly long enough for him. But maybe you've got a point. Anyway, when that half-wit of a lawman finds I'm gone, I expect the whole blessed country'll be up in arms . . . so I guess I'll have to do it fast whether I want to or not."

"How?" persisted Race, working hard at keeping the Kid's attention away from any close scrutiny of the roundabout country. He had no idea where Tim and Franklyn and Andrews actually were, but he did not plan to have the Kid see them, either, if it could be helped.

"How?" mused the Kid. "Well, a feller never knows. You know where a man is you want, an' you go lookin' for him. But after that you got to do the whole thing by split-second decisions. All I know for sure is that I'll find him. If necessary I'll hide out around here in the badlands or somewhere until Mort and Pete locate him at a line shack or a roundup, then I'll just walk into his firelight."

The Kid didn't finish. He rode along looking triumphant and bitter, as though some inner view was very pleasing to him in a tart way.

Once, as they passed along idly speaking back and forth, the Kid asked what it was that Race had against Earnest Franklyn. This was not an unexpected query, though, so Race made up a story of range troubles and boundary disputes. It sounded plausible, even to Race himself. To the Kid it seemed to fit into the pattern of behavior he thought Franklyn capable of. His face showed this, and more, for he said right back: "Yeah. Well, he tried to forget by buildin' his cow empire. You know, Dunphy, the best part of this whole plan of mine isn't killin' that old devil . . . it's takin' over what he's built up." The Kid swung his head, made a fierce smile, and nodded his head up and down vigorously. "With a man like him it's never enough just to kill 'em. You got to chase 'em right down into the grave and make 'em suffer even there."

Race kept regarding the younger man, bracing into the wild, strange hatred he saw. He looked away after a time wondering what it was that was lacking from the Kansas Kid's make-up. Something was missing; he'd felt it right from the start. This youth was a deadly gunman but he simply did not have that peculiar, electric aura genuine killers had. Mort had it, and Mort was no older than the Kansas Kid. Pete also had it, despite his sly and raffish way. But the Kansas Kid did not.

As they rode along, Race tried again, for the hundredth time, to define what that elusive something was that inherent killers possessed. And for the hundredth time he failed. Then the Kid spoke, breaking in and scattering his thoughts.

"What's his daughter like, Dunphy? Her name's Eleanor, isn't it?"

"Eleanor is right. Well, she doesn't look at all like the old man, I can tell you that much. She's tall and quiet and . . . sort of sad."

"Go on," said the Kansas Kid, his expression changing completely, looking eager and intensely interested in this topic. "Go on."

"He sent her East to boarding schools. She's been gone out of the country ever since she was pretty young."

"Yeah," opined the Kid. "Sure, he'd do that. He wouldn't ever want her to know, would he? Well, by God, Dunphy she's goin' to know. I'm goin' to tell her about her maw . . . and my maw. When I get through tellin' her, believe me, Dunphy, she'll want to plug her damned ears."

A throttled rage rang in the Kid's voice. All the pent-up agony and near-strangling hatred was there in his face again.

Race put his face fully forward and kept it that way; he was sure he'd never be able to keep up this masquerade much longer. No man could feel the thing he was now feeling and not keep at least a little of it from showing.

He wondered if the youth at his side was so blind in his wish for vengeance he could not be influenced, even to save his own life. He decided to try this, and said: "Kid, what's the sense? Kill the old man and do what you want with the girl, but don't take a lot of valuable time doin' it, otherwise Sheriff Wade may just possibly find you before you can get out of the country."

"Listen, Dunphy, you got me out, so I owe you something. But you just worry about yourself and keep your beak out of my business. You got no idea how long I waited for this . . . planned for it and practiced for it."

"I'm tellin' you, though, Wade will raise hell and prop it up when he finds you've escaped. It's not worth getting killed over, this hate you got for old man Franklyn and the girl."

"Yes it is, Dunphy, it's worth gettin' killed over."

185

Race looked around. The Kid was intently regarding him. His eyes were swimming in wetness and his lips were a brutal, thin slash over his lower face. His nostrils faintly fluttered from some violent inner turmoil. Race looked swiftly away. The Kansas Kid was far beyond any kind of influence, in Race's view; he was fanatically warped on this subject of Earnest Franklyn.

Race rode along, trying to imagine how the boyhood and childhood of this lightning-fast gunman had been. He thought he knew; it did not make a pretty picture.

"Dunphy, how much farther is this damned ranch of yours?"

Race lifted an arm and pointed ahead. "Maybe two miles." He let the arm drop. "No more than that."

"You got an extra gun there? I got to get one somewhere. I feel all naked like this."

"Yeah, there's an extra one somewhere at the house, Kid. I'll look it up for you."

"Dunphy?"

"Yeah."

"You ever shoot a girl?"

Race shook his head but did not trust himself to look around.

"Neither have I. Men, that's different. Hell, all you got to do is call a man out and he'll try to kill you. That's fine with me. But I never even hit a girl."

"You will today," said Race, still looking dead ahead.

The Kid said—"Yeah."—in a low, empty-sounding voice. "Yeah, I will today."

The land lay empty and faintly heat-hazed all around. They came across some of Race's cattle once, and again, farther along, they encountered a band of loose horses beating along in a flinging run, heads and tails high and a banner of dust fifty feet high rising in their wake.

Race thought it had to be the company he was in, but all the things that had, upon other occasions, made him feel good, such as the sight of those free-running horses, today looked somehow evil, somehow alien and suspicious and menacing. Even the sun overhead was bitterly malevolent and hostile. He shook his thoughts to clear them. He forced himself to think of Eleanor, of her haunting wistfulness and her beauty, but these things only plunged him back into the morbid depths again.

He turned to the Kid and said: "You got any tobacco?"

The Kid had. Race looped his reins and laboriously worked up a smoke. He was not a steady user of tobacco so the cigarette looked clumsy and barely remained together while he lit up and puffed on it.

At his side the Kansas Kid also built a cigarette. "Pretty poor substitute for midday eating," he said, and smiled.

Race looked at him. He seemed normal, even a little boyish in all but one way. Mention the name Franklyn and he became something altogether different. Race smoked and slouched along and felt infinitely sad.

"You'll get something to eat at the ranch, Kid."

"Dunphy," spoke up the Kid, "you're a pretty good man. You just ranch?"

Race thought to explain about his saloon. Then he kept his mouth closed and shrugged, formed fresh words, and said indifferently: "Ranch, and other things. Ranching I like best."

There was no way of knowing whether mentioning a saloon would work on Franklyn's nephew like it did on Franklyn. It very possibly could; regardless, though, keeping quiet about his saloon could do no harm, so he kept quiet.

"Yeah," mused the Kid, turning pensive in a way Race had not seen him do before. "Strange how a feller dreams of his own spread, isn't it? I always wanted a ranch of my own." The Kid stopped, looked at his cigarette. His face began to darken, to turn wintry. Even his voice changed. "I'll get it, too, my ranch and my revenge, both at the same time."

X

They were passing down the sun-lighted afternoon with a quiet and empty world all around when Race saw, far out southward, a tiny moving speck. That, he was certain, would be Earnest Franklyn. They were close enough to his ranch now for the old cattleman to join them.

It also gave Race an idea of how the others had gotten this far westerly from Lone Pine without being seen. In this rolling-to-flat country, movement stood out, particularly under a bright sun. Only by remaining beyond the farthest land swells could travelers avoid detection as they hurried along. Clearly that was what Tim Wade, Frank Andrews, and old man Franklyn had done. Clearly, too, this was their wisest course, for it would bring them in behind his ranch, down across the rolling plains, and eventually, if they were very careful, it would deliver them safely behind his barn and other outbuildings in such a way that they could not be seen from his house.

He watched that distant speck firm up into a man and a horse. The Kid had not seen any movement yet; he was looking straight ahead, wrapped in his solitary thoughts.

Race said very casually, lifting an arm and pointing: "That must be your uncle."

If he'd suddenly lashed out and unhorsed the Kansas Kid with a fisted blow, he could not have brought on the other man's astonishment or consternation any quicker. The Kid yanked upright over leather, he looked out where that slow-pacing horse and rider were angling to intercept them, and for a long while he strained for recognition. The distance, though, was as yet much too great. He hauled up his horse, stopping it, and he continued to stare.

Race could only see the youth's profile; nothing much could be read there but a bleakness. Then the Kansas Kid instinctively dropped his right hand. When his fingers touched only leather, no blued steel, he at last turned upon Race. His glare was so intense, so savage and angry, Race had to brace into it.

"What're you doin', Dunphy? You got some idea of . . . ?"

"Slack off," said Race, interrupting. "What's the matter with you? You wanted Franklyn. Mort and Pete want him, too. That's what the three of you rode this far to get, isn't it? Well, I'm givin' him to you."

The Kid's fierce stare did not diminish, but it began to turn inward, to turn analytical, as though the Kid was weighing all this. "How'd you do it?" he asked.

"Easy. Franklyn doesn't like me, but we've never openly fought, and, as I told you a mile back, we've had our range disputes. I simply sent him word to come over, that I had an idea of how we could settle our boundary-line differences."

The Kid swung, stared a while longer at that oncoming horseman, then said: "Loan me your gun, Dunphy."

Race shook his head. "One shot out here would carry for miles."

"I didn't mean I'd shoot him here," retorted the Kid. "I don't want to be the only one without a pistol. That old devil may try to kill me."

"He won't."

"How the hell do you know that?"

Race shrugged, watching Franklyn get close enough to where they sat their motionless horses to be fully recognized. "I know old Franklyn, Kid. He wouldn't shoot an unarmed man . . . not even you."

The Kansas Kid's shoulders lost some of their stiffness. He sat, watching Franklyn come on without speaking or taking his eyes away for a long time. Not even when he said from the corner of his mouth: "Dunphy, I don't really know him."

Race was surprised; he hadn't really ever given this possibility any thought; other things had kept him too occupied since the

Kid's arrival in Lone Pine. Now he began to wonder, if the Kid didn't really know his uncle, just how well old Franklyn knew the Kansas Kid.

"You saw him at the jailhouse," he said.

"Yeah. You know something, Dunphy? That was the first time. I didn't think he'd be that old, either."

"Missing your sleep for years plays hell with a man, Kid."

"It must have, with him."

"Kid, take a good long look."

"What?"

"I said take a good long look. That's you in another twenty-five years. Fifty and looking ninety. Guns destroy men, Kid, but the worst destroyer of men is men themselves."

The Kid swung around, his lips pulled down. "What are you, Dunphy, some kind of a preacher?"

"No, just a feller who's lived a little longer than you have is all."

Earnest Franklyn was two thousand yards away now. He was sitting up there straight as a ramrod, straining ahead to see Race and the Kansas Kid. He'd never been a particular man about his attire. His cowboys sported silver buckles and fresh attire, but Bear Trap's owner looked like some shock-headed old patriarch out of a stump ranch settlement. Even his hip holster was scratched and dull and worn-looking. The gun in that holster had none of its original bluing left. But Franklyn's face dispelled this illusion of stark poverty. So did his horse and saddle. He rode only the best stock and straddled especially made, very expensive Visalia saddles. His face, square-jawed, rugged as the westward mountains, showed strength, high intelligence, and what had once, many years before, been a powerful propensity for ferocity, for anger and ruthlessness. He was now somewhat anachronistic, but he was of that flinty breed who had won a continent with his fists, his fairness, and his unflinching resolve, and, although time may have passed him by and age may have blunted his great drive, he was yet a striking man to look at, especially now, when all the secret anguish from over the years was no longer hidden beneath his otherwise seamed and cultivated blankness but shown out of his eyes.

Race looped his reins and sat there, a forgotten spectator as these two warped and agonized spirits stared at one another from a narrowing distance. He could not recall ever before having been in a position so unique, so gripping in all its unspoken undertones. He could feel the electricity fairly snapping as Franklyn came on this last five hundred feet, lifted his left hand two inches off the saddle horn, and halted his mount, then sat there, not seeing Race Dunphy at all, seeing only the lean and tall and graceful younger man with the dark-ringed and dry-hot eyes, who was also motionlessly staring.

Ultimately old Franklyn kneed his horse up close and swung his eyes to Race. He seemed to wish to speak but was for the time being unable to do so. Race gently inclined his head.

"The Kansas Kid," he softly said to old Franklyn. To the Kid he said: "Earnest Franklyn of Bear Trap."

Neither of those men acknowledged this introduction, if that's what it was; they began to widen the scope of their assessments, though, to take in the build, the clothing, the mounts and holsters, and condition of each other.

"Where's his gun?" Franklyn finally said, his voice sounding thin and rough-edged.

"Back in Tim Wade's desk drawer, I guess."

"I'll get another one," said the Kid, breaking his long silence. "Don't worry, old man, I'll get another one."

Franklyn looked straight at the Kid and gently nodded. "I expect you will," he said. "I expect you will, boy." Then he said something from the heart, and Race caught some of the anguish in those words. "Boy, you look uncommonly like your paw."

The Kid swallowed. Race saw that. He looked away from the old man and back again. "You ought to know," he retorted.

"I do, boy. I know. You never knew your paw, I guess."

"You'd know about that, too, old man."

Franklyn's knuckles whitened upon his reins but he did not pursue the tangent this statement opened up for him; instead, he kept to his own line of thought, speaking almost as though the other two were not there watching him.

"When your paw was young, he was also a lean, tall feller. And a real top hand with a rope, with horses and cattle. We came north up out of Texas together on our first trail drive. In those days he was a rollickin' buckaroo." Franklyn's gaze dropped down, considered the Kid's face, and he gently nodded. "I've thought a thousand times we should've gone back after the drives were over, instead of working up our stakes in Nebraska, and finally over into Kansas. Texas was where we grew up, boy, and Texas was where we belonged." The old man's shoulders sagged as though from a great weariness. "Well, that's all ancient history now." He stopped speaking, examined the mottled back of one big, rough hand, and faintly shook his head. "Yesterday is a place no one ever finds, and yet every man makes his own yesterday by what he does today." Franklyn looked over at the Kansas Kid from beneath the floppy brim of his old hat. "That won't make much sense to you, boy. You got to live a long time before you know just how true that is. Maybe you won't live that long. I got a feelin' about that."

This last stung the Kid to quick response. "Longer than you'll live, old man. Long enough to settle things with you, which is as long as I care about livin' anyway."

Franklyn kept staring at the Kid, his eyes rummaging deeply beyond the flare of temper upon that youthful, lean countenance. He let off a long sigh after a while. "It's burned you out, too, hasn't it?" he said quietly. "Hatred is the worst poison on earth. It destroys people. It's so strong it even destroys the people you love."

"You murdering old devil," snarled the Kid. "You never loved anyone in your lousy life."

"Boy, listen to me. You don't destroy people unless you've got strong feeling for 'em. What does a stranger mean to a man? Nothing, nothing at all. What he says or does may annoy you, but he doesn't deserve your interest let alone your hatred. You've got to feel something to destroy people."

"Yeah, you feel something all right," shot back the Kid. "You feel hatred for the breath they breathe, for the ground they walk on, for the damned horses they ride. Old man, you had my paw killed. I've been waiting a lifetime for the time when we'd meet and you'd know what was going to happen for that."

"I know," mumbled Franklyn. "I'm not going to dodge you, boy. I'm not even going to try and explain how that happened. You're too young to understand how a thing like that crushes every decent instinct in a man. All I'm going to say to you is this. Go ahead and do what you figure you've got to do. I won't stop you. Only remember one thing. I'm what you'll be a quarter century from now. Take a good long look."

The Kansas Kid stared without speaking for a silent moment after Franklyn had finished speaking, then he flung around toward Race. "Two damned preachers," he snarled. "Let's get on to your ranch, Dunphy." He kicked out his livery animal; the beast sluggishly responded moving off in an ambling gait. Behind his back Race and Franklyn exchanged a brief glance and also moved out in a walking gait. The old cowman would look at the Kansas Kid, on out over the endless run of country, and back to the Kid again.

Race noticed this and privately thought how it must be with these two, struggling with their hatred and their frustration, their vindictiveness and the corrosive acid of all that inner turmoil. Life, he told himself, was never simple.

"Dunphy," spoke up the Kid. "Is that your place yonder?"

It was, and Race said so, but they were still a goodly distance off. The buildings looked hushed, looked waiting. Overhead a cloudless sky like pale blue enamel reflected pleasant sunlight downward, and yet nothing in Race's sight looked good to him. They were nearing the most trying time they had yet passed through; he could not see anything else right then.

"How much land you got, Dunphy?" the Kid asked, making a particular point of totally ignoring Earnest Franklyn. Race told him, wondering at this special interest in rangeland when ahead in his view the Kid could plainly see an end to his vengeance trail in among those dulled-out buildings.

"It adjoins Bear Trap, doesn't it?" the Kid asked, pushing this topic.

Race pointed roughly in the direction of his boundary. "It's contiguous for about five miles," he said.

The Kid looked around at him. "It's what?"

"Contiguous. It adjoins Bear Trap."

The Kid looked northward. "Why don't you just say it adjoins? Everyone else does." He didn't stop gauging this cow country until, with the ranch buildings looming close, Race, deciding the time was close for what must be done, halted his horse. Franklyn reined down, too. The Kid saw this, looked at those two, halted and put an inquiring gaze upon Race.

"Why stop? Let's get on down there."

"Kid," said Race gravely. "I don't trust your friends. They want to kill Franklyn. They want to kill Eleanor, too. It sticks in my craw that they just might have in mind doing the same to me."

The Kid's face clouded. "Nobody bothers you, Dunphy. You busted me out of that flea trap back in Lone Pine. Come on, I'll handle Mort and Pete."

Race shook his head. Off to one side of the Kansas Kid sat old Franklyn, his steady regard of the Kid unwavering. It was Franklyn who spoke next, cutting across Race's forming words. "What kind of a man fights women, boy? If you want me, I already told you I won't make any trouble. But not her . . . not Eleanor."

The Kansas Kid twisted toward Franklyn. Race saw that vicious lift come to his lips as the Kid began to speak, and Race despaired.

XI

"It hurts, doesn't it, old man!" exclaimed the Kid. "It knots your guts all up, doesn't it . . . thinking of that girl getting it. How do you like that feeling, you damned old whelp?" The Kid breathed hard; Franklyn sat still, looking steadily over at him, his face blank, his eyes solemn and dry. "Old man, I waited a long time for this. I promised myself you'd want to die long before I killed you. As for the girl, she won't die easy. First she's got to know what kind of a woman her maw was."

"Her mother," said Franklyn stiffly, very softly, "was also your mother, boy."

"Yeah," snarled the Kid. "There's a name for women like her. I'm going to spell it out for that daughter of yours, old man."

Franklyn's face turned white. His square jaw locked closed, and for the first time since those two had met, Race saw some of old Earnest Franklyn's lifelong ferocity flame in the cattleman's eyes. "You listen to me," he said swiftly, thinly to the Kansas Kid. "Your mother was a good woman. Your paw was good, too. If you try an' tell Eleanor anything against either of them, so help me, boy. . . ."

"You'll be dead, old man," said the Kid, interrupting harshly. "You'll die right in front of Eleanor, and, when that's done with, damn you, she'll hear everything, not only about her maw but about you, too." The Kid took up his reins. "Now move along, you two."

Race made no move to ride on and neither did Franklyn. The Kid looked from one of them to the other. He settled his angry gaze upon Race, something like suspicion beginning to firm up in his face.

"Dunphy . . . ?" he said, making a question of this. "You coming?"

Race had reached his limit. For a while he'd alternated between hope and despair. Now he gazed upon the Kansas Kid, thinking there could be no hope for this one, no hope at all. He had one more thing to do; somewhere behind his outbuildings were Tim Wade and Frank Andrews. They'd be waiting for the Kid's renegade friends to leave the house, and getting those two out was here and now up to Race. He had this one more thing to do. Because of this he compelled himself to continue just a little longer playing his part.

"Listen, Dunphy, you can come or stay but. . . ."

"Hold it, Kid. Like I told you, I don't trust those two in the house. Before we ride on in, you call 'em out into the yard and tell 'em about me."

The Kid's eyes faintly widened. "You're scairt," he said, this notion replacing his earlier suspicion of Race. "Hell man, you're scairt of Mort and Pete." The Kid began incredulously to wag his head back and forth. "Dunphy, you sure fooled me. It wasn't just breakin' me out of that tin trap in Lone Pine. You look tough. You look the part of a pretty good hand. And now there you sit . . . scairt like a little child."

Race clamped down hard on his control. He could not, however, prevent a little wrath from showing in his stare as he said: "Call 'em out, Kid. Tell them I've brought you back and Franklyn, too."

Race drew his handgun and covered Earnest Franklyn with

it. He even bent far over and yanked out the older man's hol-stered gun and pushed this weapon into his waistband. But neither Race nor Earnest Franklyn was a good actor. This disarming of the old cowman did not quite ring true; for one thing Franklyn made no struggle, no outcry as a surprised man might have done. For another thing Race scarcely heeded Franklyn at all. He kept his entire attention upon the Kansas Kid, who watched all this with moving eyes, with a faintly clouded expression, and with slow-growing doubt and suspicion. Race wagged his pistol barrel.

"Call them out of there, Kid."

Instead of obeying, the Kid reached for his tobacco sack, dropped his head, and went to work manufacturing a smoke. He did this with slow, meticulous attention as though to mask his thinking with this outward labor. When he finished, he popped the cigarette into his mouth, and snapped a match, star-ing straight over at Race. He inhaled, exhaled, and suddenly stepped down off his horse. His face was wire-tight now and smoothed out; there appeared to be only one thing now oc-cupying his attention. He turned his back upon Race and Franklyn, stared for a long time over at that ranch house, then slowly faced back around toward them. Now he was bitterly, very gently smiling.

"Sure," he said to Race. "I'll call them out, Dunphy. But first hand me the old man's gun."

Race did not move. Somehow, he told himself, the Kid knew. Somehow he'd figured this out as a ruse. All their careful plan-ning and hard riding had been for nothing. Well, not quite for nothing. Those killers in the house would be watching all this from windows. They would believe Race had kept his end of the bargain. They wouldn't know, even if the Kansas Kid did know. Race decided to use this only remaining advantage; the same advantage he'd privately thought of back in Sheriff Wade's office. The Kansas Kid was his prisoner. If his cronies wanted him, they would have to trade for him.

"You won't need the gun, Kid. Not yet. Call those men out into the yard."

Cigarette smoke broke out around the Kid's hat brim. His narrowed gaze whipped to Earnest Franklyn, lingered there a sardonic moment, then jumped back to Race.

"Call 'em yourself, Dunphy. It was a good try. You took me in all along, right up to now. When a feller's mad, he doesn't notice things. When he cools down, he remembers an' he figures things out. You said you and Franklyn had range disputes, yet you never mentioned 'em. You said you'd sent for him, yet he didn't look like he was ridin' for your ranch, Dunphy, and this is too big a country for him to just happen to ride up on us like he did. And now this disarming business." The Kid shook his head. "That was a lousy piece of stage-actin' by both of you." The Kid removed his cigarette, dropped it, and ground it out. He looked slyly at Race. "Mexican stand-off, Dunphy. I know what you're thinkin' . . . you got me for a hostage and my friends have Eleanor and your cowboy. That makes it a Mexican stand-off. One side or the other's got to give. It won't be Mort and Pete."

Race sagged in the saddle. He looked ahead beyond rifle range where his hushed buildings stood. There was no sign that anyone was down there at all. But they were there, all right, and they'd be watching like hawks. He withdrew the pistol from his waistband and silently handed it back to Franklyn. He holstered his own weapon. He leaned down and looked very solemnly at the Kid.

"All right, Kid. You guessed it. But it's less of a stand-off than you think."

Race said no more than this and the Kid, staring into his lowered face, appeared almost at once to get the drift of Race's meaning. He twisted, ran a long look outward over the ranch yard, and completed this inspection when he returned his attention to Race.

"Where?" he asked, simply. "Where, and how many?"

Franklyn didn't let Race answer. "I'll strike a bargain with you, Kid. Call to those men to let my daughter walk out of there, and I'll go on in with you."

No answer came back to this offer. Moments passed. The two mounted men and the solitary dismounted man stood in bright sunlight exchanging steady looks, until the Kid reached up, thumbed back his hat, turned, and leaned with one hand upon his saddle horn, gazing down at those quiet, silent buildings. It was as though, by turning his back, he had cut out the other two from his thoughts. They were each willing for it to be this way, thinking that the Kid had his decision to make.

Race felt drained by all that he had passed through this day. He glanced at the off-center sun, surprised to find so little actual time had passed since he'd encountered Eleanor in that badlands arroyo with her nickel-plated pistol. He thought that, if he closed his eyes, this day would turn into weeks and months, even years of struggle and anguish and travail. He had seen an old man's soul laid out nakedly for other men, himself included, to stare at. He had encountered depths of warped reasoning and hatred beyond his total comprehension, and he'd come face to face with a kind of sad and wistful beauty that haunted him.

These were the thoughts that occupied Race. Across from him, staring steadily over at the distant ranch house, old Earnest Franklyn had his own troubled thoughts; he sat there on his horse, looking older by far than he'd ever before looked, his gaze resolute but dull.

Neither of them was prepared for what the Kansas Kid now did. Even after it happened, they both had to dredge up their different reactions from beneath layers of near apathy.

One second the Kid was standing there with that arm resting lightly upon the swells of his saddle, all loose-looking and relaxed. The next moment he had a foot in the left stirrup, his arm curved tightly around the saddle swell, and the rest of his body hanging close as he dug his livery horse cruelly with his free hand sending the beast lunging ahead in a wild run, making his abrupt and violent break for freedom.

Race hung fire a moment just staring. Then he went for his gun, had the weapon out and swinging to bear, when Earnest Franklyn struck his hand down with a hard blow, each in his own way, according to his own beliefs, reacting to the sight of their hostage making straight for the Dunphy ranch buildings in a belly-down run.

Somewhere south of that fleeing figure a rifle exploded, bracketing the onward yard with its echoing crash. At the house another gun erupted, this one evidently replying to the first one.

Franklyn's grip on Race's wrist was vice-like as the pair of them sat rigidly, watching the Kansas Kid make his desperate bid for freedom. He went flinging down into the yard, swirling a flashing dust banner out behind. He made no attempt to slow the livery horse until, within jumping distance of Race's front door, near the low-roofed verandah, the beast's head was thrown violently back in response to a cruel jerk on the reins, the horse set up, stiff-legged, and covered the last eighty feet in a wild slide. The Kid had maintained his balance Indian-fashion on that beast's left side, showing none of his body, until that last slide. He then sprang off, lit hard, almost fell as momentum catapulted him onward, recovered at the very last moment, and cut rapidly over into verandah shade. After that, neither Franklyn nor Race could see him. He had gotten into the house; they were certain of that. He had made a wild gamble and had won. Race let his breath out in an audible rush. Franklyn's steel talons gradually relaxed, drew away from Race's gun hand, and the older man's shoulders dropped.

That same unseen gunman fired once more into the house. Race thought this was either Andrews or Sheriff Wade, and, whichever it was, he was behind the barn southward.

"They shouldn't be doing that," Franklyn muttered, looking apprehensive and uncertain.

Two fast shots came from the house. Pistol fire, thought Race, distinguishing between the gun sounds. Someone struck a glass window, breaking out the pane. This tinkling, musical sound came easily out where he and Franklyn sat.

Silence came now; it filled the ranch yard, the surrounding range, even the minds of men. Race took up his reins, swung, and said: "Come on. We tried and we lost. Let's hunt up Tim and Frank."

They made a very large half circle, keeping well out of rifle range of Race's house. When they came over a long land swell, descended this so as to come down behind the barn, those hidden adversaries traded two more gunshots, after which the silence returned.

Race was familiar with every inch of the territory where he halted, dismounted, and waited for Franklyn also to get down. From the barn's rear to the left and right were a number of smaller sheds and outbuildings. Once, he saw a man stand clear looking over toward them, then whip out of sight again, moving in their direction. He took both horses, led them into the barn, killed a little time off-saddling them, making them secure in tie stalls, waiting for that ally he'd spied to get over here.

Franklyn entered the barn, shuffled past, methodically tugged the Winchester from his saddle boot, straightened up, and leaned upon it as he turned to consider Tim Wade, who came jumping in out of the afternoon brightness.

"What the hell went wrong?" Wade demanded, sweaty and red-faced from exertion.

Race said: "It wasn't any good, Tim. He caught on about the time we got out here."

"Well," barked the lawman, scowling blackly, "you could at least have taken a shot at him like I did."

Race busied himself with their horses; he forked them feed, checked their tie ropes, shot a look over at Franklyn, and said nothing. He knew why the cowman had stopped him from downing the Kansas Kid, but Wade wouldn't understand at all. He hadn't been there when those two related enemies had come together; he hadn't seen their faces or heard their words—most important of all, he hadn't heard what they had not said to each other.

A fourth man glided in from the outside brightness. He, too, was rank with sweat, red-faced and breathing hard. It was Franklyn's range boss, Frank Andrews.

The four of them stood a little apart, looking over at each other. Wade, sensing some change here, said: "Race, what the hell, you tired or something?"

Instead of replying to this, Race nodded at some other stalled animals, saying: "They can't run out, if that's any satisfaction to anyone. They have their prisoners, but they're as much captives themselves because we have their horses."

XII

"They'll try for it after nightfall," said Frank Andrews, and swung upon his employer. "Let me go to the ranch. I can be back in two hours with the whole crew. We'll surround that place and give 'em no alternative but surrender."

The old man shook his head. He didn't look it but he was thinking clearly again. "We need you here, Frank. Besides, as soon as they figured out one of us was gone, they'd know what was coming. They'd do something desperate an' we can't afford that. Not as long as Eleanor's in there."

Race paced to the barn's front entrance. He pressed back from sight there and peered outward across the yard. Again that stifling silence lay over the ranch. Again there was nothing to see or hear.

The others crept up on either side of the opening, also peering out. "Awful quiet," said Tim Wade in an unconsciously lowered voice. "Race, is there a back way out of your house?"

"Yes, but they won't dare use it until dark. If they do, they'll have to go straight south up that land swell back there. We'd see them in a minute. To the east and west it's no better. No cover for two miles, all open country."

"The Kid'll be cussing in there," suggested Frank Andrews. "He made that fantastic ride for nothing."

"Not for nothing," said Race. "He's still better off than we are. He's got something to trade for his freedom. I'm wondering how long it's going to take him to get over his anger and think of that."

Tim Wade exasperatedly swore. He did not say why he did this but the others understood. For a while it had looked so favorable—then the entire thing had collapsed. Tim stood with a Winchester saddle gun held across his body, his rough, lined face brutal-looking in the barn shadow.

Old man Franklyn stood and looked and neither moved nor spoke. He was profiled to Race, his shaggy head looking almost leonine.

From the house a gunshot exploded. Lead struck solid wood along the barn's front a dozen feet west of the doorway. Frank Andrews knelt, raised his carbine, and remained frozen, waiting for that sniper to try again, waiting for flashing muzzle blast to give him something to sight on. It was a long wait; no one fired from the house again until Race threw up his gun, tugged off a careless shot to draw Frank a reply, and watched as an answering red lash came forth from the house.

Frank fired instantly. Over at the house someone cried out. Frank lowered his gun, levered up a fresh load, stayed down on one knee, and shook his head. "I couldn't have hit him square. The second I fired I saw him jumpin' clear from where he'd shot."

"You drew blood anyway," growled the lawman, also straining to sight a target. "Dammit, this thing could go on all afternoon and into the night."

"That's what he's hoping for," said Race. "Once it's dark enough he'll make his break. He has to, for all the Kid knows there's a full-size posse racin' out here right this minute."

No more shots came from the house. That deadly hush settled over the yard again, and, when he could no longer stand it, Race said: "I'm goin' to try and get closer. The rest of you stay here."

"Wait," commanded Sheriff Wade. He got no further with whatever else he might have said.

Race turned on him. "I know every foot of this yard. Don't worry about me. But if they get me in a crossfire, you fellers give me cover."

He turned, passed swiftly out the rear of the barn, and swung left. In that direction was a blacksmith shop and the bunkhouse where Curt Lake stayed, both buildings solidly constructed of chinked logs and thick, summer-hardened adobe.

Someone called out from the house when Race was whipping across the little intervening space between smithy and bunkhouse. He only caught a fragment of what was shouted, something about saddle horses.

Tim Wade's booming answer came right back from the barn's echoing interior: "No horses for Lake. Send both Curt and Miss Eleanor out, and you can have your horses. Don't send 'em . . . no horses."

For a moment longer this bargaining went on, those two

invisible men calling back and forth, then someone up at the house, evidently in a rage, let off two quick pistol shots, making Race think of the Kansas Kid the way those explosions sounded almost simultaneously, something only an experienced gunman could do, fire a single-action pistol so swiftly both shots sounded almost as one.

This ended all talk while half a dozen furious men exchanged brisk gunfire. Race broke off his end of this to utilize the preoccupation of those in the house while he stood poised for the longer move from bunkhouse onward.

The distance here was considerable, and, although it was not directly exposed to the front yard, nevertheless erupting swift movement would probably not go unnoticed by the Kid's friends inside. He never made the attempt.

At the house someone beyond sight yanked open the front door, shoved Eleanor Franklyn out onto the verandah with both arms lashed behind her back, with a length of hard-twist lariat rope around her throat, and a man's exulting voice roared from behind the girl.

"Hey, Franklyn, you want your daughter? Step out into the yard an' you can have her!"

Race heard a loud commotion down in the barn. Evidently Frank and Tim Wade were struggling with Eleanor's anguished father there. Up at the house this racket was also heard, and that same taunting voice cried out once more.

"Turn our horses loose in the yard or she gets it in the back of the head!"

Race could see Eleanor clearly. Her face was gray, although she seemed more drained dry of emotion than afraid. He thought that she had perhaps lived with terror for so long now—since early morning—that fear had become dull apathy; he'd seen that happen with people before. He wanted mightily to attract her attention but did not; it could not help her any, knowing he was this close, and it might jeopardize his hiding place at the southward corner of the bunkhouse.

"No horses!" came Tim Wade's savage roar from deep inside the barn. "No horses unless you cut her loose an' also let Curt Lake come out an' get clear across the yard!"

That recognizably taunting voice yelled back to the lawman: "You aren't makin' the terms, I am! I say turn our horses loose!"

Race knew that voice; it belonged to the hatchet-faced youngest killer, the one he knew only as Mort. He eased gingerly down on one knee. He could see the bare space between Eleanor's back and that opened front door. If he was lucky, someone might step out there, believing himself protected by the girl. With great deliberation Race brought up his gun, made an arm rest by utilizing the bunkhouse corner, and waited.

For a long time there was not a sound. The men in the barn were hidden from sight and the men in the house were likewise beyond view. Someone gave a sharp tug on the rope encircling Eleanor's throat. She took a rearward step, and, as that intervening distance between her back and the doorway lessened, Race's disappointment and frustration heightened. Finally, when she was almost into the house, a man's hand shot out roughly, caught her by the shoulder, and pulled her staggeringly out of sight. An instant later Race's front door slammed violently closed.

Sweat ran in rivulets down into Race's eyes. It also ran coldly under his shirt. Until he eased back a little, preparatory to standing up again, he had not known how great a pressure he'd been under. He leaned against the bunkhouse wall, breathing deeply and feeling terribly relieved. He would have fired had anyone stepped up behind Eleanor; he knew that. And yet that little distance had been hopelessly narrow, not more than four feet at the most.

He turned, retraced his way back around behind the barn,

stepped inside, and saw old Earnest Franklyn sitting upon a horseshoe keg, gray in the face. Tim Wade whipped around as Race spoke out, coming down toward the front entrance. Frank Andrews turned less swiftly. He looked only glancingly at Race and put his longer regard upon old Franklyn.

"No good," reported Race. "Maybe I could have gotten up closer. Maybe even around back, but not likely. They're pretty well concentrating on watching the yard."

Wade glumly nodded. He, too, shot a look down where Franklyn sat. He leaned close to say very lowly into Race's ear: "Frank had to cold cock the old devil. He tried to run out there when they pushed his girl onto the porch. He'll have a headache but otherwise he's all right."

Andrews glided over. He heard the last of what Wade said, looked at Race, and shrugged. "No sense in anyone gettin' needlessly killed," he muttered, then strengthened his voice to say: "I don't like it when they're this quiet. I still think I ought to ride for the Bear Trap crew."

Race was considering this when Franklyn said from over where he sat slumped: "No, none of us leaves here."

Andrews looked unhappily up at Race and Tim Wade. He did not again make this suggestion of riding for reinforcements.

After more time had passed the lawman growled: "I'd like to know what they're workin' up over there now."

"I can tell you," retorted Race. "They're just waiting. Sitting over there just waiting for sundown. That's their only hope now, slipping out in the dark."

Andrews glanced out at the visible sky that was faintly reddening. "There's got to be some way of gettin' them out of there."

Neither Sheriff Wade nor Race offered any comment on this and Earnest Franklyn got up unsteadily, shuffled over, and leaned nearby upon a barn upright.

"Give 'em their horses," he said in a fading voice.

Tim Wade looked exasperatedly around. "You know damned well they won't release the prisoners first. If we give 'em their lousy horses an' they keep Eleanor and Curt, they'll use 'em as shields until they're a mile off, then they'll kill 'em both. You know that, Mister Franklyn. You better go back an' sit down an' get hold of yourself."

"Maybe money," muttered the cowman. "Maybe they'll release 'em for money."

Wade's face brightened a little at this, but Race dampened his lifting spirits. "You heard what the Kansas Kid wants, Mister Franklyn, and it's not money, it's revenge."

Frank Andrews turned to go back across where he had been; he muttered once more: "There's got to be a way. There's plumb got to be."

Sheriff Wade looked after Andrews. He watched Bear Trap's range boss take up his Winchester, check it, and ease back in the strengthening shadows, gazing thoughtfully out into the yard, and he grumbled to Race: "Yeah, there's got to be a way . . . but what is it?"

Race turned to pass over where Franklyn was standing, slouched and vacant-eyed. He thought of a dozen things to say but at the look on Franklyn's face he said none of them, moved on deeper into the barn, and found himself a seat upon the edge of a manger.

There was a way to get Eleanor and Curt Lake out of his house. There were three renegades inside and there were only two hostages. When the renegades finally made their nocturnal break for freedom, one of those men would have to walk out without a human shield, but the other two would bring their hostages outside.

Race was confident this was how the Kansas Kid would work it for the elemental reason that there was no other possible way for the outlaws to keep from being shot the minute they left his house. And they would leave his house, he was also quite positive of this. If they did not, if they lingered overnight and into another day, every passing hour would diminish their chances of getting clear at the same time it increased their chances of having reinforcements arrive, summoned by some chance passer-by hearing gunfire, which in the end meant capture and death for the renegades.

The Kid would try it, Race thought. He would use both Curt and Eleanor as shields, too. That went without saying; he certainly dared not abandon them. They were his only passport to survival.

Up ahead where the sheriff stood, Franklyn said something too low for Race to hear. Tim Wade made a growling answer back. Outside of these sounds there was no noise to be heard anywhere.

Afternoon sunlight continued to darken, to redden with a soft saffron heat haze, to blaze out in dying glory over the buildings, the range, and the overhead skies. Race guessed the time to be close to 6:00 P.M. He got up and strolled forward, a germ of an idea forming in his mind.

Frank Andrews twisted a worried face to watch Race come forward. Earnest Franklyn looked glumly up and glumly down again. Tim Wade put aside his carbine, began twisting up a smoke, and he lit it cautiously behind his hat although it was not yet dark enough for that tiny flaring light to betray its holder. He exhaled a gray cloud and settled his solid attention upon Race. "You got something in mind," he said. "I can see it in your face. Let's have it, Race, we sure Lord need a plan, otherwise darkness is going to rob us of everything."

"Darkness," corrected Race, stopping and looking out, "is more our friend than theirs. Pretty hard for five people to slip around in the night without making noise and casting shadows."

XIII

Sheriff Wade thought briefly on what Race had said, then doubtingly shook his head. "Maybe they can't help but make noise in the dark," he said, "but that isn't going to help us a whole lot either, because shootin' in the dark's damned uncertain."

"They'll come out," Race told them. "They've got to make their move after sunset. The Kid'll know that."

Frank Andrews spoke up, approving of everything Race had thus far said. "Sure, they'll make their run for it . . . and we can anticipate 'em, can't we, Race?"

"We've got to do more than that, Frank. We've got to cover every bet they might make."

Wade and Andrews stood there, waiting for Race to explain. Old man Franklyn came up, showing interest, and halted also to listen.

Race went on speaking. "They need their horses, but as long as we're in this barn, they'd be running a big risk tryin' for them."

"Sure enough," agreed Andrews.

"If they decide the risk's too great, they'll still have to try and get clear, so, with two hostages for shields, they'll try slipping out over the range on foot."

"That'd be pretty foolish," muttered the lawman.

"Not if they could get a half mile off without being seen, Tim. If they could do that, they'd stand a good chance of gettin' to one of the southward ranches where they could pick up more mounts. Remember, there's darn' little moonlight these nights."

Old man Franklyn spoke up: "We'll have to split up and watch both routes then."

Race, who had already come to a conclusion about this, shook his head. "Only one of us goes around back and lies out there to see whether or not they try slippin' out on foot. Me. The rest of you stay here in the barn."

"Hell," growled the sheriff, "one man against three top-notch gunslingers stands about the same chance as a snowball in hell, Race."

"No, not quite that bad, Tim. I know this yard. Neither you fellers nor the renegades know it. Furthermore, it'll be dark, and, if you fellers throw a slug now and then, they may think the four of us are still in here."

"But one of us could go with you," suggested Frank Andrews. "It sure would come closer to evenin' up the odds."

"Not for the fellers left in the barn it wouldn't, Frank, and my guess is that you fellers will be the targets, not me. The most important thing to the Kansas Kid right now is these horses."

Sheriff Wade grudgingly agreed to Race's plan. So did old man Franklyn. Frank Andrews lifted his shoulders and let them fall, saying nothing, but faintly wagging his head. Race took up his carbine, considered it for a moment, then put it down again; it would be too awkward, and, if there was any fighting, it would be at close quarters. He ran his eyes over those three, mutely nodded, and stepped away, heading for the rear barn opening.

Daylight was fast fading now. The sun hung off in the smoky west, an enormous red medallion, the sky was turning gray dusty, and the hush out there was deep enough to lean into.

Race went along the barn's rear wall, faded out in forming shadows, and reëmerged over behind the blacksmith shop. Here, he remained for some time, watching the house and letting the dusk settle still more. No shots had come from southward down across the yard for some time now. He could visualize those men in the house; they'd be pacing like caged wild animals. They'd be eating in the kitchen, drinking coffee, and wandering through the rooms. In a bad situation the hardest thing was waiting. They'd be living on nerve now, and, when men were like that, they would snarl at one another over nothing.

He made the quick sprint from smithy to bunkhouse and got back to that southeastward corner where he'd formerly been. He remained there even longer, in no hurry, content to let his ally, the night, grow thicker, more enfolding all around. He used this time, too, for developing some vague notions into plans of action. By now the renegades would be aware that, when they left the house, only two of them would have human shields. He thought it probable that Mort and Pete would be thinking strongly of this. One of them would be exposed. It was something for a besieged man to concern himself with, for with relentless foemen around him, without protection he would unquestionably be shot.

There was the stillness, too. If this had worked on Tim Wade's raw nerves, then it surely had played havoc on other nerves. To test this belief Race scooped up a stone, stepped forth, lobbed it overhand, and swiftly stepped back. The stone struck upon the house roof and rattled down until it tumbled from the verandah overhang back into the yard.

Instantly someone over there fired off a shot toward the barn. The crimson flash of that gun drew two answering flashes from inside the barn.

Race smiled in the dusk. It wasn't only the renegades who had raw nerves.

He had a long stretch of open yard to cover now before achieving the side wall of the house. This same broad opening, clearly visible in broad daylight from the house, had discouraged him earlier, but now with evening down and dark to follow, he was confident of making it without being hit, perhaps without even being seen, which was what he especially hoped for. Once behind his house he knew the little depressions that would, in the night, adequately hide a man, and he was confident that, if the Kansas Kid led his contingent out afoot in their bid to escape, it would be over this rearward route that would keep the house between his party and those enemies lodged in the barn.

Darkness deepened; the sun was entirely gone now; a carpeting, stealthy sootiness deepened everywhere. No light shown from either house or barn. To any chance observer Dunphy's ranch would have appeared deserted. A young barn owl left his overhead loft in a gracefully dipping swoop that carried him down low to the ground in his nocturnal search for rodents, then up again, and over the house southward.

Race began moving westerly. It was not his intention to run directly across that open ground. He instead paced off to his right until the house was only a dark square in his sight, then stepped up his gait into a little jog, swung fully southward parallel to the house, and afterward began approaching inward again, in this manner safely crossing that lethal ground.

He was now coming up to the west wall, confident that the Kid and his companions would only be keeping a cursory watch in this direction. There were only two small windows here anyway, both opening into dark bedrooms. The advantage of knowing his ground was valuable; he kept well south of both those little windows, reached the house, and pressed flat against it, resting and heeding the stillness, the thickening darkness, the tiny sounds and scents of this twilight time.

A very faint reverberation carried to him through the wall, of booted feet moving purposelessly within. He had been correct; the Kid and his cohorts were restless. This rough pacing stopped occasionally, then started again. Once he heard the deep rumble of voices, the skidding of a chair where an impatient hand had flung it aside, and after that footsteps coming closer, coming into his wing of the house. He whipped around to dart away southward where the south and west walls joined, making a sharp corner, but that moving man stepped to a window, flung it roughly open, making movement inadvisable, and, instead of getting clear, Race had to stiffen his full length against the house scarcely daring to breathe.

A man's face appeared at the window. There came to Race the unmistakable rake of steel over wood where a gun barrel was carelessly brought up and set to rest upon the sill.

It was impossible in this gloom to make out which outlaw this was, but Race thought it was the older man, the one called Pete. He kept his hand upon his holstered six-gun, ready to draw and fire if Pete poked his head out far enough to look southward along the house wall. This was a bad moment.

Race smelled tobacco smoke but did not see Pete drag on the weed he obviously was holding. He waited stiffly for the renegade to leave. Pete, though, appeared in no great hurry. When he finally turned back into the room even after his long, casual vigil, it was not to leave; it was to answer something said to him from farther back. Race heard Pete's reply although he did not hear the question that prompted it.

Pete said: "Quiet as a church out there. . . . Naw, they wouldn't all go. They'd send one man is all. . . ." That other man said something more. Race heard the voice this time but again could not distinguish the words. Pete muttered—"All right."—closed the window, barred it, and walked away.

Race did not move until he felt, rather than heard, that bedroom door close, sending its echoes through the wall into his back. He eased down, flat-footed, controlled a wild urge to get away from there, recalled Pete's words verbatim, and concluded that the topic under discussion among the renegades was the possibility that their enemies had sent someone for reinforcements. If they believed that, it would not be very long now before they made their attempt to get away.

He turned, put one foot forth, brought up the other foot, and in this agonizingly slow, but noiseless process got to the corner of the side wall and rear wall. There, he stepped around behind his house.

Behind the house was the little level area where he'd played as a youngster. Farther back, beginning to lift toward its eventual long slope, was one of the gentle land swells of this area. Where it topped out some quarter mile farther south, a few weak stars twinkled. Closer were several depressions, probably ancient buffalo wallows, which had served Race for every imaginable kind of a hide-out during his early youth.

There was also a cellar back here. Its doorway stood on a slanting incline at the foundation of the house,. leading down into a hand-dug room some twenty feet long by twenty feet wide, used primarily for storing perishables during the hot summer months, but also used upon infrequent occasions as a place to hide when cyclones ripped across the land. This door was set nearly flush with the ground; it slanted downward away from the house so that winter moisture would not seep into the cellar. Looking at that low door now he recalled the time, when his father was living, that an old cowboy leaving the house after dark had fallen into the cellar because a young boy had carelessly left the door open. There was a sequel to this event: Race had stepped into the wood shed with his father for a rawhiding.

This entire area was full of memories for Race, but he had neither the time now nor the inclination to resurrect them. Eastward, a long hundred feet from where he now stood, was the rear doorway out of the house. This being the only exterior door except for the one around in front, he was confident, when the renegades inside made their bid for freedom, this would be the way they would try it.

For a long while he stood motionlessly. It was more difficult back here to pick up any sounds from within, but once he heard someone pass from the kitchen out into the rear pantry, stand there for a while, then return to the kitchen again.

He finally stepped clear of that shadowy rear wall, stepped out into the unprotected rear yard, and glided as far as a particularly deep depression where a man might lie concealed, entirely safe from detection as long as he did not raise up, and as long as no enemy came across to peer down. There, in the identical place he'd pretended as a child he was standing off hordes of howling Indians, he eased down, stretched out, drew his handgun, and waited. It might be a long wait or a short one, or even an entirely futile one, but of one thing he was quite certain. Whichever way the Kansas Kid chose to make his escape, whether toward the barn or around behind the house, he was due for a surprise.

Time passed very slowly. The sky, with its full darkness, lost all semblance of evening. Night was fully down now, its hush and limited visibility both a curse and a blessing. Somewhere inside a door was slammed, somewhere outside and a long way off a coyote tongued at the thin, anemic new moon that silently lifted from beyond the earth's far curving and began silently to climb toward its zenith.

A horse nickered down at the barn. Race listened to this. Evidently someone tossed the horse a flake of hay or led him over to water, for the sound was not repeated.

He lay on with his thoughts giving him a little trouble; they had a tendency to wander, to drift back down this unique day to events and people, to hopes and disappointments and fears. He constantly had to work at keeping his vigil.

He was tired and hungry and apprehensive. The Kansas Kid's youthful face appeared in his mind's eye as clear as though the Kid stood there before him. Eleanor Franklyn appeared this way to him, also. He belatedly recognized a similarity between those two faces. It occurred to him now, when he had the time to dwell upon it, that Earnest Franklyn must also have noted this sameness. What possible other reason could the old cowman have had, out there when the Kid broke away from them hanging to the side of his horse, to knock Race's gun hand aside? The old man had seen his wife in the Kansas Kid; he could not, despite all that those other people had done to him, stand by and see his former wife's son shot down.

He dwelt longer on Earnest Franklyn, making his careful judgment, forming his decisions, striving to understand how it must have been for the old cattleman, and coming up with a conviction that no matter how hard he tried, he would never really know how it had been.

XIV

Restlessness worked its subtle will on Race, made his nerves crawl and his ears imagine sounds that his eyes failed to corroborate. He told himself that, if this dragging time was bad for him, who had been through less of it, it must by now have the Kansas Kid and his companions in the house on the verge of doing anything at all but enduring more of it.

And he was right in this. Several men stepped from the kitchen to the pantry. They stood there, softly speaking back and forth for a little while. One of them even went over to the back door, pushed it slightly open, and ran a quick, cursory look over the roundabout yard.

These two returned to the kitchen, their footfalls faded out, and a moment later someone in the front of the house threw an exploratory shot down toward the barn.

As before, this solitary explosion drew two swift, crashing replies from the barn. But this time, after a short pause, two more shots shuddered into the front siding. Race understood the purpose of those last shots; Andrews and Wade, wishing to give the impression four men were still in the barn, had made their play. He doubted very much whether the Kansas Kid had been taken in by this, though, because Frank and Tim had allowed too long an interval between shots.

For twenty minutes there was no more shooting, no more noise of any kind. Race was beginning to turn angry over this delay, to squirm where he lay in that shallow depression, to look left and right and rapidly blink to prevent drowsiness from claiming him. He was so occupied with drowsiness and frustration that he did not notice anything foreign in the yonder night until, over by the back door, the last of several moving shadows cleared the opening, milled briefly, then became motionless.

The drowsiness dropped away magically. Race's heart sloshed in its hidden place. His every nerve and muscle became instantly alert. The Kansas Kid, having determined by that exploratory shot, that the barn was still adequately manned, very clearly had made his bid for escape this other way.

Race tried to separate those blurred silhouettes in the formless dark, tried to count them when he could not determine which was an enemy and which was a hostage.

It was too dark over there, several hundred feet away and with the brown rear wall of the house solidly backgrounding those people, to make out much more than that there were at least five of them; that three of them had pistols and carbines, and that one of them had a dirty white bandage around his head instead of a hat.

Race considered what must be done. For the time being, nothing; he dared not shoot, but even if he had dared, the Kansas Kid, Mort, and Pete were more than a match for anyone foolhardy enough to try shooting it out with them unsupported.

He lay bareheaded, only the top of his skull and both his eyes above the crumbly lip of that depression. For nearly sixty seconds none of those yonder people moved. They stood like stone, listening, taking the pulse of the night, their heads moving a little, their bodies quite motionless. One of them took a long forward step. This one had his left hand upon the wrist of a second person. When these two got clear of the house, Race caught two profiles. One of those profiled bodies had to belong to Eleanor Franklyn; the other, recognizable by its gracefully upcurving hat brim, by its leanness, its lithe movements, and its height had to belong to the Kansas Kid.

Race watched but made no move at all.

Two more stepped clear of the house, moving easterly. This pair, too, seemed joined together at the wrist. Only one of these men had a bared gun. The other not only seemed unarmed, he seemed unsteady on his feet. Race was confident this last one was his cowboy, Curt Lake.

The last man to move away from the doorway was stocky, slightly under average height, and moved with none of the lithe agility of the other two with guns. That one, Race felt, was Pete, the older gunman.

He let them pass entirely along the rear of his house and over to the little pale place where the house walls cornered. There, no longer aided by that shadowed tall wall, he saw them better, but still not well enough to separate them, particularly since at this juncture they bunched up again.

For a moment the leader of those people remained motionless, as though intently listening. Then he stepped clear of the house, twisted from the waist, and peered down across the yard toward the barn. For several minutes he remained like that, looking, listening, studying, before he stepped back again, bringing the others up close around him.

Race very faintly heard a soft murmur of masculine voices. The Kansas Kid pushed clear, looked back down the night where Race lay all but entirely concealed, turned his head to the left, ran another speculative glance up that gradual slope behind the house, then made his decision. Race held his breath, fearing the Kid might just decide to travel west instead of east; if he did, if that entire party of five people passed along in front of

Race's shallow depression, someone would almost certainly look down and see him.

But the Kid did not decide in favor of the west. Neither, thought Race, would anyone else in the Kid's boots. There was nothing westward for miles on end whether the Kid knew that or not.

He decided to strike out southeastward, angling along the base of that rolling land swell, which was a good move because for at least half a mile this would keep Race's house between his party and those watchers down there in the barn.

Now Race knew every foot of ground the Kid would pass over, and, knowing this, he was extremely anxious to get back to the others, get mounted, and stalk the renegades in force, for clearly, and despite his most improbable hopes, he could not do as much alone as he'd hope he might have, when he had first tried getting around where he lay.

The Kid was cautious. He not only moved quietly at intervals, pausing often to make sure his men had not been spotted, but he also kept Eleanor on his left, on the north side of him so that, if any shots came from the barn area, her body would protect him.

Race watched, and stormed at their moving slowness, and ached to rise up out of his ancient buffalo wallow. He could not, however, for as long as the others were in his sight, if he could see them moving, they could also see him moving.

It was half an hour before the stocky man bringing up the rear passed on around the slanting foothill, passing beyond Race's sight. He let another agonizingly slow minute pass to be sure of safety, then sprang up, holstered his gun, crushed on his hat, and went loping back around the house, across that open place between his residence and his bunkhouse, across to the smithy, and from there over to the rear of the barn. Here, he hissed his name into the forward dark, jumped inside, and instantly called the others.

Three rusty silhouettes came stalking through the barn's blacker interior gloom. When they halted, Race told them the Kid and his men had gone. He explained the route they were taking and said to Tim Wade that he and Earnest Franklyn should take the horses, make a wide, surrounding sashay, and get into position somewhere well eastward and perhaps a little southward where they could intercept the renegades.

"Frank," he said to the Bear Trap range boss, "you come with me. We'll go after them afoot. It'll be slow but that way we won't make a sound."

Frank started to mumble something but Tim Wade interrupted him. "I'll go with you on foot," he told Race. "Frank's got a bullet groove along his thigh. He can ride, but walkin' would be dog-gone painful for him."

Race saw Eleanor's father open his mouth to speak. Anticipating the older man's mood, Race hastily accepted the sheriff's offer, jerked his head at him, and the two of them moved rapidly toward the front barn opening. Here, Wade looked out cautiously.

"You better be sure there's no one left in the house," he grumbled before stepping forth into the yard.

Race looked back to reassure the lawman, saw wet star shine reflecting off Tim's carbine, and said irritably: "Get rid of that damned Winchester, will you? It's like carryin' a lantern."

Wade halted, looked around, obediently leaned his saddle gun against the barn wall, then hurried after Race, who did not wait, but who went scurrying across the yard on an angle that carried them both directly in front of those broken, black, and forbidding front parlor windows through which the Kansas Kid's cohorts had thrown so much lead.

Tim used enough speed getting past this spot to bring him right up behind Race. In fact, when Race halted abruptly at the

221

house corner to peer around, Sheriff Wade stumbled into him.

They whipped along leaving the house, the barn, and ranch yard well behind. Once, Race stopped up along the side hill listening for Franklyn and his range boss. When he could detect no sound of horsemen, it pleased him.

"I had my doubts," he explained to Wade. "I thought the old man might still be too demoralized, too broken up to remember how in his younger days he used to stalk Indian camps on horseback."

"I'm not worryin' about old Franklyn right now," mumbled Tim. "I'm worryin' about you an' me . . . more especially about me. Any idea how far ahead they are?"

Race did not reply. He continued on around the side hill, angling higher all the time. He thought it very unlikely that, if they stumbled inadvertently upon the Kansas Kid, the renegades would look uphill for enemies; he was sure they would be concentrating on the back trail instead, for it would ordinarily be this route others would follow from the Dunphy ranch barnyard.

The night turned still as death; weeds and tough forage grass made whispering sounds against their feet and legs. Countless little flickering stars shone malevolently and that weak little sickle moon seemed now to be deliberately casting downward more light than it should have been able to.

Race, who knew every yard of the country they were crossing, halted once in a shallow place, a little sunken place made by a striking meteor in ages gone, and turned to Tim Wade with a suspicious scowl.

"They're changing direction," he said in a barely audible tone. "Tim, they're swinging almost due north."

"How do you know that? I can't hear a thing but the damned stillness. Anyway, what difference does it make which way they go so long as we don't lose 'em?"

"This difference," replied Race. "The way they're going now, they might bump into Franklyn and Andrews. But there's something else wrong here, too. The only ranch northward and eastward where they could steal fresh horses is the Bear Trap."

Wade looked and pursed his lips and thoughtfully said: "That's no mistake. I'll bet you money that's no mistake. That dog-gone Kansas Kid's still tryin' for old Franklyn." The sheriff wagged his head back and forth. "I've run across bull-headed men in my time, but that damned fool takes the cake." He blew out a big breath, craned his neck to look carefully all around them, and relaxed where he stood beside Race. "He's askin' for it. He's doin' what no gunman in his right mind would tackle, Race, headin' for Bear Trap. He must be plumb out of his mind."

"On one subject he is unbalanced, Tim. Just on that one subject." Race turned and started ahead once more. Sheriff Wade looked a little dubious but he, too, continued on around the side hill. He tried harder to hear now, too, but he still could not pick up any sound of the party ahead of them; this annoyed him because he had to admit Race Dunphy had better ears.

He slipped along, thinking of Race, wondering why, exactly, he and Race had never been friendly. He could think of a number of minor irritations that had rubbed him a little raw over the years, but here, following Dunphy toward a shoot-out with three seasoned killers, none of those things seemed significant at all. In fact, they seemed ridiculous. Like the time Race had posted bail for three outriders passing through the country with a trail herd, who had gotten swilled to the gills in his saloon and had tried to shoot up the town. He and Race had come very close to blows over that; he had said those outriders should remain behind and sober up. Race had said if they were forced to do that, they would lose their jobs with the trail outfit.

Tim squinted ahead where Race was moving silently along.

He shook his head, feeling sheepish. Hell, that had been a silly thing to fight over. The other things they'd clashed about were no more significant, either, Tim thought now; in fact, he couldn't really recall but one or two of them. He spat aside, glided along, and was disgusted with himself.

This was the way to measure a man; by the way he laid his life on the line for someone else, not by some tomfool incident no one remembered a day after it happened—like three parched outriders in off a long and lonely trail drive.

When Race halted again, crouched and peering over the side hill's gentle curving where distantly he could make out the faint soft blur of moving men, Tim Wade tapped his shoulder, stuck out his hand, and said: "Shake."

Race looked bewildered but he slowly shook. "What was that for?" he asked.

Tim flushed scarlet. "Do I have to have a reason?" he demanded. "Let's go on."

XV

Race didn't move; instead, he put up a hand, took hold of Tim by the elbow, and brought him up where he, too, could see those indistinct dark blurs down the side hill and distantly ahead of them.

The lawman looked and came to see closer. He moved his lips as though counting, then turned his head. "They're all there, but it's hard to make out one from the other." He stepped back, motioning Race ahead again. "Let's go."

Race began now to angle downhill, and in fact the farther they progressed, the less slope lay under them; they were running out of land swell as they followed the northerly route of the Kansas Kid's party of renegades and hostages.

Once the Kid threw up an arm, halting his people. Race saw that gesture. He also saw how the Kid leaned a little as though listening. Race's heart missed a beat. Behind him Tim Wade also drew stiffly upright. It seemed to the trailers that those onward men had detected a sound of riders somewhere around them in the night.

The Kid dropped his arm, turned, and spoke briefly to Mort and Pete, started ahead once more, and now began to move more rapidly, setting a gait the others had to hasten to keep up with.

"Headin' for Bear Trap sure as it's dark," said Tim. He once more wagged his head wryly over the folly of this.

"It'll take him until near dawn to get there," grunted Race, picking up his own gait in order to keep the yonder people in sight as they passed out over the hushed and faintly lighted prairie. "I don't think he can keep up that speed, either. From the look of Curt back at the house, he wasn't feeling so good. Maybe he stood up when he should have shut up. Anyway, he was unsteady when they left the yard."

But it was not Race's range rider who began to falter; it was the renegade with the bandaged head. His steps slowed, began to drag, and, when the Kid twisted to encourage him, this outlaw could only respond with a short burst, then he began to drop back once more.

"My meat," said Race to Tim Wade. "That one's called Pete. He's vicious and deadly. I particularly want that one."

They stopped from time to time to avoid detection, because the Kansas Kid seemed troubled by Pete's inability to keep up and constantly turned to see how Pete was doing. The lot of them passed along the eerie landscape, hunted and hunters, moving in fits and starts.

Once, after the Kid's party made a rather long halt, it seemed that Pete was much better. It began to dawn on Race that Mort had a bottle of whiskey with him. He'd seen Mort tilt his head occasionally, but after this last rest halt, when Pete stepped forth with a springy step easily keeping up with the others, Race was sure how this miracle had been achieved.

Ahead lay one of those low, long land swells. Race knew this country they were passing over very well. He swung toward Sheriff Wade without halting. "You keep on the way they're going," he directed. "I'm going to try and get around that swell yonder, ahead of them."

"What the hell for?" protested Wade.

"For Pete, that's what for. Drunk or sober he's running out of steam. He'll be the last man in line, the one man without a hostage."

Race turned off westerly and began steadily to jog along. When he was parallel with the Kid's party, he waited, staying even, until another rest halt was called. He trotted on past when this occurred, got well around the renegades, and began circling back westward again, coming at last in behind that low land swell.

Here, safe for the time being, he threw himself down in dry grass, breathing hard. He was still like that when out of the murky east came an unmistakable sound—horseshoe steel striking stone. He got up onto one knee, looking along the skyline for movement lower down. He saw them, two riders coming cat-footedly in behind his land swell, both with Winchester saddle guns balanced across their laps. He waited, letting them come almost even, then he straightened off the ground, went ahead a little distance, waved his hat, and stopped, letting those two approach him.

Frank Andrews was eager. He leaned down to ask where the renegades and Eleanor were. Race told him. He also told both Andrews and Franklyn to go back, to ride farther out, because if he had heard them, very shortly now, when the outlaws came trudging along, they might also hear riders in the night. His final words were addressed to Earnest Franklyn.

"They're heading for Bear Trap. I think it's possible the Kid's doing that on purpose. He still wants your hide."

Franklyn looked bitter. "He's crazy to try that now. Why, hell, he wouldn't last five minutes, walkin' into Bear Trap with Eleanor his prisoner. I've got over a dozen men at the home place. They'd tear those outlaws to pieces."

"Not," explained Race dryly, "if the Kansas Kid had a cocked pistol in her back, they wouldn't. Now you two ride off, and be damned quiet about it."

Andrews would have asked a question, perhaps something about his and old Franklyn's part in what was clearly nearing a climax. But Race said a hard word, irritably gestured with his hand, so Frank never got to say whatever had been occupying his mind. He and Franklyn reversed their mounts and rode westerly out into the surrounding night.

Race waited. He did not think the Kansas Kid would climb up and over and down this land swell behind which he was waiting. He thought he would come shuffling around from the west, which is what happened.

The Kid was out front. At his side Eleanor Franklyn walked phlegmatically along, looking neither right nor left. Some ten or fifteen feet behind those two came Mort and Curt Lake. Race paid close attention to the way his rider was holding up. Curt did not appear to be tired or weak, although back at the house Race had gotten the impression he might be one or the other.

Finally Pete came striding along, his bandaged head looking unnaturally pale in the darkness. Pete was easily twenty feet to the rear. He seemed not the least concerned with his surroundings.

Race began moving. He meant to take a long chance now. He came even with a rare sagebrush clump, hid in its thorny density until only lagging Pete was in view, then started forward, gliding first one way, then another, utilizing each shadow no matter how insignificant, each outcropping of hillside rock, even tall patches of curing buffalo grass. In this fashion he got to within ten feet of Pete, who had by this time dropped back a good fifty feet.

Race went for him. He simply jumped up, drew his handgun, and ran at the unsuspecting killer from the rear. There was no other way to do this; the entire area through which the lot of them was now passing was as devoid of cover as ten dozen late fall burns could make it.

Pete had no warning. Race got up behind him, swung his pistol in a fierce, short arc, and Pete went down without a sound. One moment he was walking along, arms swinging, legs lifting, falling; the next moment he slumped forward, slid down upon the earth, and gently lay there.

Race took five sideward steps and faded low into a clump of buffalo grass, watching.

For perhaps two hundred feet no one looked back for Pete. It was Mort who eventually discovered Pete was not still behind him. He looked, strained around, swung completely around, then called softly to the Kid. Race heard his every word.

"Kid, Pete's gone."

"Hold up," growled the Kid, moving back beside Mort. "What do you mean, gone?"

"Look for yourself. He was back there a hundred yards or so . . . now he ain't."

The Kid made no move to go back, to investigate. He dropped his right hand to his hip. He looked; he seemed to sniff the darkness. He said: "Mort, did you hear anything back there?"

"Not a damned thing. It wouldn't be that Dunphy feller, would it? Hell, Kid, we been keepin' a close watch behind. There's been nothing."

Mort wished to say more. Race could even see that from as far off as he was, prone in the grass patch.

The Kid walked back a short distance, halted, looked around, and walked back still farther. Race noticed that he made no effort to get beyond sight of Mort, standing back northward with Eleanor and Curt Lake.

"Come on!" called Mort, getting uneasy or impatient. "Listen, Kid, I got a bottle I found in Dunphy's pantry. I gave Pete a couple of big swallows back there when he was cussin' about his head achin' somethin' fierce and his legs turnin' to water." Mort paused; he affected his raffish, mirthless smile as the Kansas Kid came slowly back toward him. "Maybe he drank too much. Maybe, him bein' light-headed an' all, the stuff. . . ."

"Give me that bottle," rapped out the Kid savagely, and swore. "Any other time and place, Mort, and I'd kill you for this."

Mort handed over the bottle. It was nearly empty. He watched the Kid raise it, dash it down, and break it.

"We'll leave Pete. There's nothing else we can do."

"*Aw*, hell," growled Mort. "There's no one around. We can fetch him along."

"Yeah?" snapped the Kid. "How? You want to carry a passed-out drunk? No? Well, neither do I. Eleanor can't carry him, Lake can't. You don't want to and I don't want to, so he stays. Maybe it'll teach him when to drink and when not to."

The Kid started ahead, up beside Eleanor again. He suddenly stopped, turned, and said: "Mort, do you have another bottle?"

Mort shook his head.

The Kid caught hold of Eleanor's wrist, shot a careless look around, jerked his head, and walked out northward again.

Race reached out, plucked a stalk of grama grass, popped it between his teeth, and thoughtfully chewed. When that diminished party passed from sight in the northward night, he rose up, retraced his steps, and found Tim Wade kneeling beside the unconscious gunman. Tim had rolled Pete over for a good look at his face.

As Race knelt, Wade straightened up, swung and pointed a rigid arm downward. "You know who that is?" he demanded. Race said all he knew was that the younger gunman had called this one Pete.

"Yeah," ground out Wade. "They call him Pete, all right. No one knows what his right name is but this one has a price on him as just plain Pete Smith. Hell, Race, he's wanted in Texas, in Idaho, in Montana, and Wyoming. Murder. That's Pete Smith's specialty . . . murder. I've looked at that hatchet face from so many Wanted posters I can see it in my sleep."

Race was not greatly impressed. "Speaking of sleep," he retorted, considering the unconscious man lying before him. "What do we do with him now? All I wanted was to even up the odds a little."

Without a word Sheriff Wade removed his own belt and the outlaw's belt. With these he bound the wanted man's ankles and his arms. He rocked back, gazing critically at his handiwork, said—"Nope."—and held out his hand for Race's belt as well. "Can't take a chance with this one."

Race handed over the belt. He reached for Pete's six-gun, hefted it, then threw it by the barrel as hard and as far as he could.

They left their unconscious prisoner trussed tightly. Race forced the gait for an hour, until they sighted the Kansas Kid again, with the others. He slowed, halted when those others halted, started up again when once more the Kid led out, saying nothing to Tim Wade at his side until, where broken land loomed dead ahead, he made a stifled groan. This was that mile-wide stretch of eroded country where, over ten hours before, he had first walked head-on into trouble.

He told Tim Wade: "If they don't cut easterly from here,

we're in trouble. We can lose 'em in those arroyos as easy as falling off a log."

The Kid halted again. Race thought the reason for this latest stop was the sighting of the badlands. He thought that until the Kid sharply hissed a warning to his remaining companion. Race heard him plainly say: "Horses ahead. Don't anyone move or make a sound."

Tim stiffened beside Race, brushing his companion's shoulder and dropping his head low to whisper: "It'll be Franklyn and Andrews as sure as hell."

Race knew this, or felt it, so he remained utterly still, straining to see what those two renegades ahead would do.

They forced Eleanor and Curt to lie flat upon the ground. The Kid and Mort also got belly down. Race could see the faint, threatening sheen of soft moonlight off gun barrels. He very slowly drew his own gun. Tim Wade also drew.

"Lord help those two if they ride in now," breathed Wade, and held his breath as Race was also doing, waiting for what must happen next.

Moments dragged by. No horsemen appeared. In fact Race heard no riders at all, had not heard any even when the Kansas Kid had heard them. Wade touched his arm.

"Listen."

Race heard them finally: two horses coming southward, side-by-side.

XVI

It was a terrible moment. Race's throat constricted, forming around a cry of alarm. Those horses were moving unerringly straight for the place where the Kansas Kid and Mort lay waiting.

Wade's breath rattled. He looked helplessly at Race and away again. He was hoping with everything in him that those animals would swerve, would change course, and go off into the night in some other direction.

But they did not; they kept right on coming, their hoof falls sounding unnaturally loud inside the head of Race and Tim Wade.

"This is sheer murder," whispered Wade. "Race, we got to . . . we can't just lie here. We got to open up regardless of your rider and Miss Eleanor."

Race reached over, caught Tim's right wrist, and fiercely gripped it. He did not look around or utter a single word. The two horses were in sight now. They were riderless.

Wade saw, and sank down. Race let go of Tim's gun arm but otherwise he did not move at all; in fact he slowly rolled his brows together in the beginnings of a perplexed scowl.

"Tim, those are the horses Franklyn and Andrews were riding. Dammit, I talked to them on that selfsame pair of animals not an hour ago."

Wade, staring ahead where the Kansas Kid rose up out of the dust and swore bitterly, making those two loose animals leery of coming closer, whispered: "You're plumb right, Race. I recognize those critters from back in your barn."

"I think," mused Race, "Frank and old man Franklyn did that on purpose. I have no idea why, but for some idea they're working out, they deliberately hazed those horses up to the Kid."

"Makes sense, like askin' for a poke in the eye with a sharp stick," grumbled Tim Wade, enormously relieved and therefore somewhat miffed, too. "Now the whole passel of us are afoot. I don't mind tellin' you my feet feel like two burned holes in a blanket from all this cussed walking."

The Kansas Kid scooped up several small stones in his anger. He threw them violently at those two loose horses. The animals at once wheeled and went running down the night. From farther back Mort let out an anguished curse.

"What's wrong with you, Kid? Dammit, them was ridin' horses, whether they scairt the daylights outen us or not. Now we'll never get 'em."

The Kid whipped around. He glared, and even Race, back in the night so far he was visible only as a dark lump against the lumpy ground, could see the fiery wrath gripping the Kid in every line of his rigid stance.

"Mort, you loud-mouthed whelp, I'm goin' to kill you yet. Push that damned cowboy up an' let's be movin'."

Mort obeyed, his movements sullen, his growls at Curt and Eleanor grim and pointed. The four of them started onward once more.

Race and Tim Wade did not immediately resume their pursuit. They sat there in the night, listening to the dragging onward footsteps, trying to imagine why Earnest Franklyn and his range boss had herded their loose saddle animals down upon the Kansas Kid.

"To frazzle his nerves," suggested the sheriff.

"That part of it succeeded," Race responded. "When he turned on Mort, I thought he was going to let him have it then and there."

"He's mad as a wet hen all right, but he hasn't lost all his sense yet. One gunshot and everyone for five miles around would know there was something wrong out here, an' maybe half of 'em would come ridin' to investigate." Tim cocked a wry eye. "That includes Bear Trap. Can you imagine what those Bear Trappers would do to the Kansas Kid if they found him abusin' Franklyn's daughter? All the fast guns in the territory wouldn't keep him from gettin' spread-eagled over an ant nest, then. You can take my word for that. Old Franklyn has a tough crew."

Race stood up, turned northward, and stood listening. From

his seated position the sheriff made an anguished grunt, pushed, got to his knees and stiffly, painfully brought himself fully upright.

"How much farther to Bear Trap?" he asked. "I'll say one thing for the Kansas Kid. He's got better feet and legs than I have. I haven't walked this much in ten years."

"About three miles," replied Race, taking up the trail again. "And we're lucky, Tim. He's going easterly out and around the badlands."

"Yeah," mumbled the footsore sheriff, "lucky as a bull in fly time." He hobbled a few feet, looked up to see Race fading out a hundred feet onward, hissed: "Wait up, dammit. I don't want to get lost out here." He hurried along on his painful feet.

The Kansas Kid stopped once in Race's sight and spoke briefly to Eleanor Franklyn. Afterward, still keeping her beside him, he angled still farther away from that broken country off on his left, striking out straight as an arrow for the Bear Trap home ranch. Race could understand Eleanor directing him in this correct route only if she had no idea what Race thought was still in the Kid's mind—killing her father before he killed her.

This puzzled him. Clearly the Kansas Kid had not said anything to Eleanor about her father yet. He'd had ample time, Race knew. He'd had all those nerve-racking hours back at the Dunphy place. And he'd made it vividly plain to Race, to old man Franklyn, to anyone who would listen, that his prime motive was to kill the Franklyns. Then why hadn't he told Eleanor? He'd described in livid detail how he meant to torture her with tales of her faithless mother, of how her father had sent a gunman to kill her uncle—his own brother—the Kansas Kid's father. He seared these details of his intentions into old Franklyn, nearly breaking the old man with the sordidness of all this. And yet now, it seemed, he had not said a single derogatory thing to Eleanor. Why? Race went along, wondering about this, trying to imagine one good reason for the Kid's silence. He thought it might be because the Kid wished father and daughter in each other's sight when he poured out his vituperation, damning one as a murderer, the other as the daughter of a faithless woman. Still, the Kid was no fool. He would realize by now he no longer held the whip hand. He was running and hiding behind Eleanor's skirts to save his life.

Somewhere ahead an owl hooted, breaking into Race's thoughts with its oddly misplaced sound. Only roosting owls hooted, and there were no trees for miles in any direction of this place.

A second owl hooted, well off in the east from where that first call had come from. Race instantly lodged the same objection against the source of this call. He went ahead another hundred feet, halted, and sank down. Tim Wade limped up and gratefully sank down behind him. Tim whispered skeptically: "If a self-respecting owl heard Frank and old Earnest imitating him like that, he'd quit the country."

Race was just figuring this out as Tim spoke. He tried to locate the Kid and his hostages, but they were beyond sight in the night. "Wait here," he told Tim, and trotted off.

Once again those owls hooted, first one off in the northwest, then the other one off in the northeast. It was an eerie sad sound in the otherwise silent night.

Race came upon the Kid and Mort, prone again, their hostages lying with them. Both Mort and the Kid had their heads up and moving, their six-guns cocked and ready. They, too, understood that those were not owls out there.

Race faded behind a scrub brush clump, watching the gunmen who lay not two hundred feet ahead. One thing he grudgingly admitted about the Kansas Kid: when he had hostages, he knew exactly where to place them so that no one, either in front, behind, or off on either side of him dared shoot. He had Eleanor pressed close to him on one side, Curt Lake prone upon his other side. Mort was on the far side of Curt. Even in broad daylight no sane man would attempt picking off any one of those four people unless he was resigned to killing at least one other in the process. Certainly no man with the interest of those hostages at heart would even think of trying a pot shot in the darkness.

Another of those mournful owl hoots came, swelling, then fading out. For a while there was total silence. Then the other owl hooted off in the west. This one sounded much closer than it previously had.

Race saw Mort yank up off the ground, swing his six-gun and hold rigid, waiting for a target. All he got was another dismal, eerie hoot. The Kid barked at Mort: "Get down, you fool. Get hold of yourself. Don't you see you're doin' exactly what they want, gettin' all edgy and reckless?"

Mort's answer to that was too low to be heard out where Race was, but its vicious tone was unmistakable. Suddenly, off behind Race, a third owl hooted. This was the most believable of all three imitations. Race could not repress a slight start as Tim Wade came gliding over to him. Tim nestled down, beamed a grim smile, and whispered: "Now that's how the Indians used to do it, real enough to fool a gen-u-wine owl."

It was clear now to everyone involved in this ghostly chase what was happening. Those two Bear Trap men, Franklyn and Andrews, had instituted a campaign of harassment. They never showed themselves, never came close enough to compel the Kansas Kid and his single remaining companion to turn their guns upon their hostages, yet they were always out there, always threatening, always ready if opportunity offered, to spring in for the kill.

Race, who had been content to keep on the Kid's trail, waiting for the opportunity he knew had to come sooner or later to free the hostages, discussed this other scheme with Sheriff Wade. "The only thing that worries me," he whispered, "is that one or the other of them, either Mort or the Kid, may get so exasperated they turn on Eleanor or Curt. They're getting awfully jumpy."

"Mort, maybe," stated Tim, "but not the Kid. He's wise enough to know the only thing that's keepin' him alive is his hostages."

"Mort's been drinking," said Race. "You saw how he nearly jumped up a minute ago. Listen, Tim, we've got to concentrate on him, even risk a shot if he goes berserk."

Wade reluctantly nodded over this. "They're movin' again," he eventually said, pointing with his chin. "We'd better keep up."

Now the Kansas Kid altered his earlier tactic of traveling in fits and starts, halting often to plumb the night. He knew his foemen were out there in the darkness stalking him so he no longer halted. He also increased his pace, pushing the others to their limit, urging them with words when they slowed. Finally he did the one thing Race hoped he would not do; he changed course, heading due west, straight for the badlands.

Race swore with feeling about this. When Tim asked what troubled him, Race explained. The lawman considered, then said: "Can we get around him, head him off before he gets down in there?"

"Not without forcing a gunfight," answered Race. He was standing still, peering ahead where those four crowding-up people were swinging westerly, when that owl-hooting man on the renegades' left made his haunting cry twice in quick succession.

Race said: "Some kind of a signal, come on."

The easterly owl did not hoot at all, which was significant.

Race and Tim swung westerly, coming in behind the fleeing outlaws and hostages. Overhead, that watery moon phased out behind a fat little cloud, plunging everything into Stygian blackness down below. Race and Tim halted to wait this out. They at once lost sight of the renegades, the hostages, and even one another.

"Hold it," ordered Race. "Stand where you are until the cloud passes."

Tim muttered something unintelligible under his breath as he ground to a halt and eased down upon one knee in the total gloom.

Behind Race an owl hooted again. He twisted, thinking this was Tim keeping up the harassment even though all of them were temporarily immobilized. He saw a dark blur, not wide or thick enough for Tim Wade, glide into sight and glide out again. Hair at the base of Race's skull rose stiffly; a quick shock of alarm ran out along his nerves. He dropped flat, bringing his gun to bear upon the site where that shadow had materialized, but the silhouette disappeared as silently, as eerily, as it had swung across his vision. Of one thing he was very certain; whoever that was out there, it was not Sheriff Wade.

He thought it might have been Frank Andrews. Frank was lean and lithe. It was not old Earnest Franklyn. He was positive of that. But there was another lean, lithe man in the roundabout night—the Kansas Kid. He was wily enough to try flanking his pursuers, to take advantage of this long moment of absolute darkness to try and catch his foeman from behind.

That sickle moon floated from behind the cloud and weak, milky light ran over the land ahead of it. Race peered over, saw Tim also lying prone, and breathed a soundless sigh of relief. Whoever that had been he'd caught a fleeting glimpse of, had, he thought, passed between the two of them and had gone on. He got up and started for Wade.

XVII

Tim was face down, flat. There was a trickle of shiny blackness behind his left ear. When Race eased him over onto his back, the lawman's lips fluttered. Tim Wade was unconscious.

Race examined that puffiness behind Tim's left ear, rocked back on his heels, and bitterly swore to himself. That had been the Kansas Kid gliding through the utter darkness. He'd come upon the lawman from behind, struck him down with a pistol barrel, and had swept briefly across Race's vision on his way back to the others.

The Kansas Kid had gone over onto the offensive in this strange war of nerves. From now on the pursuers might at any moment be the pursued, as a whipcord-tough shadow passed noiselessly through the surrounding night.

They were close to the badlands now. Close enough for Race to make out those dim breaks and upthrusts on ahead. He no longer had any idea where the renegades were, with their hostages, but this did not particularly bother him right then.

He made Sheriff Wade comfortable, used his handkerchief to fashion a crude bandage, got up, and moved off. There was nothing more he could do for the lawman. Tim would eventually recover and he'd have a splitting headache, but for now he was out of it. The odds had been effectively whittled down, and the Kansas Kid had scored again.

Race was more careful now as he criss-crossed the land, striving to pick up the trail. From time to time he shot a long look skyward to consider the likelihood of other clouds sweeping up to obscure the moon. He also kept a closer watch on both sides and behind.

That owl hooted off in the west again. As before it made its mournful outcry twice in succession. Race thought this was meant to give the other owl a bearing on where the renegades now were. Operating on this notion, he swung slightly northward, heading in the direction of those dual cries.

His surmise proved correct. Near the beginning of an erosion break faint onward moves caught and held his attention. It was the Kansas Kid again, with Eleanor beside and slightly in front of him, and also Mort with Curt Lake. Race watched those four step down, twist away, and go into that steadily sinking gulch until little more than their heads remained visible.

They were in the badlands now and only the most astute attention would keep them in sight. Here, where dozens of tributary arroyos corrugated the land, all debouching into one central, wide, and deep gulch, lay a hundred traps. Race knew this country perhaps better than any of the others. He realized how simple it would now be for the Kansas Kid to step into the dark of one of those smaller tributaries, wait until a pursuer crept past northward, keeping in the main arroyo, and either shoot him or bend a gun barrel over his skull as he'd done with the sheriff.

Easing down into the same gully the fugitives had taken, he thought it improbable that the Kid would fire at an enemy. If he did, he would give away his position. This, Race felt positive, was the reason the Kid had only knocked out Sheriff Wade instead of killing him.

It was much gloomier down in the broken country than it had been out upon the plain. Here, while there was a little of that same weak light, there also were totally dark niches, tortured twistings of the serrated land where no light ever struck down, and wiry clumps of thorny underbrush that cast man-shaped shadows.

The cry of an owl came from somewhere behind Race. He stepped into a dark place and froze. Whoever had made that noise was also down in the arroyos, moving north. The westerly owl answered this call, but Race paid no heed to this second sound. It was a long, nerve-racking wait, and, if he'd been sure

240

that oncoming man was either Franklyn or Andrews, he would not have endured it. But he was not sure any more; the Kid had amply demonstrated a canniness matching the wiles of his pursuers. Race stood firmly in his dark place, unwilling to take the risk of being caught from behind as Tim had been, motionlessly waiting, scarcely breathing, feeling that hair at the back of his neck stiffen. He did not draw his six-gun; blued steel had a way of catching light and reflecting it where scarcely any light existed.

Somewhere southward small stones faintly rattled. Moments later a crouched-over, shapeless lump, blacker, more solid than the surrounding darkness, eased out into sight, faded out where a crumbling earthen bank cut off sighting, then came on again, moving only a foot at a time.

Race kept this moving silhouette in sight by looking slightly above it, not directly at it, drawing in all the surrounding light to form a pale pattern in his sight that surrounded this darker form, giving it shape and substance. When the man was less than a hundred feet south, Race saw him halt, sink behind a scrub clump of sage, cup both hands, and make one of those eerie hooting sounds. He relaxed, certain this was Frank Andrews. He was too youthful in his movements to be Earnest Franklyn; he was too obviously a pursuer to be the Kansas Kid.

Race let the man pass to within twenty feet of him before softly hissing at him. At once that dark silhouette dropped down, twisted, and threw up a dully shining gun.

"Easy," whispered Race in a hard outward rush of breath. "It's me . . . Race Dunphy."

The man remained like stone for almost thirty seconds, his gun barrel like an eyeless socket, his face a pale, damp-looking blur. Gradually he lowered the weapon; gradually he got up to one knee, hung there until he could separate Race from the darkness around him, then the man slid over and stood fully upright. It was, as Race had guessed, Frank Andrews. He peered upward, shook his head, and made an audible, shaky sigh.

"That was almighty close," he breathed. "If you live to be a hundred and fifty, you'll never be any closer to salvation, Race, damned if you will."

"Tim Wade's out of it," said Race, speaking softly, giving Frank time to recover. "When that cloud passed over the moon, the Kid slipped back, flanked us, came upon Tim from behind, and busted him over the head."

Andrews's face was shiny with oily sweat. He put up his gun, considered what Race had just said, and puckered his forehead. "He's not just runnin' then," he said of the Kansas Kid.

"No, he's doin' a little stalking on his own."

"Maybe we could bait him, get him to try it again . . . get him away from Curt and Miss Eleanor." Frank looked up. "What do you think?"

Race pondered. "Maybe," he conceded. "But first we've got to find them again."

"That won't be hard," said Andrews. "The old man and I been keepin' track of 'em with owl hoots. He's west somewhere, stayin' ahead of him. The idea is for him to keep 'em in sight and hoot every once in a while so I can come in behind 'em."

Race nodded; he'd already figured this much out. Now he said: "How come you fellers to do that trick with your horses?"

"The Kid heard us. We accidentally got too close. As soon as we heard him say he'd heard horses, we figured the only thing left to do was make him think it was loose stock, so we off-saddled and eased the critters up where he'd see 'em." Andrews shrugged. "It was a good idea, but as it turned out he wised up to us being around him anyway, so in the end all we really accomplished was to put ourselves afoot. Still, we got to play this thing as the cards are dealt."

"How is the old man?" Race asked, recalling how Franklyn

had been earlier, cowed and tormented and torn apart with his anguish.

"Better," said Andrews, understanding how Race's thoughts were running. "A lot better now, Race. Sometimes inactivity takes everything out of a man, while activity puts it back again. Anyway, he's his old self again . . . well, almost, anyway."

Race stood a moment listening to the silent night. Frank ran a soiled shirt sleeve over his whiskery face, and, when Race nodded at him, Andrews cupped his hands, made the hooting call, and stood with his head cocked, waiting out the answering sound.

It came, far northward and faint-sounding, as though Franklyn was still up on the prairie somewhere, had not gotten down into the broken land.

"Lead out," directed Race. "But be damned careful. There are a dozen places we can be ambushed down in here."

Andrews bobbed his head and stepped away, stepped out into the main pathway leading up through catclaw and rocks and willowy cottonwood shoots northbound. Race followed him at a distance of thirty feet until, where the trail widened, the arroyo's sides dropped swiftly back, easterly and westerly, he hastened up, touched Frank's shoulder, and said: "There's a pool of water around the next bend. You'll have to keep well to the right where there's a game trail. It's narrow and it's exposed. If the Kid's on across the pool, all he'll have to do is hide in the underbrush and wait until we're halfway over, then knock us off like birds on a limb."

Andrews nodded, glided ahead until he could see weak moonlight glimmering off a broad, still sheet of water, then he stopped, looked ahead, moved over sideways into darkness, and hunkered down, waiting for Race to get in beside him. He turned a worried face toward his companion, saying nothing.

Race understood both the look and the silence. Frank Andrews was waiting for a decision to be made. He was a tough, resolute, and loyal cowboy, but he'd developed a lifelong habit of taking orders. In the position he was now in, he shrank from taking the initiative.

Every inch of that onward area was thoroughly familiar to Race; he'd explored it as a boy and he'd plumbed the cool depths of that pool under blistering yellow summer skies. What he had to determine first was whether or not the Kansas Kid had passed around the pool. To do this he had to leave cover, crawl over where that little buck run angled narrowly along the arroyo's bare west wall, and seek footprints in the porous earth there. He explained this to Frank, told him to watch the onward brush clumps for sign of shiny barrels, then zigzagged until he ran out of cover.

He went the last hundred feet in a crouched-over trot, dropped to all fours where the trail began its encircling way out and around the limpid pool, and crawled ahead as far as the first disturbed, damp earth. There were the tracks, smudged and scuffed, but recently made and showing haste by their makers.

Race lifted his head, looked straight ahead across the pool where that curving trail returned to the central arroyo's continuing northward run, and several things happened at once. An owl hooted very close by and overhead, upon the rangeland above him westerly. Simultaneously with this sudden breaking of the silence he saw a clump of sage across the pool quiver and metallically glisten. A shock of warning struck down through him, making him drop like stone one second ahead of the blasting gunshot that flung its crimson muzzle blast out of that sage clump.

He was too exposed; there was no time to draw and fire; there was not even enough time to whip around and try for that cover he'd left a hundred feet back. He had only one alternative before the second shot came and he took it. He pushed mightily with his left arm, heaved his body sideways, and crashed down into the water reaching desperately for the depths of it. Before a murky, green world closed entirely over him, he heard two more gunshots. Something plucked at his shirt, but only for a second, then the silence was deeper than ever, the light more diffused, and he swam powerfully for the opposite shore where a tangle of ancient plum thickets hung over the bank. The same plum thickets where, as a youth, he had rummaged for sweet, wild fruit.

It seemed a lifetime before he got across, although the pool was actually neither long nor wide. With lungs near to bursting he eased up very cautiously, making scarcely a ripple, caught at rough, wiry branches, and ran a quick glance all around.

There were no more gunshots. In fact there was nothing, neither movement nor sound. The night was as bland as it had ever been, as treacherously bland, he thought, planting booted feet down deep into the slime underfoot, getting enough purchase this way to be able to ease himself up into the thicket, and waiting until he was sure it might be safe to do this.

The water was not cold where Race stood, and he was careful to make no ripples. He could, by twisting his head, see back where he'd left Frank Andrews. By looking across from where Frank was, he could also see that onward thicket where someone had fired at him. There was no gun barrel visible in that underbrush now.

Water lapped at him from the ever-widening circles whipped to life where he had plunged into the pool. He pushed stealthily deeper into the plum thicket and waited.

There were six people in the roundabout night. At least four of them, not counting Race, were seeking good clean shots. He eased his right hand over to his hip holster, three feet down. The holster was empty!

A man can become philosophical under stress while he waits out whatever must ensue, as long as he is himself, at least for the time being, quite safe. This mood came over Race where he stood with little more than the top of his head and his eyes, showing through tangled undergrowth. The Kansas Kid, since seizing the initiative, had put two men out of action: Tim Wade first, and now unarmed Race Dunphy.

Race felt a little grudging admiration for the Kansas Kid, and continued to stand in nearly six feet of water, just waiting.

XVIII

The very thing that had contributed to Tim Wade's being put out of the fight came now to put Race Dunphy back into it. A scudding cloud floated before the moon; everything became instantly and totally dark, and Race was able to climb safely out of the pool into the plum thicket. This was not altogether gratifying for that underbrush was full of thorns. Still Race was back on land again, and with his knowledge of this area he turned and pushed his way stealthily northward around the pool toward that distant place where someone had fired at him some little time before.

Now neither Earnest Franklyn nor Frank Andrews were using their mimicking calls. Now, too, the moon glided into the clear once more, fresh, ghostly light flooded the world, and Race had to slow his onward progress, to move more cautiously so as not to draw gunfire by rattling the underbrush.

He had never before tried encircling the pond by the route he was now forced to use, and evidently no animals larger than rabbits had ever done this before, either. There were tiny trails where rodents had passed along, but none large enough to accommodate a man.

Still, after losing complete track of time, Race made it, came to the final last tangle of underbrush, poked his head through, and saw, not fifty feet ahead of him, that still, dusty, and dark-green sagebrush plant where an invisible gunman had tried to pot-shoot him. There was no way to get across that intervening faintly moonlit distance other than just jumping out and making a wild dash. Race, who had until now been coldly calculating and shrewdly thoughtful, dropped those attributes from his thinking. He got upright, planted one foot well clear of his shielding thicket, balanced forward, and sucked back a big breath. If there were still a gunman behind that sage bush, he was about to get the surprise of his life.

Not a sound broke the stillness. Back around the pool where Frank Andrews had been—still was, although Race did not know it—only softly lapping water dully sparkled under the hushed heavens. Onward up the main arroyo not more than a thousand yards was the place where Race had ridden down earlier this same day trailing a rider he'd thought at the time was Curt Lake, and who turned out to be someone altogether different. That was the same place those two grimy outlaws had come up, disarmed both him and Eleanor Franklyn, and brought down upon nearly a dozen people the wild events that had followed.

Race knew that country onward from the sage clump as he knew his own hand. Between the sage bush and the more northerly reaches of the central arroyo there was no cover until he came to that same earthen wall he'd stopped behind hours before, when Eleanor had fired her nickel-plated pistol. After he cleared the sage clump, unless he encountered a gunman there, he would be totally exposed to gunfire as far as that earthen barranca.

All these things ran through his mind as he eased clear of the plum thicket, heard water squish in his boots, set himself forward on the balls of both feet, and ran. He ran swiftly and without any attempt at rendering himself a smaller target by crouching forward.

He hit that clump of sage like a charging buffalo bull, rose up in a powerful leap, and crashed down behind it. A man's sudden outcry, terrified and astonished, rang out. Race had a glimpse of a blurred, oily face twisting, of a pair of bent legs fighting to straighten up. Then he hit the man and the pair of them went tumbling furiously sideways, tearing sage limbs, scuffing up clouds of dust, and gradually coming to a straining halt as each of them lost momentum.

Not until he wrenched clear of his adversary's clawing talons did Race see who his adversary was. It was the younger gunman, he of the ice-cold eyes, the perpetually sullen mouth, and the bitter, harsh tongue. Race jumped away from a wild kick, rolled sideways, and got up. He lunged. The gunman rolled, fought up onto his knees, and pawed at Race with both hands outstretched. They made scarcely any noise at all in the dust, in the ancient sand of this insular place. Race stepped in then as the gunfighter got fully upright and rushed him. He sidestepped, swung a powerful blow, sank a fist wrist-deep into the gunman's belly, brought his other fist down with the force of a high-swung axe, caught the gunman at the base of the skull, and dropped him straight down. That was the end of it.

Race stepped warily into some westerly shadows, shot a quick look northward where he thought the Kansas Kid might materialize, breathed deeply for a moment, then peered around for the downed man's six-gun. He never found it; undoubtedly the gun was there somewhere, but it was not in plain sight. Race considered it probable that in the scuffling his weapon had been covered by sand. He could not take the time to search for it; on ahead up the arroyo the Kansas Kid was undoubtedly probing ahead for a safe hiding place or a way out of this erosion maze.

Race padded along as far as that earthen barranca. Here, he

paused for a little while deeply breathing, letting the tension run out of him somewhat, pushing away wet leaves and dirt from the area around his eyes. Far back and sounding much more distant than it was came Frank Andrews's hooting call. Race became intent, waiting for the answer from Earnest Franklyn. It never came.

Andrews tried again. Still there was no answer from Eleanor's father. Race abandoned hope for further aid from either of those two, eased gingerly around his crumbly earthen outthrust, and at once sighted the Kansas Kid with his hostages.

This was the end of the trail. The Kid had obviously decided to end the running fight here and now. He might or might not have guessed what had happened to the last of his hired gunmen, but the position he now presented to Race showed very definitely that he was through with running, was through with everything but the showdown, the final fight. He had his back to the easterly arroyo wall. Eleanor stood ahead on his left; Curt Lake stood ahead and on his right. From three directions at least no one could approach the Kid and certainly no one would dare risk taking a shot at him from in front or from the north or south.

Race raised his eyes. Behind the Kid, where the arroyo wall abruptly ended upon the overhead plain, he saw why Frank Andrews had gotten no reply to his hooting calls. Stealthily crawling up there, moving no more than an inch at a time, was Eleanor's father. He was bareheaded, did not have his gun in hand, and was drawing himself forward to drop upon the Kid with his fingers. It was an agonizing moment for Race. If old Franklyn made one sound, if he even rubbed over a stone or breathed too loudly, the Kid would whip around. He instantly thought of doing something to divert the Kid, anything at all that would hold the Kid's interest forward and downward. But he was not himself in too good a position. If he'd had a weapon, he'd have felt much better. The Kid had his six-gun out; it shone dully between where Eleanor and Curt stood, their faces gray and stone-set, looking numb and resigned and hopeless.

"Kid," said Race quietly, holding his voice level, making it sound as natural as possible, "your pardner back by the pool is out of it. That evens things up for you bustin' Tim Wade over the head back on the plain."

Race paused to give the Kid a chance to speak, to move, to focus his whole attention upon the place where Race's voice was coming from but where the Kid could see only bare earthen walls.

"It's gone far enough, Kid. Let Eleanor walk out of here. Don't do anything we'll all regret as long as we live."

The Kid finally spoke and he, too, kept his voice almost casual-sounding. "Is that you, Dunphy? You fooled me again. You weren't scairt after all, were you?"

Race let his breath out loudly. "Sure I was scairt, Kid. I've been scairt a dozen times tonight. So have you. So has everyone else. But that part of it's over now."

"You think it is, do you, Dunphy? Listen, you got a gun . . . step out where I can see you. We'll settle it in a matter of five seconds."

"Can't oblige you, Kid, because I lost my gun in that pool back there."

For a long moment the Kid said nothing. Then he made a brittle little laugh. "That's the oldest dodge on earth, Dunphy. I'm surprised at you."

Race knelt, poked one side of his face around the earthen outthrust, saw Earnest Franklyn balanced up there to drop, and called forth: "Kid, end it. Let it stop here and now. Listen to me. You don't want to kill anybody. I know that and you know it. I've been all night tryin' to make sense out of some of the things you've done."

"An' you've got it figured out, have you, Dunphy?"

"I think so, yes."

"All right!" called back the Kansas Kid. "You got it figured I don't want to kill . . . then step out where I can see you. That ought to be the acid test for your theory, hadn't it?"

Race balanced this decision in his mind. He peered around again, saw Eleanor's father bending, pushing his center of balance forward, beginning his drop. Race stood up, stepped out where the Kid could see him, and for the space of several wild seconds his heart did not beat.

The Kid saw Race at the same instant some sudden alarm caused him to half twist, to jerk his head around as he brought his handgun upward. He was standing like that when old Franklyn's falling body struck him, knocked him violently forward into Curt and Eleanor, sending those two to their knees in the dirt and sand, while the Kid and old Franklyn struck down, bounced and rolled, both of them wrenching, one to break clear, the other desperately to hang on.

Race ran forward. He had no hint that the Kid had control of the situation until a boot lashed out, caught him flush in his soft parts, dropping him to his hands and knees in the identical spot where he and Eleanor had been disarmed a lifetime ago.

He hung there, gasping, trying to clear his head and hearing as though from a great distance Eleanor's and Curt's outcries as the much younger and tougher man fought out from beneath old Earnest Franklyn, still with his gun in hand.

Race pushed his hands hard into the sand to gain purchase for an upright, onward lunge. His right fingers curled around something cold and bright and steely-hard. He brought this object up in his fist. It was Eleanor's nickel-plated pistol, dropped here at the orders of those gunmen hours and hours before. Race blinked at it, believing with difficulty this thing had really happened. It was Eleanor's agonized scream that brought his head up in a whipping way.

The Kansas Kid was free of Earnest Franklyn, was standing over the older man his six-gun pointing downward as steady as a rock. Curt Lake, who had been in the act of scooping up a stone to join the fight with, stopped in mid-motion, staring at the cocked gun. Eleanor, too, after her one anguished outcry, was motionless. She had both hands over her mouth, both her eyes fixed in horror upon the Kansas Kid's dead-white face.

Every detail of this tableau was indelibly imprinted upon Race's brain. He could see each detail, each small line and shading and scored place upon the ground and in the postures and faces around him. He did not know then or later whether it was that kick in the stomach that had made time so definitely stand still for him. He only knew that it did stand still. Then he spoke, forever breaking that strange interlude.

"Don't do it, Kid."

He pointed the nickel-plated gun with his right hand while continuing to support himself against the ground with his left hand.

"Take my word for it, Kid. It will be the worst thing you'll ever do in your lifetime. It'll damn you and haunt you for as long as you live."

The Kid's head moved very slightly. He saw the nickel-plated gun. He looked above it into Race's face. At his feet Earnest Franklyn did not move at all. He simply lay there, brokenly breathing, looking steadily upward.

The Kid let silence run on to its maximum limit before he very gently eased off the hammer, very gently straightened up, looked over at Eleanor on her knees, down at her father, then back over to Race.

"Dunphy," he said, speaking wonderingly, speaking so softly Frank Andrews who had just come up scarcely heard his words at all, "I couldn't do it."

He threw aside his gun.

Race reached far down for one more ounce of energy. He got upright, let the nickel-plated gun hang at his side, and stepped over to help old Franklyn to his feet. He stood with Franklyn in front of the Kansas Kid. For a moment no one spoke and only Eleanor, getting to her feet beside Curt Lake, made any sound at all.

Race reached out with his free hand. He gripped the Kid's arm, then let his fingers drop away. "I want to say something," he murmured so only old Franklyn and the shaken youth before him heard. "It takes a mighty good man to know in his heart when he's wrong, and it takes an even better man to know that in this world two wrongs never made a right." He then turned away, leaving Franklyn alone with the Kansas Kid, crossed over where Eleanor stood, and held out her little nickel-plated pistol.

"If anyone had told me this morning when you dropped this thing, that when I picked it up I'd be ten years older in about that many hours, I'd have thought he was crazy. But it's true."

Eleanor took the gun and looked at it. She raised her eyes to Race a moment later; they shimmered in the moonlight. She stepped up, leaned forward, and kissed him squarely on the mouth.

Curt Lake and Frank Andrews looked appalled. They also swiftly looked away.

ABOUT THE AUTHOR

Lauran Paine who, under his own name and various pseudonyms has written over a thousand books, was born in Duluth, Minnesota. His family moved to California when he was at a young age and his apprenticeship as a Western writer came about through the years he spent in the livestock trade, rodeos, and even motion pictures where he served as an extra because of his expert horsemanship in several films starring movie cowboy Johnny Mack Brown. In the late 1930s, Paine trapped wild horses in northern Arizona and even, for a time, worked as a professional farrier. Paine came to know the Old West through the eyes of many who had been born in the previous century, and he learned that Western life had been very different from the way it was portrayed on the screen. "I knew men who had killed other men," he later recalled. "But they were the exceptions. Prior to and during the Depression, people were just too busy eking out an existence to indulge in Saturday-night brawls." He served in the U.S. Navy in the Second World War and began writing for Western pulp magazines following his discharge. It is interesting to note that all of his earliest novels (written under his own name and the pseudonym Mark Carrel) were published in the British market and he soon had as strong a following in that country as in the United States. Paine's Western fiction is characterized by strong plots, authenticity, an apparently effortless ability to construct situation and character, and a preference for building his stories upon a solid foundation of historical fact. *Adobe Empire* (1956), one of his best novels, is a fictionalized account of the last twenty years in the life of trader William Bent and, in an off-trail way, has a melancholy, bittersweet texture that is not easily forgotten. In later novels like *Cache Cañon* (Five Star Westerns, 1998) and *Halfmoon Ranch* (Five Star Westerns, 2007), he showed that the special magic and power of his stories and characters had only matured along with his basic themes of changing times, changing attitudes, learning from experience, respecting Nature, and the yearning for a simpler, more moderate way of life. His next Five Star Western will be *Guns of Thunder.*